I0823953

A GIFT BEFORE DYING

A GIFT BEFORE DYING

A NOVEL

MALCOLM KEMPT

CROWN
NEW YORK

CROWN
An imprint of the Crown Publishing Group
A division of Penguin Random House LLC
1745 Broadway
New York, NY 10019
crownpublishing.com
penguinrandomhouse.com

Library of Congress Cataloging-in-Publication Data
Names: Kempt, Malcolm author
Title: A gift before dying: a novel / Malcolm Kempt.
Description: First edition. | New York City: Crown, 2026.
Identifiers: LCCN 2025008909 (print) | LCCN 2025008910 (ebook) |
ISBN 9780593801000 hardcover | ISBN 9780593801017 ebook
Subjects: LCGFT: Detective and mystery fiction | Novels | Fiction
Classification: LCC PR9199.4.K455 G54 2026 (print) |
LCC PR9199.4.K455 (ebook)
LC record available at https://lccn.loc.gov/2025008909
LC ebook record available at https://lccn.loc.gov/2025008910

Hardcover ISBN 978-0-593-80100-0
Ebook ISBN 978-0-593-80101-7

Editor: Shannon Criss
Editorial assistant: Austin Parks
Production editor: Abby Oladipo
Text designer: Andrea Lau
Production: Heather Williamson
Copy editor: Maureen Clark
Proofreaders: Hilary Roberts and Nicole Ramirez
Publicist: Elora Weil
Marketer: Hannah Perrin

Manufactured in the United States of America

9 8 7 6 5 4 3 2 1

First Edition

The authorized representative in the EU for product safety and compliance is Penguin Random House Ireland, Morrison Chambers, 32 Nassau Street, Dublin D02 YH68, Ireland, https://eu-contact.penguin.ie.

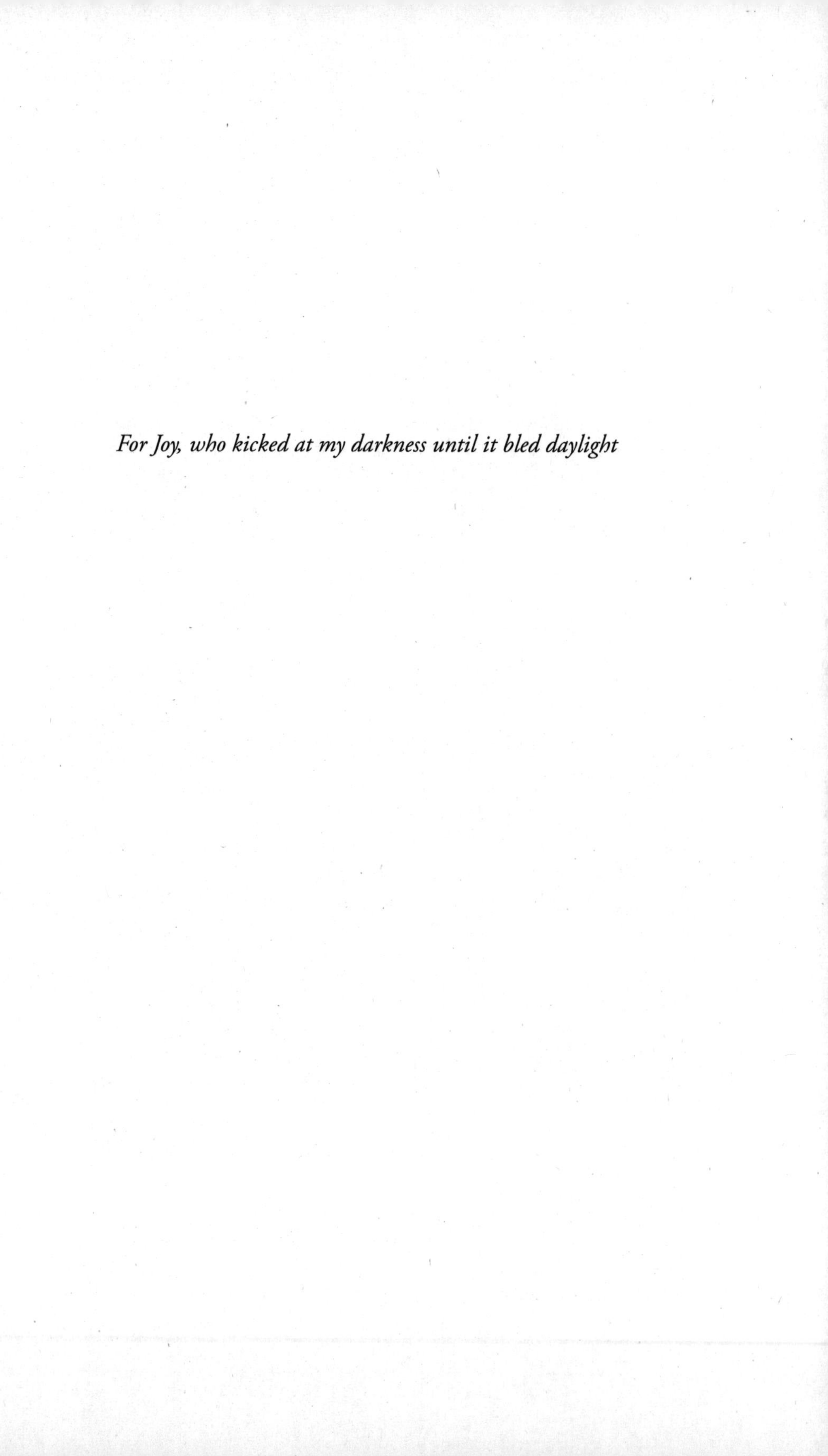

For Joy, who kicked at my darkness until it bled daylight

A GIFT BEFORE DYING

CHAPTER 1

Sergeant Elderick Cole pulled back the hood of his parka and switched on his flashlight. Dead. The bulb flickered once and the silhouette of the girl lingered on his retinas. He removed one tactical glove using his teeth and fumbled with the battery casing; icy pins and needles pushed deep into his bone-white fingers. The furnace must have been out for hours. He swore aloud, his warm breath crystallizing in the Arctic air. Cole whacked the frosted device against his palm in frustration. It flashed again, illuminating the crime scene for a heartbeat.

The body of the girl hung in the center of the kitchen, her head bent downward at an unnatural angle, concealing her features in its shadow. It didn't matter. He didn't need to see her face. Even from the far end of the hallway in the unlit apartment, he knew exactly who she was. Resignation set in, a feeling of deep sorrow stealing over him. It was the fourth suicide he'd responded to this year in this little Arctic town. December was only hours old.

Standing in the darkness, giving his eyes time to adjust, Cole allowed her image to fade, dreading everything that lay ahead. How did it all come to this? Sliding his bare hand along the cold surface of the wall, he found the light switch for the hallway and flicked it upward. Nothing. Before he could even consider the reason for the outage, a frigid gust ripped through the inner door behind him, so he forced it closed against the howling wind.

As he tightened the cap on his flashlight, it mercifully sparked to life. He brought the beam to bear on her corpse. An electrical cord had been tied around her throat in a crude slipknot. Stiff arms and legs dangled from her tiny frame. She was frozen solid. Her toes were level with Cole's knees, bringing them face-to-face. He stepped closer to her, touching her hair with his gloved hand. Was there anything he should have done differently for her in the past few weeks? He pushed a rigid strand back off her face, but it fell forward again. She looked angelic in the artificial light, crystals of frost on her pale cheeks, her eyes open, lost and vacant. He whispered her name as if to wake her.

"Pitseolala."

Cole rotated her body with a soft touch, turning her face away from his. He unzipped his parka and reached inside for the handset buckled to his tactical vest.

"This is Sergeant Cole, Dorset detachment. Do you read me?"

A distant voice crackled over the airwaves.

"This is Iqaluit dispatch. I read you."

"I'm at the location and I've found the body. It's a suicide. Over."

The operator acknowledged him and he shut down his radio. No need to get his partner out of bed for this. He pulled out his smartphone. No one had told him two years ago, before he flew into Cape Dorset to start his placement, that there was no cell service in the town. No infrastructure, they told him. Too remote, they said. The device had become an overpriced dictation machine. He activated the voice recorder app. As he got older, he'd found himself relying more often on recordings to write incident reports. His memory wasn't what it used to be. That, and he wrote so many of them now. Crime never seemed to sleep here, and as of late, he hadn't either.

A violent wind shook the house while he spoke into the phone, the wooden frame cracking and shifting in the otherwise silent darkness.

"The deceased is wearing a black T-shirt with a silver butterfly design on the front, black jeans, green belt. Barefoot. Toenails painted red, fingernails blue. Hair is normally black, recently dyed blond, traces of pink on the ends. No visible injuries except for numerous dated scratches, bruises, and a few hickeys."

It had been less than a week since Pitseolala slept off a night of heavy drinking in the holding cells. Cole had found her staggering around without a parka or mittens during a night when the temperature had dropped well below –31 degrees with the windchill. This scenario had become a regular occurrence for her in recent months.

He leaned in and inhaled deeply through his nose. Cheap flowery perfume, no smell of decomposition. He exhaled a cloud of icy frost. No telling how long she'd been hanging there. His hands trembled as he searched her pockets, her frozen body turning slightly at his touch. Nothing but lip gloss and chewing gum. Just a minor, a kid who had nothing. The tension in his neck increased. He realized he was clenching his teeth again, so he closed his eyes and recalled the exercise he had read about on the internet. *Open hands, breathe in. Close fists, breathe out.*

He slipped past the body to clear his head and survey the room. It looked like every other kitchen in every other prefabricated unit in the area. No signs of a struggle. An overturned chair near the body. A single plastic tumbler and an open bottle of vodka on the table. Nothing notable except the young girl's blue jacket on the back of a standing kitchen chair.

He pulled a small point-and-shoot camera from his pocket and took a dozen pictures of the room from different angles. Then he squatted down to peek through the hole in the glass of the back-door window. Forced entry. No damage except the shattered pane above the knob where she must have gained access to the apartment. A small drift of snow had formed on the tiles among the shards of glass. He stood up, walked to the counter, and picked up the cordless phone. No dial tone. It was tied to the power supply; some fuses must have blown and knocked out the furnace along with them. He reached for his mobile radio unit again and dialed Bert Miller, the local justice of the peace. The regional office had also designated him as a lay coroner.

Ten rings later, a somewhat sober Miller mumbled into the receiver.

"Miller? That you?"

"Yeah, yeah," he whispered, before breaking into a coughing fit.

"I got a body. House 273. I need you to confirm it so I can cut her down."

Seven seconds of silence. "I'll get dressed."

At the sound of the disconnection, he cursed under his breath and hoped that Miller wouldn't roll over, fall back asleep, and leave him standing in the cold for the rest of the night.

He braced himself for a long wait and climbed the stairs to investigate the rest of the residence—a two-bedroom apartment in one of the five-unit housing complexes at the edge of the hamlet. Each had an identical layout, so he knew the floor plan. He turned left at the top of the stairs into the bedroom, instinctively reaching for his gun when his own darkened reflection in the mirror startled him. He paused, releasing his grip on his still-holstered firearm, then swept the flashlight around the room. Empty, as expected. He strode carefully through the unlit room to the lone window and turned off his flashlight, wiping the frost from the pane with the sleeve of his parka.

Outside, through the ice-covered glass, the tiny community of Cape Dorset, with about eleven hundred Inuit and two hundred *Qallunaaq,* or non-Inuit, like himself, looked almost peaceful. He knew better. In the early 1900s, the Hudson's Bay Company established an outpost in this location, offering tobacco, sugar, and ammunition in exchange for animal hides and pelts. It didn't take long for the nomadic Inuit to become dependent on the goods and services offered by the company and move from their hunting camps on the tundra to settle around the company store.

More than one hundred years later, despite its small size, this isolated town had one of the highest violent crime rates per capita in North America. Harsh weather, rampant substance abuse, lack of treatment resources, and pure isolation created a pressure cooker of social ills. Violence lingered as a potential solution to every problem.

He flicked the flashlight on again. A photo stuck out from the mirror frame above the dresser—a group of girls on a hiking trip. The teacher who rented the unit stood third from the left. Smiling, happy, elsewhere. She'd been on vacation for the past three weeks. The neighbor who reported the body noticed all of the lights extinguished and used a spare key to check on the place.

He tucked the photo back and stepped out across the hallway. Cosmetics and hair products cluttered the tiny bathroom. The flashlight beam revealed a toilet bowl full of ice; a long crack extended from the flush handle to the base of the tank. He turned the hot water tap on, but nothing came out. The pipes in the house would have frozen when the furnace died, most of them burst. Checking his watch, he wondered if he had accidentally locked the front door on Miller. He descended the stairs and made sure the dead bolt was open before sitting on the couch in the living room. Cold had begun to seep into his joints. When he was a senior in college, a promising career in professional hockey had been derailed by a poorly executed check from a careless defenseman. Two surgeries and three titanium implants later, he would relearn how to walk. He rubbed his bad knee hard with two hands to warm it before taking out a pencil to make notes. Years ago, his instructors had taught him to always use a pen, but up here, the ink kept freezing.

Cole heard Miller long before he saw him. The lay coroner stomped his feet on the outside stairs several times. The front door opened and slammed shut against the wind, shaking the whole house. Most buildings at this latitude were raised on steel frameworks with posts driven deep into the ground; the residual heat from a regular concrete foundation would melt the permafrost and cause the structure to shift and collapse. Cole leaned toward the table and finished writing out his last timed entry before closing his notepad and putting it back in his vest pocket. Miller held on to the doorknob for support and cursed loudly as he tried to keep his balance while removing his boots. He didn't spot Cole until his first one was halfway off.

"Leave your boots on. It's not a murder. There won't be anyone flying in for forensics."

Miller rose, nodded in appreciation, bent again at the waist, and pulled his boot back on. He looked like many Southern men who spent a long time in the North—overweight, red-faced, and heavily bearded, a Falstaff in winter wear. Cole smelled the stale liquor before Miller stumbled five steps from the living room door, but he couldn't really complain since he'd dragged the poor man out of bed on a weekend without warning.

He nudged past the coroner and down the hallway toward the body. The older man followed, using the officer's flashlight as a guide. The legs of Miller's snow pants swished loudly against each other as he pulled off his fur mitts and adjusted his matching hat. Cole stood off to the right of the girl, knowing that Miller might need a chair for support in his condition. Miller let out a resigned sigh, his breath crystallizing from the cold as he stood in the kitchen doorway. Balancing himself with one hand against the frame, he looked up at the hanging girl.

"One can only hope it was quick," said Miller, making the sign of the cross on his chest before contorting his face and closing his eyes. He took a deep breath in through his nose and let it out through his mouth in a cloud of frost before he opened his eyes again. Fearing that the drunken man might vomit, Cole stepped back.

Miller rallied and composed himself. "Well, she's frozen solid, so I don't need to check her pulse. I'll do the paperwork tomorrow. You're good to cut her down."

Cole nodded and placed his hand on Miller's shoulder, turning him to face the exit. Miller gave him a weak thumbs-up, lowering to one knee with great effort to pick up a dropped mitt, and shuffled back toward the front door.

"You need a hand with her?" he asked half-heartedly without stopping.

"No, I'll be fine."

Cole waited until he heard the outer door slam shut before he pulled out his jackknife. He dragged a chair over behind the hanging girl, stepped up on the seat, and slipped his left arm firmly around her waist. The knife took less than a minute to cut through the taut cord. Careful to keep the blade pointed away from her body, he wrapped his right arm around her as the cord gave way. He eased her feet to the floor before stepping down carefully to avoid twisting his weak knee. Despite her small size, Pitseolala's lifeless body felt heavier in death. He strained to release her gently. He positioned her flat on her back on the floor before he took her jacket from the chair and draped it over her face.

He pointed his light toward the remainder of the cord tied to the exposed pipe above him and reached up with one arm to gauge the height of the ceiling, but his fingertips fell well short of the knot. The flashlight beam moved down the height of the kitchen chair and then along the length of her shrouded body. *Need to bring a measuring tape.* He squeezed the back of his aching neck and closed his tired eyes with a despondent exhale. Sleep would be a gift.

When he stood at the front door, preparing to lock up and leave, he noticed a tiny pair of shoes on the rubber mat. Tattered blue sneakers with pink laces. He'd temporarily removed the laces from the same footwear when he'd placed her in a cell only days before—standard procedure to prevent prisoners from harming themselves. From the end of the hall, Pitseolala's bare feet seemed out of place, yet somehow significant, with her stiff toes now pointing toward him. He snapped a picture of the shoes before taking one last look at her body.

Cole stepped outside into the blackness and pulled his hat down low against the biting wind. He could barely see the truck through the blowing snow, despite it being only twenty yards from the building. Before he came to the North, he had worried about the constant darkness of the winter. He never thought he would get used to it. Now, the never-ending night was somehow comforting. Like the thick blankets of constantly drifting snow, it hid the ugliness around him.

CHAPTER 2

Maliktu Kullu stood motionless in the moonlight, far out on the frozen ocean. The oversize parka, stained with blood and fat, hung down below his knees. Disfigured skin covered the boy's entire face from untreated burns he had suffered as a toddler. He cradled a weighty rifle wrapped in caribou pelt in his spindly arms. Next to him, his grandfather, Pingwatsiak, sat on the snowmobile with his own gun slung across his back. The long fur trim around the old man's hood wicked away the moisture of his breath, creating a halo of ice around his weather-beaten face.

"I will circle you at a distance and drive the seal toward its breathing hole," Pingwatsiak said in Inuktitut, his mother tongue, over the rumble of the idling engine.

Maliktu pulled the trim away from his mouth with his caribou mitt. "And watch for bears."

They were not hunting alone. A polar bear making a meal of a ten-year-old boy and his grandfather was not unheard of in this territory. When seals were scarce, the huge beasts were often lured great distances by the smell of potential food as it drifted on the wind.

"Let me worry about the *nanuq*. You worry about the seal." His grandfather revved the engine and pulled away. The boy was on his own.

Maliktu trod cautiously, deliberate in every footfall. This form of hunting demanded silence and darkness. Seals could hear better than sled dogs, even through thick layers of ice. He puffed out his little chest inside his parka, clutched the rifle tight with both hands, and moved the last few feet toward the *aglu*—the seal's breathing hole. He squinted at the taillight of his grandfather's machine as it blinked in and out of view behind the snowdrifts in the distance. He already seemed so far away.

The boy knelt, removing his headlamp and pressing it against the side of the ice cone that had formed above the *aglu,* peering into the small opening he had created in the top with his knife. Open water, no foul odor. Big male seals often stank, and their meat was fit only for feeding the dogs. His family, like many in Cape Dorset, had only human mouths to feed.

Unfurling the caribou pelt from around the barrel of his rifle, he retreated from the icy mound. The seal could hold its breath for nearly an hour, but it would have to breathe eventually. And he would be waiting for it. Planting his feet wide to keep his balance, he stuck his harpoon and his *niksiq*—a makeshift hook strapped to a broken hockey stick with some black electrical tape—into the snowdrift beside him. The M1917 Enfield bolt-action was still too big for him, but less so now than three years ago when he'd used it to kill his first seal. Fewer and fewer children his age hunted anymore. Families found it easier and cheaper to buy corn dogs and pizza pockets at the local supermarket.

He checked the safety and cocked the gun before shifting the rifle in his arms to change the burden of its weight. It would be a long wait. There were no northern lights tonight to entertain him, so he counted stars, giving each one a name—Killiktee, Piita, Maata, Goo—until he ran out. The longer he stood, the more the cold seeped in, despite his heavy clothing. He couldn't feel his feet and his back had grown stiff. To keep the blood flowing through his legs, he squatted up and down several times. Every itch, every tingle in his toes, was surely frostbite setting in.

A gasp erupted from inside the *aglu* beside him. He refocused and readjusted his grip. A short, sharp breath erupted and then a little splash—a cautious seal testing to see if any danger lurked above it. He bit his lower lip in an effort to breathe silently through his nose. Another short breath, another hushed splash, the inhalation longer this time, but not long enough to fill the seal's lungs. He removed his right fur mitt with his teeth; the thin glove beneath allowed him to better operate the trigger. The longer he remained silent, the more confident the seal would become.

He eased the safety off without letting it audibly click, then extended the rifle with one hand. The tip of the barrel hovered less than six inches from the side of the *aglu*. He bent his knees slightly to take the change in weight distribution. His outstretched forearm burned under the tension. The seal broke the surface fully, inhaling deeply. He tried desperately to remain steady while his shoulder ached and his lower back spasmed. If he waited too long, the seal would slip beneath the waves with its lungs filled for another hour. He let the mitten fall from his teeth into the snow. His lungs burned, starving for air as he held his breath in silence. His entire body trembled, acid burning in his veins. The seal took another full inhale. And then an exhale. Maliktu's strength faltered, the gun barrel drooping. As its third breath began, he let his own breath go and squeezed the trigger. The gunshot echoed out across the tundra as the *aglu* exploded. His rifle jerked backward, knocking him off balance. Blood and seawater sprayed across his scarred face as he crumpled to the ice.

His grandfather dismounted from the snowmobile and hit the kill switch on the aging machine. The engine died with a chugging sputter and the headlight faded out with it. Maliktu bent at the waist and grabbed the seal by its lower flippers with two hands, mindful of the razor-sharp claws. The boy dragged it toward the wooden *qamutiq*—the sled hitched to the snowmobile. Steam rose up from the hot carcass in the lamplight, its ringed coat sparkling in the glow. A bullet hole in the side of its head oozed blood, its shiny musculature twitching sporadically.

Maliktu shouted in triumph, eyes wide, before smiling from ear to ear.

"Turn it over," Pingwatsiak instructed.

The boy dropped to his knees and heaved the seal onto its back. His grandfather knelt down beside him. He clicked on his headlamp, running the tip of his knife from one end of the seal's tender belly to the other. "Good shot," he said, tapping his blade against the dark hole in the seal's skull.

Pingwatsiak removed his beaver mitts and worked swiftly without the benefit of undergloves, his thick fingers calloused and worn from decades of toiling in frigid conditions. He cut and trimmed with fluid motion, muscles moving with the memory of a thousand seals caught in his lifetime. Maliktu stood next to him, observing carefully, noting every step. His stomach growled in anticipation. It had been a week since he'd had a proper meal of country food. Eating the spoils remained the best part of *aglu* hunting, especially the tender liver and the warm juice from its eyes. Blood pooled on the ice around them, staining the white snow, appearing black and purple in the light of their headlamps.

His grandfather held the liver up in the light, dark and rich with fresh blood. He cut a piece for Maliktu as his reward, allowing him to savor it before taking his own. The warm offal in the boy's mouth brought heat up through his face. They ate another piece together, sharing smiles as they cherished the moment and the flavor as long as it would last.

"Life does not get better than this," Pingwatsiak said.

Once the seal had been butchered and packed into plastic tubs on the back of the *qamutiq,* his grandfather made the last-minute preparations for the trip home: tying ropes, securing containers, and taking inventory. The meat had to be sealed tightly or exhaust fumes from the snowmobile would taint the flavor on the long journey home.

When Maliktu stood to stretch his exhausted legs, a quiet splash brought his attention back to the seal's breathing hole. Bloodstains and jagged shards of ice lay all around the dark opening. Maliktu stood at its edge; the water inside was calm but impenetrable. Strange music began without warning, its distant, haunting melody drifting toward him. The boy looked toward the unseen mountains in the dark distance with trepidation. He'd been hearing this song since summer ended. It was like no other music he had ever heard, an eerie fugue with interweaving, overlapping tones repeating endlessly. Sometimes when he hunted alone, he'd catch himself humming its mournful refrain, then clap his hand over his mouth for fear of triggering the uncanny tune.

A splash, another seal perhaps, brought his gaze downward. He knelt on the ice, shoving his *niksiq* back into the hole. Shadows moved beneath the water, ripples forming on the black surface. The hook snagged on something beneath the ice. Maliktu gripped it with both hands and tugged hard against the unseen catch. The slushy opening frothed and splashed in the light of his lamp, the icy spray stinging his frost-burnt cheeks. His head sank forward, inching closer and closer to the surface of the dark water.

"I've got something!" Maliktu shouted between desperate gasps. He lifted his eyes enough to see the old man toiling away at a stubborn knot on the sled, unaware. The howling wind carried his frantic cries away from his grandfather's ears. The boy struggled to maintain his grip on the shaft of the hook. His eyes widened as thin black tendrils slithered up the handle in the light of his headlamp, slick ribbons of darkness, creeping upward over his hands into the sleeves of his parka, wrapping around the burning muscles of his wiry forearms. Terror enveloped him. He dug the toes of his boots into the snow but continued to slide toward the hole. The tips of the seaweed-like filaments had reached the soft flesh of his armpits, coiling around his chest, constricting until he felt his ribs would crack.

Retching sounds broke free from his throat, and he struggled to breathe as the black strands wound themselves tight around his neck, his eyes bulging in their sockets. The muscles of his back spasmed and his body crashed headlong into the frigid blackness. Acrid seawater burned his throat as he submerged, filling his starving lungs. In the silence underwater, a pale face emerged from the depths. Her eyes blank, her mouth gaped wide. Long black hair swirling in the icy water around her, surrounding her in a swarm of effervescence.

Maliktu heaved backward out of the hole. He gasped for breath, lying in a heap between the bloodstains and the shattered *aglu*. The music had disappeared. The sleeves of his parka were as dry as caribou bones bleached in the sun, the *niksiq* still in his hands.

"*Atii!*" his grandfather shouted. The old man pulled the rip cord and the engine roared to life. "Let's go!"

Maliktu ran to the snowmobile and leapt aboard, clutching his grandfather tightly around the waist, tears streaming down his cheeks in the icy wind. As they rushed off, the girl's face beneath the ice lingered in his mind's eye. It seemed clearer now. His sister's face.

Pitseolala.

CHAPTER 3

Cole killed the headlights and shifted the transmission into park. *Home sweet home.* Thick layers of platinum frost blanketed the front of his house like the inside of an old freezer. Ghostly swirls of blowing snow haunted every porch light and streetlamp around him. He shut his eyes and rested for a moment in the driver's seat, soothed by the warmth of the dashboard vents and the rumble of the idling engine. The police detachment needed to be unlocked in less than two hours. Yet another night without proper sleep.

When he finally exited, a raven launched itself from the rooftop and swooped down over the truck. Black on black, invisible. Only the startling flutter of its wings gave away its presence. He struggled to insert the frost-covered block heater plug into the outdoor receptacle. Without it, the police truck would be dead within hours. The icy roads of Cape Dorset lay empty in the deep quiet of early morning. He grabbed the railing and pulled himself up the staircase, cursing softly with every step. His aching knee throbbed in time with his heartbeat. The key turned, but the front door refused to budge. *Idiot.* He had left the porch heater off when he responded to the call. If he had been gone any longer, it would have frozen completely and he would have needed a blowtorch to get back inside. Just like the last time.

Wrenching the knob, he slammed his broad shoulder repeatedly into the jammed door with all his weight. The stubborn ice yielded with a startling crackle on the third try. Once inside, he kicked off his snow-covered boots and slumped onto the porch bench, hating the accursed door, his injured leg, and the bitter cold. He hung up his fur hat and police-issue blue parka before limping into the darkened house. The overhead lights buzzed to life over the racket of the rattling windowpanes. He unbuckled his gun belt, tossing it on the couch.

A dust-covered stack of impulsive online purchases sat unopened at one end of the coffee table, one of many pieces of unremarkable used furniture provided by the local cooperative. Unread mail lay neatly piled at the other. Wall decorations were sparse—a few photographs of his former sports teams, a pair of old boxing gloves hanging from a nail, and a well-worn hockey jersey tacked up with pushpins. All were items from before he'd gotten married and had a child, long predating the intervention and their split. Artifacts from the golden age of a life that had since unraveled. Loneliness saturated his surroundings, but trying to improve it felt pointless.

He limped into the bathroom and opened the medicine cabinet where his pain medication and anti-inflammatories waited. Necessary crutches. Closing the cupboard, he confronted his haggard reflection and leaned on the sink, his stiff hands with their scarred knuckles gripping the edge of the counter. He rolled up his sleeves and splashed warm water on his face in hopes of revitalizing himself. Initially, he had visualized his placement here as a monastic one—penance for his sins, service to the people, a secluded time of introspection and discipline. But now, after months of isolation and hardship, he saw himself instead as a prisoner in solitary confinement on a frozen, distant planet or perhaps as a ghost haunting an abandoned house.

While putting away the pill bottles, he rubbed his thumb against the inside of the third finger of his left hand, spinning a phantom ring. Strange being without it, even after years. He withdrew the missing wedding band from the breast pocket of his uniform and laid it on the empty soap dish. Reaching into the other, he pulled out a picture—Danny Carter, a little boy lost and found. Five years ago this past October, the six-year-old floated face down in a river in Northern

Alberta, a few miles from the backyard where he'd gone missing. Cole's albatross, a botched investigation. He could have been fired, but the disciplinary committee cleared him. The downward spiral that followed led him to this frozen wasteland, two thousand miles from everything he cared about, waiting for a transfer that might never materialize. He was a pariah. No one wanted to work with a condemned man. Since his arrival in Cape Dorset, the boy's father had filed a lawsuit, and the resulting bad press intensified pressure on the higher-ups to fire Cole. He placed the boy's photo upright next to the ring and swallowed two blue and two white pills without water before turning out the lights.

Three fingers of scotch in hand, he collapsed onto the couch and placed the remainder of the bottle of Laphroaig on the coffee table. He opened his laptop. While he waited for it to boot up, he shuffled through all his neglected bills, junk mail, and work-related forms. One envelope caught his eye: a last-will-and-testament kit he had ordered. He swirled the ice around in the glass and drank deep, holding the liquid in his mouth, letting it warm his tongue and burn his nostrils. No new emails. No new messages. The faces in the framed photos on the side table glared at him and he tried to avoid their eyes. His ex-wife, Rebecca, and his twenty-six-year-old daughter, Chloe. Eight days past his birthday and still nothing from either. He had kept his expectations low but felt empty all the same.

Notifying Pitseolala's family tomorrow would be tough. Throughout his career, he had told many strangers that their loved ones had died, but never at the frequency of this posting. Homicides, suicides, accidental shootings, hunting parties swallowed up by blizzards, drunkards frozen in snowbanks—the people of Cape Dorset encountered death often, and by more ways than most. His thoughts drifted to the portraits of the slain officers hanging in the police detachment, reminders of the fragility of life. He flipped the envelope containing the will kit over and over in his hands. What would Rebecca and Chloe think if a stranger told them he'd been killed in action?

Rebecca would care, even if he tried to convince himself she wouldn't. In an attempt to stave off melancholy and nostalgia, he'd fashioned an armor of bitterness. He had treated her poorly until eventually she'd returned the favor. Their sporadic exchanges—less than a dozen in the past few years—usually occurred when Chloe had fallen off the wagon. His daughter's last message, thick with curses and incoherent rambling, remained in his voicemail. She contacted him only when she needed money or was too intoxicated to know why she'd even called. He had financed both of her failed attempts at a college education and taken a week of unpaid leave every time she'd attempted drug rehab. He struggled to reconcile his responsibility as a parent with the certainty of disappointment. She had become a symbol of his failure as a father and husband, a source of shame. He was done with her. Nothing he could do for Chloe would be enough to save her from herself. More likely, he'd be the one getting the bad news someday.

He lay back and shut his eyes and thought about the last time he had spoken to Pitseolala. A week, maybe more? Days and nights blurred into a long black smudge of undifferentiated time. All his regrets about the dead girl echoed in his burnt-out mind.

Pitseolala perched on a plastic chair in the interview room with her feet tucked up beneath her: bloodshot eyes, no makeup. Hard and worn-out despite her youth, fragile despite her combative expression. She wore ill-fitting jogging pants and an oversize long-sleeved shirt. At sixteen—a decade younger than his daughter—her face bore the damage of a life that ran roughshod over her. A bag containing her soiled clothes lay between them on the battered tabletop.

"I'm sorry I couldn't find you anything better to wear," Cole said.

She didn't respond. They both knew she was lucky to be alive: weighing less than a hundred pounds and having consumed the better part of a forty-ounce bottle of vodka he'd found in her possession the night before. She peered at Cole through the eye that wasn't swollen shut, jackknifed her knees up to her chest, and wrapped her arms around them. The gold cross on her necklace jutted out from the corner of her wind-burnt lips. Lifting a long rubber band from the tabletop, she dangled it between two fingers at arm's length like a used condom.

"Can I have this?" she asked.

"Only if you tell me where you got the booze."

Pitseolala sat upright and pulled her tangled hair back into a slipshod ponytail. Her closed eye fluttered partially open. She coughed in a spasm and the cross fell to her chest.

"I don't remember," she mumbled, nestling it back into the corner of her mouth.

"Don't, or won't?"

"Maybe both."

She pointed at the adjacent coffee room through the open doorway. "Can I have one of those?"

Cole left and returned with two mismatched mugs. Her hand trembled when she brought the piping hot coffee to her lips, spilling it on the tabletop. Before he could offer her a tissue, she mopped it up with her sleeve.

"I'm not drinking as much as I used to," she claimed after another messy sip. "I'm doing okay."

"You didn't seem okay last night."

Leaning forward, she set to work threading the pink laces back through the eyelets in her shoe. "I'm not gonna hurt myself, even drunk," she said without lifting her eyes. "I'm not gonna burn forever like my cousin, Piita."

His name lay heavy in the silence between them, the specter of a man who had succumbed to his own demons long before Cole's arrival. "You think he's in hell?"

"My *anaanatsiaq*—my grandma—says that people who kill themselves meet the devil when they die." She picked up the other shoe and then looked at Cole directly for the first time, irrational fear in her deep brown eyes. "I don't wanna end up like him."

He felt a chill pass through him and unconsciously touched his forearm where she had bitten him during her arrest. Only the thick sleeve of his duty coat prevented her from breaking the skin. Had it been another girl, Cole might have charged her with assault. But he knew that her parents had been killed in a tent fire when she was a child. He knew she had been bounced around in foster homes without counseling or therapy until her uncle Etidloi had taken her in and terrorized her for years with his own psychotic delusions. He knew her ex-boyfriend Silas had controlled her every movement and taken out his own frustrations on her tiny frame. Cole had seen both men sent to prison. Everyone who was supposed to be taking care of her had been hurting her. Nothing he could charge her with would remedy any of that.

"Silas will be out in three months," he said.

"I got a new boyfriend," she replied with a slight smirk.

"Anyone I know?"

She hesitated, pondering the possibility. "Maybe, maybe not."

"Are you worried about when he comes back?"

She shook her head. "I've got someone to protect me when he gets out."

"This new guy you're dating?"

"No," she said, locking eyes with Cole once more. "You."

He smiled despite himself. She tucked the cross into the corner of her mouth and smiled back at him like a mischievous child.

The cross. Cole retrieved the camera from his jacket in the foyer and slid the memory card into his laptop. She always wore the cross and he couldn't remember seeing it at the crime scene. He polished off his drink and poured another while he waited for the memory card to load. He scanned through the images—her shoes by the front door, the vodka bottle and tumbler on the table, the cord, the broken window, her discarded jacket—until he reached the shots of her body lying on the kitchen floor.

"Makeup, perfume, newly dyed hair," he whispered to her photograph. "Why go through all of that to meet the devil?"

Opening a password-locked folder labeled "Injuries," he scrolled down to a cache of older victim photos: bruises, lacerations, and bullet holes. Officers weren't supposed to take confidential pictures from the files. Sometimes late at night he'd look through the grisly images, staring into their eyes, recalling their names, their stories, searching for something he couldn't articulate. He dragged a picture of Pitseolala's lifeless face into the folder and closed it.

Cole rubbed his eyes raw and shut down the computer. Time enough to grab an hour's sleep. He drained the bottle into his glass, threw the gun belt over his shoulder, and limped upstairs to bed.

CHAPTER 4

A dense shroud of ice fog formed early that morning near the *sinaaq*—the precarious floe edge where the open water met the sea ice still attached to the shoreline. In centuries past, some referred to it as the "white death" and wrongly believed that breathing its fine crystals would bring pneumonia into their lungs. Within hours of its creation, the icy mist had crept across the frozen ocean until it slithered up over the snow-covered beach into the empty streets of Cape Dorset, coiling itself around the weatherworn buildings beneath the sparse glow of the streetlights.

By the time the fog had closed in around the old hotel, Lorraine Hingham stood watch over the propane range in the kitchen of the dilapidated lodge. She had been the owner since the mid-1980s, when she acquired the place from the local authorities. She clutched a spatula behind her back, surveying the bacon and sausage sizzling on the griddle while Cole waited in the near-blackness of the empty dining room. Her apron bore brown and yellow stains from a year's worth of grease. A faded corduroy baseball cap roosted on her head; silver wisps of hair poked out from underneath, sticking to her sweaty forehead where a wide, ugly scar ran down the left side of her face. Cole never dared to ask her how it happened.

Over three decades, she had assumed almost every role in the little Arctic hamlet. Her husband, Martin, succumbed to a heart attack during the five-day blizzard of 1993. Despite having numerous suitors, she couldn't bring herself to remarry, dedicating her days to maintaining the forsaken hotel and tending to its sporadic guests. Originating from parts unknown and lured by a twelve-month contract at the local airport, like many Northerners, she fell in love with the place and never left. There was something ineffable about the Arctic that captured people's hearts and minds. Lifers would suggest its stark beauty and quiet isolation, but its allure was more complex. Every local expatriate Cole had asked, no matter how articulate, found it nearly impossible to put into words.

Cole ate breakfast at the hotel every morning he was able. A dust-covered lamp in the corner provided the sole source of light in the empty dining room. He could have asked Lorraine to turn on the overheads, but darkness was easier on the eyes. He could pretend that work was still hours away. The warm aroma of cooked bacon wafted past him, carried along on the muted melodies of the kitchen radio. His stomach rumbled in anticipation. The thermostat had been cranked since Lorraine arose in the middle of the night, and the baseboard heaters ticked erratically in the silence of the room. If he leaned back and closed his eyes, he could be sitting in any greasy spoon in the South.

Cole's attention shifted upward at the sound of muffled voices and footfalls from the floor above. Lorraine came out of the kitchen and slid his usual breakfast across the table.

"You look awful," she said matter-of-factly. A gruff voice, even for a chain-smoker. Nicotine stains on her fingers, appearing bruised and yellow, revealed themselves as she wiped the perspiration from her face. "No offense."

"None taken," replied Cole, shaking out a paper napkin into his lap and surveying his meal. A thin sliver of light from the kitchen door split the table in two. She poured herself a coffee, then stepped up on a chair three tables away from him with a labored grunt and deactivated the smoke detector on the low ceiling.

"My exercise for the day," she announced. He had seen and heard this act at least a hundred times. Settling in across from him, Lorraine lit a cigarette and took a long pull, turning her head to blow the smoke away.

"What's all the news?" she asked.

"You know I can't talk about work," he said half-heartedly, their early-morning exchanges almost scripted.

"I'll find out anyway," she said, right on cue.

He forced a smile before the grimness of the situation set in. "Death last night. Looks like suicide. Kid broke into a teacher's place."

"Firearm?"

"No, a girl," he said. Female victims rarely used that method, despite rifles being readily available. "Hung herself."

"Easier for you to clean up," said Lorraine, devoid of empathy.

If it was anyone else, he might have been offended, but he knew about her own battles with depression and the emotional armor she'd built up over the years. He tore off a piece of toast and dabbed it into a soft-poached yolk.

"Bit early," she added. "Christmas isn't for a few weeks."

Emotional stress and heavy drinking during the holiday season heightened the risk of suicides in Arctic towns. Strangely, rates surged highest in the endless light of summer rather than the bleak winter. Men were more likely to do it when the days first started getting longer and women later, when the sun refused to set. No one had offered Cole a decent explanation.

"Who was it?" she asked.

He hesitated, reluctant to bring her name out into the room. "Pitseolala."

She tapped ash onto the linoleum, lost in memories. "Our oldest tried to kill himself once on Boxing Day. Pills and vodka. Martin found him passed out in the snow."

"I didn't know about that," he confessed.

"We never really got the why part out of him. Most likely over a girl, I guess."

He realized he'd lost track of time and shoveled back the last of his eggs. She lit a second cigarette, tossing the first butt into the dregs of her cup.

"We don't understand what's going on in our own heads," she mused. "So how can we expect to know what some drunk girl is thinking?" Lorraine took a hard drag and blew smoke out the side of her lips. "You should worry more about that visiting preacher and his crew. Harassing people, spewing their hellfire and brimstone over the local radio."

"I've had complaints already," he grumbled. "He's making a lot of people uneasy."

A snippet of the preacher's sermon had played in the police truck on the way to a call the previous morning. The homily railed against sinners and the godless, blaming them for all the world's ills, all the while asking for money. Evangelists like him could be manipulative, narcissistic, and, given the circumstances, dangerous. Many people here were desperate, poorly educated, and susceptible to anyone claiming a divine connection.

Cole recalled a case from the 1940s, when a string of deaths ripped through another community not far from Cape Dorset. Two Inuit men, emboldened by missionary teachings, proclaimed themselves to be God and Jesus, convincing their newfound followers that certain other residents were evil and deserved to die. Nine people were brutally murdered before the federal authorities intervened to prevent more deaths.

"Someone said they were taking their suppers here," suggested Cole.

She scoffed as she removed his empty plate: "God don't eat here."

He let out a melancholic chuckle that left him feeling drained at the end.

Cole swore the ceiling in the detachment office had lowered since his arrival. No windows that opened, no air vents: a place of stifling discomfort. Fluorescent overheads hummed, their clinical white light rendering the room shadowless and casting faces in a deathlike pallor. Stacks of paperwork monopolized every cluttered surface, and the photocopier had been broken since September, with no repairman for a thousand miles. The clock in the holding area had died weeks ago, but no one seemed to notice.

He removed his winter gear while staring at the pixelated human shapes on the cell monitor that had once been cutting-edge technology. Spectral blurs of grays and blacks slept blanketless on concrete beds. Each cell stood a little larger than an elevator with a thick door. Walls covered in etched graffiti, a seatless toilet, and a meal slot just big enough for a microwave dinner or for someone to fling feces through. Blood, piss, shit, vomit. Cole tried to convince himself it was all part of the job, that he'd gotten used to it, instead of acknowledging the bitter truth.

A roster of civilian guards held down the fort during the graveyard shift, when officers were meant to sleep. But most nights required after-hours calls and resulted in a full lockup. The howling of the drunks faded as their internment dragged on. By morning, they'd reverted to their civilized selves, werewolves transformed once the moon had gone down. Many detachments in the territory were manned by only two officers. Positions were difficult to fill. They were on call at all hours with little in the way of resources. No support staff, no cleaning staff. Relief constables often had to be flown in when injuries, duty travel, or vacation time left officers unavailable. The work was grim and burnout was common, but there was lots of lucrative overtime, and those who stuck it out could pretty much name their next post when they finished their contract.

He checked messages while guzzling down his fourth coffee of the morning. Still no responses to anything he'd sent out. One curt voicemail on his work line from his ex-wife. No mention of his birthday. Another over-caffeinated morning before the chaos of the day. Traces of a nightmare during his half hour of shallow sleep resurfaced. He dreamed he was slipping down into an icy crevasse, clawing desperately at the sides, unable to slow his descent. Even hours later, he remained plagued by a sense of dread, imagining what unseen horrors had waited for him at the bottom.

Constable Veronica Aningmiuq stepped in out of the cold. Like all the officers, she wore a beaver-trimmed hat, black gloves, and a drab blue uniform with her last name embroidered in Inuktitut syllabics. The Inuit had no written language prior to the arrival of Europeans, who foisted a writing system upon them. It was developed by Christian missionaries in the 1800s to teach the Gospel. Even after all this time in Dorset, Cole couldn't decipher a word of it, not that he'd ever really tried.

Veronica was roughly thirty and stood five foot seven, tall for an Inuit woman. She rarely laughed but would softly chuckle out of nervousness. Her mother moved her to Iqaluit from Cape Dorset when she was six, before dying at the hands of a boyfriend when Veronica was barely eleven. After completing her police training, she was offered a placement in Dorset. She'd confided to Cole that she'd hesitated before accepting. They had now worked together for months, and Cole had never had a more reliable partner. She could handle anything the job threw at her. *Growing up hard makes you hard when you grow up*—his grandmother's words.

"We had a death last night while I was on call." He paused to let the message sink in.

"Pitseolala," he said, using her full name, instead of the usual "Pits."

Veronica didn't respond but absorbed the information with her head down, as if taking in a dead bird left on her doorstep. A long stillness uncoiled between them, the partners sharing an unplanned moment of silence for the girl. The overheads flickered; a strong gust of wind rattled the lone windowpane. She barely raised her eyebrows, indicating she understood. If he wasn't familiar with her, the gesture would have been imperceptible.

"I didn't want to wake you," he said. "Figured we could deal with it today."

Taking off her gloves and hat, she laid them on a desk before staring out the window through her own reflection into the darkness beyond. On the unseen horizon, distant headlights of snowmobiles returned from the weekend hunt. She wished she was among them, or somewhere even farther away.

"I thought I'd let you make the call," Cole said.

Her face tightened as she glanced toward the telephone in the interview room. "Her grandmother will be crushed."

From his desk, he watched her leaf through the community listings with the receiver in her hand. While her background had its advantages, it also brought her closer to every tragedy. The cell area remained quiet, the switchboard silent. A thick manila envelope containing the Carter lawsuit documents lay like a stone near the edge of his desk, souring his mood even further. Potential damages, solicitor fees, future unemployment, bankruptcy. He decided it would remain unopened for another day.

That missing-child investigation was supposed to have been another rung on the ladder of his rising career. As lead detective, he'd had the resources, the manpower, and the faith of the department. But he'd been stumbling toward a messy divorce, struggling to help his troubled daughter, and self-medicating on top of it all. He had focused on the boy's father as the perpetrator despite a lack of evidence. A gut feeling based on an interview. The man had seemed confident, less distraught than the mother, avoiding questions and asking too many of his own. In all his years of investigative work, Cole's intuition had never let him down. Until it did.

Three months later, a neighbor with a history of mental illness and criminal convictions involving children turned himself in. Cole's team had wrongly ruled him out as a suspect after only a single round of questioning. In the end, the man led them to Danny's corpse, which he'd wrapped in plastic and dumped in a nearby river. Overcome by guilt at failing to prevent the boy's death, Cole had lifted the little body from the water himself, inadvertently tainting the forensic evidence. The defense attorneys had a field day punching holes in the flawed investigation until they convinced the jury to acquit. Following his demotion, Cole endured a disciplinary process that dragged on for months before the boy's father filed a civil lawsuit against him. Cole drank heavily to cope, rarely spending time at home—nails in the coffin for both his struggling career and his failing marriage.

While Veronica spoke into the phone, voice hushed, face toward the floor, Cole headed to the break room to clear his head. The civilian guard had left an hour ago. He took a clean mug from the shelf and poured from the cheap coffee percolator he'd purchased, casting a glance at the pictures of the two fallen officers, then toward a wall of missing-person posters, each one outdated beyond hope—an audience of the dead. He slumped for a long while half conscious, sipping coffee in an uncomfortable chair, mesmerized by the gurgle of the percolator and the relentless wind, before withdrawing the night binder from the filing cabinet. During a shift, the guards would make a note on each prisoner every fifteen minutes. He found the page with Pitseolala's most recent entry and slid his index finger down each column. No threats of self-harm.

Before he could consider what that meant, the scanner crackled to life with the loud voice of the dispatch operator. He listened to the details—domestic assault in progress, child present—while eyeing the community map on the wall. The streets in Dorset had no names, but each house was numbered, although they followed no pattern he could discern. When he left the break room, Veronica stood in the main area, putting on her outdoor gear.

"Her *anaanatsiaq* couldn't stop sobbing," she said as Cole approached, her expression grim as she double-checked her gun and reholstered it. "Hung up before I could finish."

The pair zippered up and braced themselves before stepping outside into the biting cold.

CHAPTER 5

Maliktu allowed the wide strap to slip from his aching shoulder. The canvas sack outweighed him and hit the plywood floor hard and loud. Relieved of the burden, he stood up and stretched, arching his stiff lower back. The stagnant air in the cabin stank of wet fur and mildew. Out of the wind, the interior was silent and unlit. He withdrew a sealed canister of kerosene from the bag and tossed it onto an unmade bed in the corner. Fishing his sister's lighter from his pocket, he sparked it to life and the butane fumes crept up into his sinuses. His condensed breath sparkled in the dim, uneven light. He stood, transfixed, watching the flame sway rhythmically with utter fascination, lulled into a momentary trance until an unsettling sensation of dread crawled up over his skin. Unnerved by the shadows writhing on the walls around him, he rummaged with one hand through the wooden chest in the corner until he located the battery-operated lantern. His sister had found it last time when they had broken in together.

"Shine it over here," Pitseolala said. "I can't see what I'm doing."

He obliged begrudgingly, shuffling over with the flashlight in his hand. From her knees, his older sister unearthed a lantern out of the jumble in the chest, sending random objects clattering to the floor. She activated it, holding it high above her head; a dreamlike glow filled the cabin.

"Ta-da!" she said, laughter ensuing until they exchanged a high five.

Though the siblings had driven by the shack on the tundra a hundred times, they had never been inside until this moment. Local children would joyride around on the endless playground of ocean ice that surrounded the town, breaking into hidden caches of supplies and vandalizing cabins at their whim. It was rare to find a kid in Dorset who hadn't hot-wired a snowmobile or at least ridden one that had been. Their stolen rides inevitably ran out of gas and had to be abandoned, forcing them to trudge home together in search of another. Under Canadian law, children under twelve lacked the necessary understanding of their actions to be held responsible, so they couldn't face criminal charges, and the justice system was lenient on those under eighteen.

Pitseolala surveyed the place—a single-room shack with unfinished walls and yellowed insulation stuffed between rough-hewn studs. A bed large enough for a family, crudely fashioned from compressed foam and discarded wooden pallets, took up half the room. There was a makeshift kitchen on an old countertop; a table and chairs occupied the center of the room. A simple place, but exceptional among the other cabins they had broken into.

"Pretty cool," she said and lit the remains of a ratty cigarette, taking a drag before handing it to him.

"You shouldn't smoke, you know," she said, exhaling. "You're too young."

"You smoke."

"I'm old enough."

Maliktu took two quick puffs, worried she might take it back. His sister chuckled as he coughed uncontrollably, pounding his little fist against his chest, gasping for breath. She snatched the cigarette from his flailing hand and took a long drag before snuffing it out on the vinyl tabletop. It left a perfect black dot on the otherwise unmarred white surface.

"I'm trying to quit," she confessed. "I might be having another baby."

"When?" he asked, wondering where it would sleep in their overcrowded house.

She lifted her shirt and looked down at her bare belly as she puffed it outward. "If it's true, I'm gonna give it away again."

"Who's the father?" he asked, hesitating with each word, wondering if the question would irritate her.

"Someone you don't know." She smiled mischievously. "Someone secret."

He recalled when Pitseolala flew to Iqaluit to have her last baby, and how happy everyone was when she came home with it, especially their aunt Lizzie, who adopted it. The wind rocked the cabin hard, testing the nails that held it together. For a moment, he wondered if it would come apart if the gusts were strong enough. The pair looked at each other wide-eyed, giggling with every groan of the old building.

"Maata said this place was haunted," she said, turning serious. "Her real dad told her."

Both of them knew that if Maata's biological father, William, learned that they had trespassed in his cabin, he would string them up like animal hides.

Maliktu rubbed the rough surface of the burn scars where his left ear should have been. "Do you think he really killed Maata's aunt?"

"Maybe," she replied, picking dirt from under her bright blue nails. "I heard it was with a gun."

The boy tried to imagine what it would be like to die from a gunshot wound. He dropped his head forward as he fingered an imaginary hole in his abdomen, contemplating an exit wound in his back. He looked behind himself, visualizing where his guts would end up in the room if he had just been shot.

"Cops got him," she said, lighting a joint she pulled from inside her jacket. "He'll get murder. Go down south to jail."

He looked up from his nonexistent wound, watching her spark up again with interest. His sister tilted her head back, blowing smoke to the ceiling. The smell of cannabis wafted overhead.

"I thought you were quitting."

"This is *milutsi,* not a smoke," she said, as if he couldn't be more stupid.

He sat on the floor in front of her and picked up an empty metal tin that had fallen out of the chest when she removed the lantern. He spun it between his fingers; the reflected light blinked over him like a strobe across his face.

"Her aunt's snowmobile is really fast," he said.

"They'll probably give it to Maata's mom. When you die, they give your stuff away."

"I don't want other people to have my stuff," he said, taking inventory of what little he owned.

"Me either," said Pitseolala. The pair sat, smoking quietly, handing the joint back and forth, until Pitseolala made a decision.

"If I die before you," she said, talking with the smoke held in her lungs. "I want you to have all my stuff."

He looked horrified at the suggestion.

"Not even! I don't want girl stuff!"

Pitseolala laughed so hard she choked. Pot smoke billowed out of her mouth, obscuring her features. He laughed too, though he didn't understand what was so funny. He really didn't want her things.

"Then you can burn it all," she said, looking up into the shadows of the rafters, draining the last of the joint as it burned her fingers. Her face relaxed as the marijuana took effect. "I won't need anything in heaven."

Maliktu extinguished the lighter and the room fell into darkness. Breathless, jittering with anticipation, he scanned the barren landscape through the frosted window for headlights of passing hunters.

Hours earlier, he'd woken on the makeshift bed his grandfather had constructed out of foam in the bottom of his sister's closet. Winter clothes dangled above him; a tattered blanket served as a door. His little refuge in the crowded house, but this sanctuary was becoming too small for him with every passing night. He slept in the fetal position since the previous winter, with all his precious possessions tucked beneath the corner of the foam.

He had lain there this morning, reflecting on his visions at the *aglu,* trying to make sense of it all. Then, the faint ring of the telephone drifted in from down the hall, followed by heartbroken moaning. Maliktu peeked out from behind the blanket toward his sister's empty bed. A massive weight bore down on the back of his neck and shoulders. He didn't know who the caller was, but the message was clear—Pitseolala was gone. He covered his head with a pillow, trying to drown out the anguished wails of his grandmother echoing through the house.

That keening still reverberated in his mind as he stood in the silence of the cabin. Perhaps he should have stayed at the house and grieved with her, held her tightly, cursed toward the ceiling with her. But he couldn't. He had a promise to keep. He packed his sister's things and left before the mourners came and the cries intensified, as he knew they always did after a death.

Before leaving home, Maliktu discovered a half pack of smokes next to the lighter in Pitseolala's jewelry box. One of those cigarettes now hung from the corner of his crooked, burn-scarred mouth. He flipped the lighter end over end in one hand, clicking the lid open and closed with the other. His thoughts floated back to the seal's breathing hole. *Maybe she tried to take me with her?* His heart fluttered in his bony chest, and his hands trembled with foreboding. He reached into his pocket and fondled the bright orange, snub-nosed flare gun and cartridges, stolen three weeks ago from a fishing boat overwintered on the snow-covered shoreline. His breathing slowed as he gripped the gun, the weight of it bringing him comfort. He swept his other arm across the counter slowly and deliberately, hearing items smash in the darkness on the wooden floor. There was no anger in his movements, only satisfaction. Action, reaction, some kind of certainty. His skull pounded with pumping blood. An emptiness consumed him as he stood in the unlit room thinking about the seal he shot in the head lying on the ice with all its organs exposed.

He switched on the lantern, placed it on the window ledge, and put his hood back up to protect him from the cold. No one would see the lamplight. Out here on the land, he was miles away from everything. He took a deep breath and closed his eyes, imagining Pitseolala next to him, sitting behind him on one of the kitchen chairs. He finished the cigarette, walked to the table, and snuffed it out on the same black dot.

Maliktu unzipped the duffel bag and dumped the contents on the floor. Her clothes, magazines, and all the pictures from Pitseolala's portion of the room spilled out. He kicked at the pile, spreading it out with his boot. Shivers overtook him with a sudden need to urinate. Tucking his mitts under one arm, he pulled down the front of his snow pants with one hand and lifted up his parka with the other. He shuffled to the corner of the room and pissed. The hot stream spattered loudly on the floor, steam rising up from the plywood. Maliktu remained where he was when he finished, watching the steam dissipate near the ceiling, feeling as if he were in two places at once, like watching himself in a movie.

He withdrew two pill bottles from his pocket—the greens and the pinks. A week had passed since he last swallowed one. The doctor said he had to keep taking them to keep the ghosts away, but he'd grown weary of the constant churn in his bowels and the unsettling sense of strangeness that lingered long after the pills went down. He tossed them on the floor and picked up the kerosene canister. He unscrewed the metal cap and cast it aside. The fumes hit him, burning his nostrils. Inhaling through his nose from the container, he wanted to feel the vapors inside him, savoring the moments before ignition. He coughed, dizzy and slightly faint, his eyes welling up. The can tipped forward, splashing kerosene across the pile on the floor, soaking the cardboard boxes and plastic bins by the door. He doused the sheets of the unmade bed and the chest in the corner, throwing fuel up onto the insulation of the unfinished walls before discarding the canister behind him. It landed with a clang. Tension released its grip on him; the heavy burden fell from his shoulders. The labor of his breathing vanished. He walked to the stove, weightless, and turned on the propane tank without engaging the pilot light. The hiss told him there was no turning back and he stepped out the door.

Outside, with his hands in the wide pockets of his parka, Maliktu gazed up at the stars. They shone brighter than when he'd arrived, and the moon seemed larger than during the long ride out. The *aqsarniit*—the aurora borealis—danced above him in a curtain of rippling light, anticipating the magic to come. Fat snowflakes whirled around him, pricking the skin of his frozen cheeks, forcing him to squint. He breathed deep, the icy crystals in the air burning his sinuses, his throat. He counted twenty-five steps from the doorway, a safe distance. The ozone smell of the crisp night air erased the lingering scent of kerosene. The dark music drifted in from the hills, filling the air, as if he'd willed it to arrive. It was *his* music.

Maliktu peered out toward the lights of his distant community. The soft glow of the hamlet washed in and out of view on the horizon. The noise of the shifting sea ice reached him, crackling under the pressure of the rising tide. It was as if the *Qallupilluit* were pulling their scaly bodies out from the long crevasses that stretched across the frozen ocean, their giant caribou *amautiit* encrusted with snow. His grandfather told stories of these ravenous creatures living beneath the ice who kidnapped careless children who wandered too close to the water and stuffed them headfirst into the pouch on the back of their parkas, where a woman would normally carry her nursing infant. He could not see them in the blackness, but he felt their presence. The noxious stench of the filthy beasts wafted to him on the drifting wind. But this time, he was not afraid of them. He wanted them to come. He wanted them to witness.

Maliktu faced the shack, aware of other dark creatures that seemed to lurk within the doorway and windows. Grays moved within blacks, blacks within grays. *Taqriaqsuit,* the shadow people. Observing them, he sensed their anxiousness, the stench of kerosene within the tiny shack still fresh in his mind. The building appeared to quiver before him, its fear rising up through the floorboards and into its walls. No mythical creatures could harm him now. He wanted them to feel his power. He was in control.

Maliktu withdrew the orange gun from his parka, extended his arm toward the door, and pulled back the hammer with his thumb. Tears welled in his eyes as he squeezed the trigger. The hammer snapped forward. A white-hot flare burst from the short barrel, streaking like a Roman candle into the open doorway. The flames blossomed with a rush to match the sound of the wind, overtaking the space inside the wooden building, lashing angrily out the doorway, and licking at the rooftop. The fire within the shack lasted only a minute before the propane tank exploded outward. A window ruptured, shooting glass and fiery debris into the surrounding snow. A wall of heat rushed past him.

The blaze ascended into the night sky, fueled by the rushing wind. Swirling air currents drew the flaming debris upward, forming a maelstrom high above the burning cabin. He stood as still as a statue, dwarfed by the inferno. The stars disappeared in the black smoke. He dropped the hot gun into the snow, tossed his mitts down, and ran his fingers along the scars on the edges of his face. Tears streamed down his disfigured cheeks. From the corner of his eye, he saw a vision of Pitseolala. Standing to his right, ten steps away, she ignored the fire, watching him instead. If he turned to speak, Maliktu knew that she would disappear. He smiled through his tears when she came to stand beside him and cupped her hand to the side of his head.

She whispered a single word into his ear.

Kuukutsi.

CHAPTER 6

Veronica drove the police truck as fast as possible, navigating between the steep snowbanks that lined the icy street. As they moved westward toward the edge of town, the headlights cut a wedge in the thick darkness. Kids in Cape Dorset roamed outside at all hours regardless of the weather. Cole expected one to spring out of the shadows at every turn. Thoughts of a child's fragile body being crushed beneath the unforgiving wheels left a sour taste in his mouth. The weight of that imagined victim pressed him closer to the dashboard as he struggled to see through the blinding snow squalls. Over the years, he had learned that the corpses of children, no matter how they came to die, could never be unseen.

As Veronica accelerated into the tail end of a hairpin turn, a snowmobile shot across the road. She instinctively pumped the brakes, narrowly avoiding a collision. Cole swore under his breath, visibly frustrated by his lack of control in the passenger seat. He placed both palms on the dash to steady himself as they crested the top of the blind summit above the valley.

From the hilltop, the isolation of Cape Dorset was starkly revealed. Where the streetlights ended, the nothingness began. A thousand miles of barren tundra and frozen ocean smothered in darkness. Veronica tapped the brakes again as she prepared to make the slippery descent. As they rolled over the top, Cole spotted a rare pedestrian drifting like a phantom through the blowing snow. A fur-lined hood concealed the stranger's face; the body remained engulfed in a cloud of cigarette smoke and condensed breath that sparkled in the truck's headlights as they passed.

The area of Cape Dorset dubbed "the Valley" featured two long rows of identical social-housing units equidistant from one another, nestled in a hollow on the western edge of town. Each home had at least one working snowmobile parked out front and at least one broken-down machine nearby that had been cannibalized for parts. Residents often installed chicken wire or plywood sheets between the steel posts that elevated the houses to prevent children from playing beneath them. Lastly, there was almost always a dog, tormented by a chain just short enough to keep the ravens out of reach as they maneuvered for its food.

This house was no different. An emaciated dog awaited their exit from the vehicle, pacing back and forth, hackles up, tail between its legs. Its uninsulated doghouse stood barely visible behind it, entombed in a towering drift. Cole squinted through the frosted windshield, attempting to discern the length of its chain. He cursed the swirling snow and the polar night and recalled the last time he was bitten by a dog. He unconsciously rubbed his long-healed thigh. As he stepped out of the truck, the harsh wind lashed the exposed skin on his face and neck. He tucked his head down and dark patches of snow revealed themselves in the headlights of their idling truck—either animal blood from a recently butchered carcass or antifreeze from a leaking vehicle.

Taking the lead, he rapped hard on the battered front door and yelled, "Police!" The curtains remained drawn, lights on within. Veronica stepped to the side of the door, both officers silent and hunched against the bitter cold while they waited for a response. Thick ice coated the plywood landing, making for unsteady footing should a confrontation lead to violence. Every house in town had at least one firearm, many unregistered, most kept loaded. Cole's thoughts drifted to the dead officers on the wall when he knocked a second time.

The front door opened partially to reveal a wiry Inuit man in a bloodstained tank top. Hollow cheeks, thin facial hair, empty eyes glossy and bloodshot. He held a sleeping infant wrapped in a bath towel in one arm, and with the other he pressed a crimson-stained dishrag against his bleeding right eyebrow. Veronica pushed the door open farther with her boot. The raw odor of stale alcohol on the man's breath hit Cole as soon as he stepped inside. They didn't need his permission or a warrant, given that an assault in progress had been reported. A rare example of when lives were more important than paperwork.

"*Kinauvit?*" asked Veronica, unfamiliar with the man. Cole's knowledge of Inuktitut was limited to "Thank you" and "Good morning." Despite half-hearted attempts to learn the language, he still butchered the pronunciation of both. *Auk* was the only other word that stuck with him, given how often he encountered blood in his day-to-day life. On bad days, the spilled *auk* was his own.

"Peterloosie," the man responded with flat affect and slurred speech. They followed him into the warm living room, which was in shambles: clothing and toys strewn over the tattered linoleum floor, a cheap glass coffee table overturned and smashed in the center of the room. The stench of sweat and cigarette smoke was oppressive. Slowly and painfully, the wounded man sat on the couch and tucked the child beside him next to a balled-up blanket.

"I had to hit her," he mumbled. "She was gonna cut me again."

Veronica stood watch over the man in the living room, asking questions in Inuktitut to keep him focused on her while Cole checked the rest of the house. His hand never left his holstered firearm as he moved from room to room.

Dirty dishes filled the kitchen sink and half-full pots and pans lined the countertop. The oven had no door. A garbage can overflowed with rotten food and filthy diapers. The yeasty, fruity odor of home brew hit him long before he found the fermenting bucket of moonshine on the shelf in the pantry closet. The sorry state of the man and the child left him disgusted and angry. He had grown weary of the overwhelming poverty and dysfunction in the North; a stream of hopeless victims caught up in an endless cycle of violence.

"She's locked in the bathroom," Veronica shouted to Cole after a brief exchange with the man on the couch.

He cleared the rest of the house in haste—two bedrooms and a utility room—before knocking sharply on the only closed door. He situated himself off to one side to await a response.

"*Unakinauva?*" Veronica asked Peterloosie, pointing to where his spouse was hiding.

"Marianne," he answered without lifting his injured head, gasping heavily and grimacing in considerable pain.

Cole rapped hard on the door again. "Are you okay in there?"

No response.

"She cut me with glass," Peterloosie mumbled to Veronica in Inuktitut, gesturing vaguely toward the mess on the floor.

"How did the table get broken?" asked Veronica.

"She started jealousing," he said in English. "Wouldn't stop bitching at me, so I told her to shut up. Then she smashed the table." He gestured to the television remote lying among the shards before pulling the dishrag away from his face, staring at its bloodstains with a confused expression, then returning it to his head. Veronica unsnapped and snapped the clasp on her sidearm, a nervous tic.

She shouted to Cole: "Possible weapon. Could be broken glass."

"How old is the baby?" she asked Peterloosie.

He scrunched up his face behind the bloody rag and mumbled something she didn't catch before pointing again at the chaos on the floor. He began to drift in and out of consciousness, rambling incoherently. Veronica considered the blood loss and the level of alcohol consumption. She used her vest radio to contact the health center to prepare for him. Pulling the man to his feet, she tried to encourage him to maintain pressure on the cut. She shuffled him across the room to another chair and squatted to check the baby on the couch—sleeping soundly, breathing normally, no sign of any injuries. She paused a moment, her stomach in knots, watching the child's chest rise and fall, trying to reassure herself that even if the baby woke up, it would likely be too young to remember any of this.

She walked over to the bathroom door and stood next to Cole. The flimsy knob turned freely, but the door wouldn't budge when he pushed on it. This likely meant the woman had wedged a butter knife in the jamb. He had seen this technique used many times in local houses when doorknobs were broken. There were no hardware stores in these isolated towns and even simple repairs could take months waiting on replacement parts.

"Marianne," shouted Veronica. "This is the police. You need to come out."

A loud moan issued from inside the bathroom.

The two officers shrugged at each other, exchanging a glance, abandoning any hope this would be an easy task.

"At least we know she's alive," Cole deadpanned. Veronica ignored his attempt at humor.

"We're not going to leave until you come out, Marianne," she said.

"Fuck you!" boomed the voice from the other side of the door.

"I'll take him out to the truck," he said. "Then you can gather up the baby and take it to the health center with the father. He'll need to get that eye stitched up."

A bloodcurdling scream erupted from the living room behind Veronica, prompting both officers to reach for their sidearms. Peterloosie lay face down in the remnants of the shattered table. He had clearly pushed himself off the chair and stumbled toward the baby before falling. Cole rushed to him and rolled his unconscious body onto its side, the man's face a dog's breakfast of blood and broken glass.

"Cover the bathroom," shouted Cole. "I'll be right back."

Cole grabbed the man under his armpits and dragged his limp frame out onto the landing, wincing with every step from the extra weight on his bad knee. The wind had picked up since they arrived, stinging Cole's bare cheeks and forehead. The dog barked relentlessly, lunging at them in a sudden frenzy, testing the limits of its chain. The drunken man's bloody head drooped forward; his limbs were flaccid. Cole struggled to secure him in the back seat of the truck in the recovery position. He cursed at the prospect of having to clean blood and vomit out of the vehicle later in the freezing cold.

When he returned to the house, Cole glanced at the couch, satisfying himself that the tiny infant remained safe. Veronica stood in the now-open doorway of the bathroom with her gun drawn and pointed inside. He examined his palms in the light of the living room, realizing they were covered in the man's blood, and swore again, wiping them as best he could on the back of the couch as he passed.

"You need to put down the weapon," Veronica shouted. The fluorescent bathroom bulb flickered erratically, creating a disorienting strobe effect in the darkened hallway. "Drop the glass."

He stepped cautiously over the threshold. A woman slumped forward on the toilet, her long black hair hanging inches from her knees. She was naked from the waist up, her skin mottled with bruises new and old. Her hand was in her lap, holding a large shard of glass. Spatters of blood streaked down the drywall into a puddle on the white floor.

"She wouldn't stop screaming, so I forced the door," whispered Veronica, never taking her eyes off the woman slouched on the toilet.

Cole raised his hand slowly and eased Veronica's pointed firearm downward. "Grab the baby and get the guy to the nurse. I don't want him bleeding to death or choking on his own vomit."

The drunken woman lifted her head at the sound of his voice, and it lolled backward under its own weight. She tilted her face sideways, trying desperately to focus on the strangers in her bathroom, her left eye swollen shut, blood dripping from her open mouth, and a small gash bisecting the bridge of her nose.

Veronica hesitated, looking from Cole to the woman and back again. "Are you sure?"

"She's not going anywhere," said Cole. "And if she tries to, I can deal with it."

The woman leaned forward and spat more blood before falling backward, her head pounding against the wall behind the toilet. The glass shard slipped from her grasp and clattered on the tile floor.

The officers stood in silence for a half dozen breaths, anticipating her resurrection. When she didn't regain consciousness, Cole and Veronica each grabbed an arm and hauled the woman out of the cramped room, her legs dragging behind her. She came around enough near the end of the hallway to stumble compliantly. In the living room, the woman started to resist and made a half-hearted attempt to bite Veronica's face.

"Handcuff time," said Veronica. She spun Marianne around toward the wall and pushed her up against it. The woman turned toward Cole, smearing her bloody face across the wallpaper in the process.

"You let the girl die," she whispered through bloodied teeth as the first handcuff clicked into place.

Cole stiffened, puzzled by her statement. She locked eyes with him, appearing lucid and sober for the first time. She twisted her arms violently behind her back, causing Veronica to struggle with the handcuffs. She whispered again: "Just like you let the little boy die."

He tried to breathe but realized he couldn't inhale, as if all the air had already been sucked from the room. The hallway spun out of control in the strobing light. He forced a swallow and pulled at his tightening collar with one hand.

"What the fuck did she just say to me?" he asked.

Veronica pulled the woman away from the wall and eyed him with a perplexed look. "I didn't hear her say anything."

His mind flashed to an image of Danny's corpse floating face down in the river, then to Pitseolala's fragile frame hanging from the pipe in the kitchen, their lifeless bodies blending together. He tried to speak again. His lips and tongue moved to form words, but no sounds emerged.

When the second handcuff snapped closed around her wrist, Marianne's eyes closed and her torso went limp against the wall. She let loose a mumbled stream of Inuktitut that sounded like a strange incantation to his ears. When she opened her eyes, she spat a mouthful of blood. The hot fluid struck him square in the face. He stumbled backward at the impact, bumping into the wall behind him and nearly falling. The woman renewed her struggle to escape from Veronica's grip and burst into a demented cackle. White heat spread up through his face when he realized what had happened. His features twitched with rage and disgust in the flickering light. He squeezed the pepper spray canister on his belt to the point of breaking it. Marianne kept cackling louder and louder while she stared at him, her features contorting into a deranged scowl, her eyes gaping and frenzied. His jaw seized, fists clenched, and body tensed as he tried to resist the overwhelming urge to lash out at her hideous laughing face. The room tilted and shifted as his balance failed him. He reached out to the opposite wall for support, temporarily dazed, only anger and adrenaline keeping him upright.

Before he could fully compose himself, Veronica pressed her forearm into the back of Marianne's neck and plowed the woman's face into the drywall using her body weight. The drunken woman slumped to her knees, silenced by the blow, leaving a mess of blood down the wall.

Veronica stood still, heaving, trying to catch her breath after her struggle. Once she had, she looked at her partner, who was covered in the blood of both suspects, and her expression shifted to one of revulsion: "Jesus, you're a mess."

Cole looked down at his soiled parka. He smeared his fingertips through the fresh blood spattered on his face. His rage had burnt itself out, smoldering under a blanket of exhaustion. Veronica flashed him a wide-eyed expression that reassured him she had the situation under control, keeping the half-conscious woman on her knees with a firm grip on the back of her neck. She gave a subtle flick of her head toward the bathroom sink. An extended silence passed between the two officers before Veronica escorted the woman away. It took a long time before he found the will to move.

CHAPTER 7

Cole stood over Pitseolala's corpse on the kitchen floor of the vacant apartment with his black boots straddling her narrow hips on the linoleum. He wasn't sure how many hours had passed since he'd cut her down. The furnace remained off, which kept her body from thawing. Beneath the thin latex of his black surgical gloves, his fingers had gone numb. A coppery tang of tainted blood still lingered in his mouth despite a warm shower and a change of uniform. He squatted down and steeled himself, not ready to see her face again.

Veronica unpacked the cardboard boxes in the faint glow of the propane lantern. Forensic baggies, labels, folded white sheets—everything spread out on the kitchen table. Next to the corpse lay two brown paper bags for covering the girl's hands to protect possible evidence under her nails. A black two-layer body bag for transport lay crumpled at her feet. Cole lifted the jacket covering her face delicately with his fingertips, revealing the young woman's emotionless expression—drowsy eyelids, mouth slightly open, eyes vacant. A once-vital teen replaced by a bruised wax mannequin.

Guilt from his failure to prevent her death had spread throughout his body, metastasizing like a rotting cancer, until he was entirely consumed by it. He had worked many murders over the years. He knew the burden required. No one spoke for the victims once they were dead—no one but the men and women hunting their killers. They carried that person's spirit with them until the case was closed, or for the rest of their lives if it remained unsolved. An intangible responsibility, yet so heavy.

Veronica cataloged the jacket while he fished lip gloss and chewing gum out of the girl's jeans. He hooked his finger in the V-neck of her shirt, pulling it down far enough to reveal the lace of a cheap rose-colored bra. No necklace, no cross. His hands started to tremble. The windowpanes rattled in the relentless wind. He scanned the floor using his flashlight, under the table and along the bottom edge of the kitchen cupboards. Nothing but dust and crumbs.

"If the chain broke, it would have been caught in the cord or be down in her shirt."

Veronica either didn't hear him or didn't understand. He stared into the darkest corner of the room, scenarios swirling, theories building. His eyes, puffy from lack of sleep, strained under the low-light conditions. He straddled the corpse on his knees and attempted to loosen the stiff knot of the noose before swearing aloud in frustration. Veronica passed him a set of industrial shears. Careful not to puncture skin, he snipped near the base of the slipknot. Once it was removed, he caressed her hyoid bone with his thumb.

"Out in a minute, brain-dead after five." He spoke in a matter-of-fact tone, tracing the thick red line of discolored skin around her neck with his index finger. "Hanging leaves an inverted V, as opposed to a ligature strangulation."

"Well, we know she was hung," said Veronica.

Her sudden sarcasm snapped his focus. "The small stuff is important."

She mumbled something he couldn't make out before returning to paperwork. Cole's lack of sleep prompted a sudden migraine. He squeezed his eyes shut and the pain spiked behind his left ear. Breathing shallowly, he struggled to compose himself, his hand shielding his face until the headache relented. It was possible to make a strangling look like a hanging, or even to hang a person unwillingly; he trawled the seabed of his memory for related case names and details without success.

"Everybody panics when they drop," he continued. "Even when

they want to die. They claw instinctively. But there are no scratches on her neck, and she's got decent-length nails. But no restraint marks on the wrists either."

His analysis of the forensics smoldered, all smoke but no flames. Someone could have drugged her and hanged her while she was unconscious. Possible, but there was no evidence to suggest it. The migraine flared again, and he pressed on his eyelids with his fingertips in an effort to somehow alter the pressure in his skull.

"You might have an infection after that blood in your eyes," Veronica said.

He ignored her comment, struggling to particularize, drowning in uncertainties. Scrutinizing the rest of the room, he searched for a clue that could make it all make sense, pausing at the plastic tumbler on the table. He leaned forward, palms down on either side of Pitseolala's head. He sniffed at her parted lips; a puzzled expression was followed by a slow shake of his head.

"What is it?" asked Veronica.

"The glass," he said. "Smell it."

Veronica stuck her nose in the tumbler and sniffed once. "Nothing, like plastic."

"It should smell like vodka."

"Maybe the alcohol evaporated."

"Not at this temperature."

She appeared unconcerned. "I have to meet the family in an hour. They'll want the body for the funeral."

He didn't respond.

"What's your point about the vodka?"

"The bottle is full. She's an alcoholic who brings liquor but doesn't have a drink before she kills herself." He pointed his flashlight toward the smashed kitchen window they had covered with cardboard and duct tape. "She broke in through the back door." He pushed his thumb and index finger into the inner corners of his closed eyes. His speech slowed. "So why are her sneakers out front on the rubber mat with the laces tucked inside? And who takes their shoes off during a break and enter?"

An interim plan coalesced in his mind. He would request an autopsy, then speak with the girl's relatives and her schoolteacher to better understand her circumstances at the time of her death. More puzzle pieces would emerge; he would figure out how they all fit. The migraine spiked again, and he gripped the doorknob to steady himself. Nausea struck like a rogue wave, bringing with it an overwhelming urge to lie down.

"You should go home," she said. "Or to the health center."

He wiped his hand down his face and twisted the kinks out of his neck. "Get the cord down. My fucking knee is killing me."

Irritated by his rudeness, Veronica snatched a chair and stepped up.

He struggled with the closure tab on the plastic bag for the shoes, flashlight tucked in his armpit. "We'll need an autopsy for her alcohol levels," he said. "And a toxicology report."

Veronica blew a breath from the side of her mouth, frustrated by the thought of complicating an already delicate situation. "What about the funeral?"

"It'll have to wait," he said.

"We don't have to *solve* this, Cole. This one solves itself."

"Shoes off, missing cross, untouched booze," he said. "Tell me it's not weird."

"Odd, maybe. But the family will just want closure." Veronica struggled to reach the knot above her, holding her balance on her tiptoes, her voice wavering. "They won't authorize it anyway. And if they ask me, I'll tell them an autopsy is a waste of time."

He stared at the dead girl on the floor. His stomach churned, heat sweeping up into his face. He rubbed at his tired eyes with gloved hands, the friction of the latex burning his eyelids. He pulled a measuring tape out of his pocket and extended it toward Pitseolala's feet.

"No one is *going* to ask you."

"I can't reach this," Veronica said, ignoring him, barely touching the pipe above her. "You're going to have to get it down."

He stood up slowly without taking his eyes off Pitseolala's body. "How tall are you?"

"Five seven," said Veronica after a moment's hesitation.

"Well, she's five three." He retracted the measuring tape with a tinny clatter. "If you can't reach it, then how did she get it up there?"

CHAPTER 8

The stolen snowmobile died less than a mile from the edge of town. Starved of gasoline, its engine sputtered out. Maliktu pulled out a cigarette remnant he'd been saving. Everyone his age smoked, but no one in town would sell them to a ten-year-old, so he collected discarded butts from the ground outside the local store. Marijuana could be acquired from a half dozen dealers who had little qualms about providing a psychoactive drug to minors, but tobacco was another story. His fingers trembled with desperation as he brought the filter to his chapped lips. He shook his sister's lighter hard before sparking up, closing one eye in an effort to maintain his night vision. His thoughts drifted to his grandfather, who would be disappointed to know he was smoking again.

Three long drags and the cigarette stub was gone, sailing with a flick from the end of his finger. A rush of calm washed over him as the nicotine went to work. He donned his oversize dog-fur mittens again before his fingers got frostbite and stepped off the machine. He stared at the faraway glow of the town on the horizon, then looked back into the distance toward the cabin he had destroyed; the sense of calm and control he felt at the fire was already fading.

The stillness on the return trek unnerved him; everything seemed quieter in winter. Thick blankets of snow absorbed all sound. Normally, he would've listened to his portable player, but the cold had drained the battery again. His earbuds remained tucked down into the neck of his parka, the headphone cord frozen like a stiff white twig. Without his music, he had only the crunching of his boots on the compacted snow to keep him company.

As he trudged homeward, his sister's apparition replayed in his mind. Was it just an illusion? Was he unraveling again, like last summer when the flames first whispered his name? He questioned his decision to stop taking his pills, to burn his medication, trying to rationalize the hallucinations of her, to reshape the experiences into something that made sense. He unconsciously rubbed his arms through the fabric of his parka, recalling with unease the grip of the tendrils that tried to drown him. So real, and yet impossible.

He recalled a story his grandfather had told him. Sedna, a young Inuit woman, unhappy with the men her father had selected for her, married a dog to spite him. Her father, enraged at what she had done, came to kill her and the half-animal spawn of this union. To spare them from his wrath, she set her dog children adrift on the sea. They grew up to become the ancestors of the *Allait,* the Native peoples of the Southern lands, and the *Qallunaaq,* the white men.

When Sedna's father caught up with her, he dragged her out to sea to drown her. She fought back, but he overpowered her and pushed her head beneath the waves while she clung to the side of his kayak. Wanting to be rid of her forever, he cut off her fingers with his knife and she slipped beneath the surface of the frigid water. Her severed fingers drifted with the current and changed into sea creatures—the first seals, walrus, and belugas—while her body sank to the bottom of the ocean, where she remained forevermore, a divine being of the sea.

Without fingers, she could not comb her hair, so a local shaman would transform into his spirit body composed of many animal parts and descend into the depths to comb the tangles from it. As a reward, Sedna would provide him with more seals for the people of his community.

His sister couldn't be trapped beneath the ice with Sedna, he reassured himself. He had seen her at the fire since the seal hunt. He heard her speak to him as clearly as if she'd been alive. *Kuukutsi*—her pet name for the white policeman. But what could it mean?

After more than an hour of walking, he shuffled over the last of the hummocks onto the snow-covered beach. His hands were soaked with sweat inside his mitts. His stomach grumbled. He pulled the hood of his homemade parka down tight with both hands. Farther down the shoreline, headlights of hunters on snow machines blinked in and out as they rode up and down over the jagged hills of the pack ice.

Were those creatures really there at the cabin fire as well? He was getting too old to be afraid of such things and tried to convince himself they were a trick of his mind. But if his sister's ghost was real, then those creatures had to be real too. Panicked at the thought, he rushed up from the darkened seashore toward the lights of the houses.

As he passed the nearby graveyard, dozens of white wooden crosses cast long shadows on the snow from the porch lights of the houses beyond. Flurries painfully stung his exposed skin. He adjusted his knitted cap to better cover his lone ear, his numb hands tingling with pins and needles. He cast a worried glance toward the mountains that loomed over the little community. The music came, soft at first, then rising in volume. Its strange sounds swelled above the clamor of the sled dogs chained near the shoreline—a high-pitched wailing that rose and fell as it echoed off the surrounding mountains. The dogs howled along with it, and the music soared in and out of the intermittent screeching of the wind, like an unholy orchestra, its musicians out of time and their instruments out of tune. He tried to block out the eerie tones with his fur mittens, but it was no use; the music played inside his head.

When he stopped to catch his breath, he realized he had no idea what time it was—near dawn or the dead of the night. Snakes of snow dust slithered between his feet. Irrational fears surged like the swell of a whale passing beneath a lone kayak. He tucked a mitten beneath his armpit and clutched the *ulu* inside his coat. Its curved blade gave him comfort. It was a woman's knife, he knew. But his *pana*—a man's snow knife—would not fit, not even in the oversize pockets of his cousin's hand-me-down parka.

He stood as tall as he could manage in the rushing wind, puffing out his pigeon chest and glaring into the deepening shadows around him. He looked out into the surrounding nothingness, tightly gripping the handle of his knife with one hand and his flare gun with the other. Then he saw them.

The sinister figures—five in all—materialized without warning from behind the community center. A streetlight in the parking lot threw their elongated silhouettes out over the drifting snow, morphing them into shadowy ogres stretching out to devour him. Three boys, two girls, as far as he could tell. But the identity of the tallest one was unmistakable even from a distance. Markoosie Ukiaq, two years his senior, took particular pleasure in abusing anyone weaker than him at school. Maliktu had been one of his favorite targets before he stopped attending.

Maliktu stood frozen, desperately hoping they hadn't seen him. He surveyed his surroundings for an escape route. Beneath the flickering streetlight, he was exposed. The pack of shadows altered their course and headed straight for him. Realizing they must have seen him, Maliktu bolted between the buildings, half running, half sliding on the frozen ground in hopes of losing them. Their laughter and shouting bounced off the nearby structures, concealing their whereabouts. It was impossible to tell if they were pursuing him, but he swore he could hear their heavy footfalls on the deserted road. As he ran, he imagined them right behind him, as if monsters pursued him, their razor-sharp claws nipping and grasping at his heels.

In the distance, a particular house shone like a beacon, illuminated by the twin headlights of a stationary truck. He cut across the open road but caught his foot on a stone hidden beneath the snow and fell to the ground within shouting distance of the illuminated building. Maliktu's hopes sank as he saw the pack turn the corner ahead of him and then make a beeline straight for him. They hadn't been chasing him; they had been strategically cutting off his escape.

Markoosie, the ringleader, clutched a pouch of tobacco, the others either still chewing or wiping dark spittle from their chins. The youngest, Saila, laughed harshly before unleashing a flurry of unspeakably cruel names related to his scarred face. She lunged, a feint to intimidate him punctuated by an angry grunt, while a younger boy in a green parka threw a chunk of hardened snow in his direction, barely missing his head. They fanned out, surrounding him. Markoosie pocketed his stash, stepping forward to confront him while the others watched in silent anticipation. Maliktu's eyes darted everywhere but toward their faces, avoiding provocation, silently searching for a way out of the tightening circle.

Markoosie spat a wad of tobacco. As Maliktu wiped it off the sleeve of his parka, the first punch struck him near the temple and knocked him reeling into a hard-packed snowbank. He fought for purchase on the slippery ground, managing to right himself only as a second blow wrenched his jaw sideways. The impact sent him sprawling down onto the hard and unforgiving ice. His sense of balance lost, he remained down, throwing his arms up to shield himself and curling into a fetal position. The group swarmed him like a flock of hungry ravens; fists and boots rained down upon him. Through his fingers, he saw their true forms—wan, emaciated demons with distended bellies, wild eyes, and hideous fangs, snarling and barking, frothing blood from their gaping mouths.

When the onslaught was over, he played dead, staying down until he was certain they had gone. Peeking cautiously, he watched as the group—their need for violence satisfied—wandered off toward the parked truck. He stood up cautiously and dusted the snow from his clothing. A dull pain blossomed in his lower back as blood pooled in his mouth. He stumbled out into the center of the empty road. Stars littered the night sky. To the east, the *aqsarniit,* the aurora borealis, danced in a rippling curtain of emerald light. He caught movement across the street from the house that had been lit up in the darkness. Two figures loaded a large black bag into the bed of a pickup truck.

As their engine rumbled to life, Maliktu shuffled toward them. The vehicle pulled away, its red taillights fading into the distance. Bright yellow tape stretched across the doorway of the illuminated house. Up close, the simple building seemed to grow larger, sinister, and more menacing. It was then that Maliktu realized the black bag in the departing truck contained his sister's remains and that this terrible house was where Pitseolala had died.

CHAPTER 9

In the dim light of the bedside lamp, fresh blood pooled around the man's body as if made of red wax and melted into the mattress. Cast-off spatter from a swung knife zigzagged across the walls like a macabre abstract painting. Several gaping slashes extended down his back from shoulder to buttock. His right Achilles tendon had been severed, the calf muscle retracted in a large mound below the back of his knee. Upon closer examination, one could see a multitude of superficial cuts on his scalp.

Cole and Veronica had assumed Benny Pudlat had ceased to exist. But when Cole pressed his fingers into his neck to confirm his lack of a pulse, the dead man moaned, a muffled, ghostly wail that still haunted both officers. Thinking back, Cole found it hard to say what was more terrifying: the initial shock of his resurrection or the subsequent realization that the poor bastard was still alive.

They loaded him into the police truck—the town's equivalent of an ambulance—and rushed him to the health center and then up to the airport to be medevaced to a hospital in the South. His wounds were too serious for the Northern facilities, so he spent weeks recovering in an intensive care unit in Ontario.

Now, months later, sitting across from Cole in the interview room, Pudlat looked miraculously like a man on the mend. With no evidence beyond the horrific injuries, Cole had asked Pudlat to come in for an interview to put the unsolved case to rest.

"How are your back and your legs?" asked Cole.

"Good. I took some of the stitches out myself." Pudlat wiped the sweat from his forehead with his hand. CAPE FEAR was tattooed on his knuckles in crude, faded letters.

"You probably shouldn't have done that," said Cole.

Pudlat shrugged, looking indifferent.

"You remember anything that happened that night?" asked Cole.

Pudlat's face dropped, his gaze drifting about the room, hovering on the tape recorder for a moment to make sure it wasn't running. "I was blacked out."

"Blacking out" in the North didn't mean being unconscious, as it did in the South. It always meant being too drunk to remember what had happened. Many people in Dorset drank not to enjoy themselves but to escape, to drown out reality. Particularly when liquor was scarce, it would be consumed as quickly as possible to avoid losing it to someone else. There was little social drinking here and moderation was rare.

"Well then, I guess you can't give me much of a statement anyway."

Pudlat looked visibly relieved.

"Have you talked to Betty about it?" Cole asked.

"Social services flew her down to visit me in the hospital. We're back together now, with the kids."

"Did she tell you she did this to you?"

"She doesn't know."

Cole took a stack of color pictures from the file and slid them across the table. "Did you see the photos?"

Pudlat moved them around with his fingertips but didn't look down at them. The officers found no weapon, no third-party witnesses, and his spouse had no memory due to intoxication. If Pudlat was unable to make a statement, the file would be closed.

"Any idea why this happened to you?"

"Maybe we were fighting. I don't know."

The Inuit used the word "maybe" more than anyone Cole had ever dealt with. Cole reckoned it might be the language barrier, but sometimes they appeared hesitant about the reaction their answer might bring. Sometimes it was shame. "Maybe sleeping" was a common response when he asked witnesses why they didn't show up to their appointments with him. He could see Pudlat was guessing, pulling out shards of memories from the last few times the couple had fought to try to come up with a coherent narrative. He closed the file and put his pen down. Assessing the situation at Pudlat's home and doing damage control were the new priorities.

"Were you working when this happened?"

"No job. Maybe six years ago, I was a sewage truck helper."

Every house in Cape Dorset had a sewage outflow pipe. The permafrost made putting pipes underground impossible, and the weather was too cold for aboveground pipes. A large vacuum tanker truck drove around all day, sucking the waste from people's homes and pumping it into the sewage lagoon above the town. The water truck worked the same way but in reverse, sucking water out of the lake above town and pumping it into homes. The helper rode on the back all day in the freezing temperatures. They were well paid, but there was a high turnover.

"Does Betty work?"

"She looks after the kids."

"How many kids do you have?"

The Inuit were not as possessive about their children as Southern people. Adoption was very common in the communities, and children often lived with other family members for long periods, depending on the circumstances at home. Inuit weren't required to follow standard adoption laws and could adopt informally and openly, with biological and adoptive parents sometimes filling the same roles. A fourteen-year-old might be encouraged by her family to have a child, which would then be given to an older family member to raise. Unlike Southerners, the Inuit had a more timeless understanding of maturity; young teenagers were considered adults because not so long ago their nomadic hunting lifestyle meant they had to be to survive.

"Eight," said Pudlat, with a good degree of certainty. "Three adopted, five from me, but two of those are not mine."

"Three adopted by you, or three adopted out to other people?"

"Other people."

"So, five in your house."

Pudlat raised his eyebrows. "One of them is Betty's and another one is adopted from my nephew."

Cole didn't bother trying to make sense of it all. The structure of Inuit families like Pudlat's was complex, fluid, and often impenetrable to outsiders like him. Lines of kinship were sometimes unclear, with many individuals having multiple children with different partners within the same town. This, combined with constantly changing living arrangements due to limited housing, made for an intricate web of familial relations. The fact that it was overcrowded in the home was all Cole needed to know.

"You hunting or fishing at all?"

Pudlat scrunched his face up tight.

"How do you feed the kids?"

"Friends, family give us food sometimes. Northern Store."

"Do you smoke weed?" he asked, knowing most people in town did.

Pudlat raised his eyebrows again, leaning back, more comfortable as the easy questions kept coming.

"Sometimes. When it's around."

"Pot is forty dollars a gram around here. Where do you get the money?"

"Sometimes friends give me some. Or checks."

"Social assistance?"

"Yep."

Cole was suddenly hit by the tragedy and absurdity of it all. He let out a long, slow breath before asking, "How is Betty doing?"

"Good. We're getting married soon."

"Congratulations," said Cole, his sarcastic tone slipping right over Pudlat's head. "You both still drinking?"

"Little bit. Sometimes."

Cole leaned way in, switching to a serious tone. "I don't want to get a call and come to your house to find you dead. Or find her dead, and see you go to prison for the rest of your life while your kids grow up without a father." He put extra emphasis on the word "dead" both times he used it. Pudlat nodded his head vigorously.

"We're doing good," said Pudlat, eyebrows up. Cole looked toward the frosted window, leaning back, unconvinced. The complete lack of treatment for addictions frustrated him daily. The government had been promising a drug-and-alcohol rehabilitation facility in the territory for decades, but other political agendas always seemed to take priority.

"Twelve years," added Pudlat, rolling up his sleeve and pointing to a faded, homemade tattoo on his shoulder. A crudely drawn bird carrying a banner with BETTY written across it in block letters. "I need her. I love her too much."

Cole didn't say anything more. Pudlat asked if they were done, and the officer nodded.

"I heard about the suicide," he said while putting on his parka.

"Yeah," said Cole. "It was Pits."

Pudlat nodded, his mouth forming a tight frown. "I'm pretty sure I saw her that night."

He suddenly had Cole's full attention. "Where?"

"Walking up to R.C. with a guy."

The R.C. was an area of town up on the hilltop that was named after the old Roman Catholic church that once stood there; it was a stone's throw from the place where she died.

"Did you speak to her? Did you see where she was going?"

Pudlat scrunched up his face.

"Did you see who the guy was?"

Pudlat scrunched up harder and shook his head. "Kinda looked like Jardin. But they were pretty far up the road, and I'd had a couple sips before that."

Pierre Jardin, a recent import from Quebec, had set up shop as a bootlegger in the town shortly after his arrival. He had already been run out of another Northern community for selling illegal liquor, and word on the street had him moving into the drug trade. However, "a couple sips" was local slang for when someone wanted to downplay how much they'd consumed, so Cole was sure he couldn't rely much on Pudlat's observations.

"Do you remember what time it was?"

Pudlat blew out a breath through pursed lips. "Maybe seven, maybe nine. Before the hockey game, for sure."

Cole looked at Pudlat's wrist. No watch. That estimate was likely the best he would get.

A moment of silence passed, both men deep in thought, before Pudlat stepped out to use the washroom, leaving Cole sitting alone. Without a useful statement from either Pudlat or Betty, he would have to close the file. He stared down at the photos from the crime scene spread out on the table. He tried to imagine his former wife coming in while he was passed out, then proceeding to butcher him like an animal. He tried to fathom how he could have possibly forgiven her. Elsewhere in the detachment, a cell door slammed shut. Cole put his elbows on the table with his palms covering his tired eyes.

CHAPTER 10

Taibhse. Cole's grandmother had used that word for ghosts when he was a child. She spoke only Scottish Gaelic when she talked of the dead, or when she scolded her dog. She insisted they were somehow entangled, canines and spirits, but she never explained the connection. He always swore at her dog in English and it seemed to understand him just fine.

As a ten-year-old, he would sneak from her house on clear summer nights, drawn to the edge of the woods by an inexplicable force. The night air electrified his skin. An eerie presence lurked in the shadows and the damp soil beneath his feet, both frightening and comforting to him. His communion with the spirit world felt almost palpable then. A gift in his blood, she often said. *Touched.*

As he grew up and moved away, farther from her guidance, he believed less in such things. The son of an overworked coal miner and a mentally ill homemaker, he was eight years old when they took his mother. Flashes of that rainy afternoon still haunted him—his father's desperate attempts to calm her, the men in white coaxing her up the hospital steps, while Cole sat huddled with his siblings in the back seat of their run-down car.

As an adult, he thought his grandmother foolish for talking about the old ways—spirits in the woods and lights in the fog. She marked every picture that fell from the wall and every bird that crashed into the window as a harbinger of some inescapable tragedy. She believed that certain spirits were not bound to the places they were connected with in life. They resided in the blood, generation after generation, searching for a way back into the world they had left behind.

As far as he was concerned, and he rarely was, ghosts clung to places they remembered. He imagined his grandmother still milling about the kitchen of their old house, opening cupboard doors, cooking phantom meals, and sweeping the floors. He could think of no other place she would rather be, in this life or the next.

Cole sat in the idling truck near the storage shed behind the detachment. His thoughts shifted from his grandmother to the task at hand. Pulling on his beaver hat, he stepped out, relieved that the bitter wind had died down. The twilight of midday had faded, which he welcomed; difficult tasks always felt easier in the dark.

The old shack, bathed in the blood-red glow from the taillights of his vehicle, wasn't much to look at. Its wooden frame had tilted from years of brutal weather. Battered shingles littered the surrounding snow. Bert Miller, the lay coroner, lowered the tailgate of the police truck while Cole fumbled with the keys for the outer padlock. Even without wind, the crisp air burned inside their noses and throats, and the exhaust fumes made their eyes water.

"Do you really think it might be a murder?" asked Miller, his unlit cigarette bouncing up and down in the corner of his mouth.

"I don't know," said Cole. "At the very least, someone helped her end it."

"Who helps someone kill themselves? I mean, if someone was old or dying, fine."

Miller seemed embarrassed that the remark had slipped out. Head down, he grabbed the nearest end of the body bag. Cole knew the man's wife had been diagnosed with Alzheimer's more than a year ago. He understood the painful struggle Miller endured with her deterioration.

"Maybe they wanted Pits to die for a reason," said Cole. "I'm not sure."

He shoved the truck keys into his pocket and gripped the other end of the bag. An excited raven danced along the top edge of the shack, its talons clattering across the exposed part of the steel roof. It let out a series of low, gurgling croaks, rising in pitch from the back of its throat, one of dozens of unique sounds Cole had heard from the peculiar creatures. Distracted by its call, he paused to watch the cavorting bird.

"How can you be sure?" asked Miller.

"Well, for one, the pipe was too high for her to reach. You'd have to be at least six feet tall with a chair to get that knot tied up there."

"So it was probably a white man?"

Cole touched a gloved hand to the thick stubble on his chin, wondering how he had missed such an obvious inference. The Inuit people were shorter than most races, about five foot five on average. Adapting over a millennium to survive in such a cold climate with a diet limited to marine mammals, fish, and land animals had made them much stockier than their Southern counterparts. He'd never met an Inuk even close to six feet. With one observation, Miller had cut the list of potential suspects in town down by more than two-thirds.

Laughter out in front of the truck interrupted Cole's reply. Five school-age children stood at the road's edge to watch the men unload the body, spitting tobacco into the pristine white snow beneath the streetlight. He'd once scolded some kids for chewing it outside the Northern Store, but they seemed unconcerned and even offered him some. Cole scanned their unfamiliar faces, barely visible in their winterwear. The town had been plagued this winter by gangs of feral kids vandalizing property and terrorizing residents at night. *Little demons,* he called them. The tallest one in this crew couldn't have been more than twelve, cigarette dangling from his mouth as if mimicking Miller. He'd seen a similar group throwing rocks at a dog down near the waterfront.

"Who owns that dog chained to the pole by the beach?" Cole asked Miller.

"Toonoo. He's out until spring. Not sure who's looking after it."

"The kids keep torturing it with rocks."

"They're always doing that," said Miller with a resigned sigh. "They're kids. Boredom, no supervision . . . What do you expect?"

Cole grunted in reluctant acceptance of the grim reality. He made a mental note to try to get the caretaker to move the dog indoors. Too much to do. Getting a decent sleep kept slipping down the list.

The two men dragged the body bag off the truck. Cole shuffled backward to the narrow door, cautious of the icy terrain underfoot. His bad knee twinged at every step. Once inside, they laid Pitseolala down on a long plywood workbench with rusted metal legs—her temporary resting place before they used the town excavator to dig her a shallow grave in the permafrost.

A single bulb hung in the unheated space above. Cole pulled its chain to turn it on. The cramped space held two old four-wheel ATVs, assorted wooden crates, and tarp-covered pallets. A cluttered workbench with tools, paint cans, and other hardware odds and ends filled the back of the room.

"So who do you think did it?" Miller arched backward in a stretch, palm pushed into his lower back. "And why?"

"Not sure," said Cole, his hand resting on the leg of the dead girl through the body bag. "Like I told you in the truck, everything feels staged—her shoes by the front door, the jacket on the chair. Everything too neat and tidy."

Miller took a long drag on his cigarette and held it, considering Cole's words before exhaling.

"I'm gonna start by asking around," said Cole. "Talk to her teachers, her relatives, her friends."

"Where's Veronica?"

"Out on the land. Shack fire this morning near the point."

"Anybody die?"

"Empty as far as we know. Kids lit it, most likely. Only a matter of time before one of them rats the others out."

"Speaking of ratting, Jardin might be your man for the vodka. Likes the younger ladies too."

Cole swallowed his anger, staring at the dirty floor. "He's currently at the top of my list. I'd love a reason to throw that piece of shit out of town." Miller flashed him a look that said he agreed.

"Any other gossip I'm missing out on?" asked Miller.

"Aside from the Holy Rollers coming to town and driving everyone crazy?"

"They've been riling people up since they arrived."

Cole sighed deeply. "A few complaints, minor disputes so far. But I'm sure the preacher will find a way to piss me off before they're done here."

"You hear about Normie?"

Cole winced. They had arrested Norman Tiriaq twice in as many weeks for drunken mischief. "What's he gone and done now?"

"Got himself medevaced from the airport just after midnight. Fucked up real bad by one of the out-of-town workers building the new fourplex. Aiden, that big skinhead from Manitoba with the tattoos, worked him over pretty good, I guess."

Cole didn't recognize the name but recalled seeing a big man who fit that description around town. Construction crews often flew in skilled workers from outside the territory. Underage girls having unsavory relations with visiting laborers was an ongoing concern. Hard men with steady paychecks and illegal alcohol and drugs to ply for sex. But was Aiden capable of killing a young girl? Cole made a mental note to find out.

"We didn't get a call about that last night," said Cole.

"Normie was not exactly up for giving a statement when they brought him to the health center. Drunk as a skunk and beat to a pulp."

"I'm sure I'll hear all about it soon enough." Cole remembered that he had to see someone at the health center about the antiretroviral cocktail. An unexpected taste of blood filled his mouth. He wiped a gloved hand across his lips.

Miller dropped his cigarette butt onto the floor and withdrew a crumpled pack from his pocket. "So, when's her funeral?"

Cole shrugged. "I'm gonna put in the request for an autopsy today. Not sure how long that will take, or if I'll even get one."

"What're you looking for?"

"Honestly, I'm not sure. Mostly buying time to figure out who was with her, to process it all, maybe put the pieces together."

"Don't write those as the reasons on your request form."

Cole managed a half chuckle, more from exhaustion than amusement. "Thanks for the tip. You need a lift home?"

"Nah, you've got shit to do. I'll walk," said Miller, pausing to light up another cigarette. "What will they be able to tell you when they look at her?"

"Exact cause of death, if there was liquor in her system, if she had sex that day. Things I can't determine on my own, anything that might help." The weight of all the possibilities flooded his fogged brain. Leaning on the table for support, he closed his eyes, the sudden lack of visual stimuli momentarily dizzying.

As he opened his eyes, Miller patted his arm on the way to the exit. Cole shook the cobwebs from his head, unsure of just how long he'd been standing there in silence. The room seemed darker than before.

"Well, when Veronica gets back, you should think about taking a day off," suggested Miller, pulling on his hat and raising the collar of his parka at the door. "You know where I am if you need me."

When Miller left, Cole tried to visualize his to-do list. No leads and a million questions. His breathing grew labored, his chest heaving as if the air had grown thicker when the door shut. He gripped the edge of the table with both hands, letting his head drop toward the girl's corpse. His joints creaked and popped with every subtle movement. His limbs had stiffened and seized. He tried to remember a time when he felt worse, and it brought a storm of bad memories whirling into his mind.

Cole's heart stuttered and he looked toward the door. *Too much coffee. Not enough sleep.* He strained to hear Miller's footsteps hidden beneath a rising wind buffeting the walls of the shack. Once he was sure he was alone, Cole removed a glove despite the cold and unzipped the body bag, hesitating only to consider why he felt the sudden urge to see her face again. The opening revealed her head—a lifeless imitation of the girl he knew. He touched her icy face, sliding his finger down from her cheekbone to her chin.

"I'm sorry," he whispered, surveying the cluttered shack, noting the stench of spilled gasoline and motor oil. "You deserve better than this place."

Cole hunched over to examine her eyes—milky and vacant, rife with red spots he knew to be petechial hemorrhaging. Deep inside her iris, he thought he saw a glimmer of something he couldn't register. As he leaned in closer, a waft of flowers engulfed him. The scent startled and confused him, out of place in the dingy shack, until he realized it was her lingering perfume.

Cole stuffed his bare hand, already stinging with the cold, into his parka pocket. *Who did this to you?*

He stared at her wind-burnt lips, partially open, waiting to see a puff of exhale crystallize in the cold air like his own. Waiting for her to answer.

Her dead eyes remained fixed on the ceiling. A loud clatter shocked him back to his senses. The raven dancing across the rooftop. He zipped the bag carefully and stepped away.

As he stepped outside, the now-unseen bird squawked in the darkness above him. Cole shut the door of her makeshift tomb.

CHAPTER 11

A group of ravens is collectively known as an unkindness. Cole considered this as he stared at six of them stenciled above the urinals. An artistic vandal had used a permanent marker to draw a burning cigarette in each of their beaks. He zipped up and rinsed his hands, then fumbled with pills before fishing them from his pocket—two blues, one white—before washing them down with a handful of cold water from the faucet. The headaches were getting worse.

In the shatterproof plastic mirror, his face appeared distorted, almost grotesque, where the surface had been warped and scratched. The harsh lighting accentuated his bloodshot eyes and the deathlike pallor of his face. His attempt at a nap in the vehicle when he arrived early had been futile; his overactive brain resisted any efforts to rest. A subconscious fear nagged at him while he dried his hands—perhaps he was too afraid that he would never wake up again.

The high school was less than a year old and the place was in rough shape. The previous building had been burned to the ground. Understaffing made it difficult for the teachers to conduct classes, let alone monitor for damage. Most of the flush toilets were plugged, and the bathroom stalls no longer had doors. Hand-sanitizer dispensers had been abolished after a springtime epidemic of overdoses.

Struggling to recall the principal's name from their earlier conversation, Cole found himself standing in front of the middle-aged woman in the hallway, her shoulder-length dreadlocks tied back in a ponytail. A recent hire, she guided Cole down the long corridor lined with gray lockers and uninspirational posters, walking slightly ahead of him because his compromised knee slowed his gait. Their footsteps clacked on the polished concrete floor over the indistinct murmurs from the classrooms around them. It had been decades since he'd done the death-row-style march to the principal's office under escort, but the associated dread haunted him nonetheless.

She knocked on a door midway down the hall and apologized for interrupting the teacher who answered, then volunteered to take over the class while he spoke with the police. Curtis Reynolds stood a little over six foot, eye to eye with Cole, but not nearly as heavily built. Young and handsome with shoulder-length hair, a chiseled jawline, high cheekbones, and an inviting smile. Cole pegged him at no more than thirty-five.

Silence shrouded their walk to the teachers' lounge, and Reynolds seemed vexed by Cole's sudden request to meet. He paused to eye the surveillance cameras outside the break room with suspicion. Cole assumed the administrative staff would be watching and gossiping in real time.

The lounge itself had one window, reinforced with a steel screen. Practical furniture was surrounded by a tidy kitchenette, bookshelves of worn-out trade paperbacks, several dead plants, and a bank of storage bins. A stale stench of cigarettes emanated from the coatrack; a basket of wrapped candies sat on the table. A middle-aged, obese woman, caught off guard by the sudden presence of a policeman, hastily left the room without being asked. "I appreciate it," acknowledged Cole while she packed up her things. Reynolds became agitated once she left.

"Was this necessary?" he asked, irritated. "I could've come to your office after class instead of parading me through the whole school."

"There's been a misunderstanding," Cole replied. "I'm not here because you're in trouble."

Cole waited, notepad still unopened, letting the silence settle. Sometimes in interviews it was best to make space for them to do the talking. But Reynolds remained reticent, his hands folded over his chest.

"Pitseolala is dead," said Cole after a prolonged silence.

"Oh God." The color drained from Reynolds's face. "What happened?"

"We're looking into it."

"Jesus." Another silence unfurled between them. "The administration told me when they hired me it was always something to brace for, but I honestly didn't think it would happen so soon. Losing a student, I mean."

Cole wished someone would've warned him about such things before he started as a policeman but knew it wouldn't have prepared him either. "You were her homeroom teacher, so I was hoping for some background info."

Reynolds thought for a moment about the girl. "She was outgoing and enthusiastic sometimes. Distant and angry other times. They don't give us the resources or the training to tackle what these kids are going through."

"Did you notice anything different about her behavior recently? Any problems at home?"

"No offense, but that describes over half my students. And her attendance was spotty at best; I didn't know her that well."

Disappointment settled into Cole's expression. "Did she ever mention anyone she was having issues with, or talk about anyone in particular? Boyfriends? Girlfriends?"

"Not that I can recall." Reynolds mulled over the question. "Her aunt made a scene recently, came to the school accusing her of sleeping with her husband. He worked here as a janitor. She had to be physically removed by the staff."

After jotting down some notes, Cole ruminated on the incident with Trina, the aunt. He'd forgotten about it until now. He had arrested her a while back. A visiting judge subsequently placed her on a peace bond stipulating she was to have no contact with the former principal or trespass on school property. Trina had accused several other local women of the same crime since then.

"Is this a murder?" asked Reynolds, interrupting Cole's thoughts.

"We haven't determined the cause of death yet. We're still investigating."

The answer seemed to satisfy Reynolds, who nodded solemnly while staring at his hands. "She also mentioned appointments with a social worker. She used it as an excuse for missing class a few times, but I never bothered to get in touch with him."

Cole made a note to follow up on that. Small talk ensued about Pitseolala's attitude in the classroom and the challenges of teaching in an Arctic town. During the conversation, he couldn't shake the feeling that something had eluded him. Despite looking fresh, with no apparent signs of burnout, Reynolds seemed anxious and distracted. "How long have you been here?" asked Cole.

"Almost a year and a half. My wife and daughter were planning to move up from Ottawa in February, but I've decided not to renew my contract."

"How old is your daughter?"

"Two and a half."

Cole's thoughts drifted to his own daughter as a toddler, another lifetime ago. "That's a good age. Exhausting, but they're at their cutest."

Reynolds rambled on about childcare struggles, but an exhausted Cole barely listened. He had never recovered from the slow dissolution of his own family. Deeply damaged by the raw trauma of his childhood, he found the weight of being a father and a husband nearly unbearable. He was absent during his daughter's early years—the beautiful, precious ones that mattered most—burying himself in his work. And as his marriage drifted from emotional distance to physical separation, his daughter stumbled through her teenage years in a haze of drugs and self-harm. Unable to face that pain, he turned to old familiar vices to numb his aching heart. And when his once-promising career faltered, and then crumbled, he was left standing in the ruins of everything he had ever loved.

The rush of difficult memories triggered the aura of another migraine, prompting Cole to bring the interview to a swift end. As he thanked Reynolds and turned to leave, he paused for a moment before asking the man about his initial standoffishness.

"Rumors can kill a career," said Reynolds. "And I've had bad experiences with police in the past." A nod followed but no further explanation. "If there's anything more I can do, please let me know."

"I think I've got all I need," replied Cole. "And if there is a next time, I'll call you first."

On the drive back to the detachment, Cole didn't notice the children until he was almost past them. Two young boys, roughly ten years old, had climbed onto an oil tank to reach the rooftop of a nearby building. He slowed down and watched them scramble up the shallow pitch of the snow-covered roof. He realized that there were several more kids up there, five or six silhouettes backlit by the rising moon, oddly motionless as they waited for their friends.

Cole decided not to interfere. He hoped they would content themselves with playing on the roof, but he knew that break-ins and vandalism were everyday occurrences, frequently in extremely dangerous circumstances that all too often led to accidental death.

Given the law pertaining to children under twelve, all Cole could do was return them to their parents for discipline. The adults sometimes greeted the police at the front door with indifference, less often with outright hostility. Many cared deeply for the children they looked after but confessed that they couldn't control their behavior. Lorraine had once called him in the middle of the night when a pair of smoking nine-year-olds had crawled in a window at the hotel and raided her refrigerator. On another occasion this past summer, he came across three kids under seven pelting a downed woman with fist-sized rocks in the center of the roadway. They set upon her after she had scolded them for trying to break a window.

Cole was aware of the underlying causes: the fact that their deep connection to their land and culture was being eroded by modern influences like television, video games, and the internet. They suffered from a loss of identity and belonging, surrounded by social ills including overcrowding, poverty, substance abuse, and violent crime.

In his more reflective moments, Cole questioned the value of what he was doing. Was he helping, or just part of the irresistible grind of change that was destroying their culture? He consoled himself by focusing on people as individuals. He clung to small victories, hoping that some of the kids could be pulled from the wreckage of their young lives, as he had been, and that some children would manage to survive even these darkest of times.

CHAPTER 12

Cole shut the door of the rear office to call his ex-wife in private. The flickering lights in the cramped space seemed to intensify as the latch clicked closed. The mercury had crept upward since he'd returned to the detachment, but rasping wind had gained momentum, causing the building to shiver—both signs of a coming storm. Outside the frosted window, only a black void existed.

Hesitating, his fingertips inches from the receiver, he mentally prepared himself for the dreaded conversation. Years of unresolved problems and unwanted emotions clawed their way to the surface. Closing his eyes, he drew deep breaths, meditating on the tension rising in his neck muscles and the subtle clicks of his jaw. *Open hands, breathe in. Close fists, breathe out.* Even after years of separation, the anxiety never seemed to fade.

On impulse, he dialed the health center to avoid making the call. Janet, the head nurse, answered on the third ring. Cold and frank as usual, wasting no time on pleasantries.

"I'm shutting down if this wind keeps up," she said, her voice cutting through the static like a razor. "The power shorted out twice already." The antiquated building, a relic from the 1960s, groaned under the pressure of the growing community's needs and lacked the resources and equipment to deal with severe trauma or major medical procedures. Anyone who required serious attention could be stabilized only until an evacuation plane was arranged to fly them to a larger facility hundreds of miles away—if they could survive that long. Patients who remained faced power outages, a routine occurrence during the long and stormy winter. A replacement facility had been promised by the government for nearly a decade.

"I don't blame you," he said. "They really need to upgrade the electrical."

"Spit it out, Cole," she snapped, impatience dripping from her tone. "You never call unless you want something."

Cole shook his head at her ceaseless bad attitude before diving into his request: "Did Marianne have hepatitis or TB or anything?"

Having come in contact with her blood, he faced a mandatory cocktail of post-exposure antiretrovirals. The side effects of those drugs meant more headaches, fatigue, and general misery. His insomnia-induced headaches and exhaustion made him reluctant to add to his torment.

"You know I can't give out patient information."

"I don't want her medical history, just a yes or no. She spit blood in my face. Do I need to take the cocktail?"

"You need a written consent form. You know the drill."

"I just don't want to wait until she finishes sobering up to ask her for it. And we're really busy right now."

"We're all busy," she retorted.

"It's just that I'm having headaches and I'm worried about being infected or something."

"Take a Tylenol. Then get her to sign the form. Or take the cocktail. Your choice."

"I just want—" The nurse hung up.

Before he could even feel frustrated, he heard the main door chime. He cursed himself. He'd forgotten to lock it. He cringed at the thought of dealing with another needy resident, given everything on his plate.

An unfamiliar man stood behind the frosted security glass. Tall, Caucasian, bundled into a government-issue red parka. His leather satchel looked out of place, far too fashionable for the Arctic. He brushed snow off himself, then removed his fur mitts and knitted hat and tucked them under his arm. He made eye contact with Cole and grinned knowingly. Cole struggled for a name or any flicker of recognition.

"We've never formally met," the man said, extending a hand through the narrow gap in the security glass. Cole shook it, noting his firm grip and expensive watch. Up close, Cole pegged him at roughly fifty, his age betrayed by the wrinkles around his eyes when he smiled; otherwise he was aging much better than Cole. The rosiness of the stranger's frost-burnt cheeks contrasted with the pale skin of his clean-shaven neck and face. His brown hair with too little gray for his age was slicked straight back, an obvious dye job. He had a weariness in his expression, typical of Northerners, but it somehow lent him an air of refinement rather than exhaustion.

"You look familiar," Cole said. "But unless you're in trouble, I don't meet many new people."

"You said you wanted to chat about Pitseolala. I'm Felix Bauer."

Cole recognized the name from numerous files. He had messaged the social services office earlier in hopes of setting up a meeting.

"I'm Elderick, but everyone calls me Cole." He unlocked the secure inner door, motioning for Felix to enter. "I didn't expect to hear from you so quickly."

"I was about to run some errands when I got your message. I'm free now if you have time to talk."

"Of course," said Cole, the irritation from his call with the head nurse still lingering. "But I need a change of scenery."

December was an unforgiving month in the Arctic, the harsh environment at its coldest and darkest. The desolate old hotel served as a place of refuge for Cole, its common areas often vacant and always quiet. Lorraine had given him a spare key to the main door last summer while she was out of town. She never saw the need to ask for it back. Cole would dress and come down to ruminate in the empty lounge during nights when he couldn't sleep and had grown weary of his little house. The self-serve coffee maker ran all night long for the guests and the internet connection was reliable. On rare occasions, fate would provide a weary fellow traveler, another insomniac, to share a conversation.

Lorraine welcomed Cole and Felix from the kitchen door with a cursory wave, then gestured toward the dining room. A young Inuit couple with their infant daughter was eating lunch near the picture window. An unfamiliar middle-aged woman sat alone at a nearby table, drinking coffee and reading a paperback. Likely a government worker passing through town, thought Cole. The two men maneuvered through the empty tables to the back corner, away from inquisitive ears.

Once seated, Felix produced a thick file folder bound in elastic bands from his satchel, handing it to Cole. "Pits was in regular counseling with me. I thought this might be useful."

Cole accepted it with one hand and turned it so he could see the front. A white label bore the dead girl's name.

"I ran into Veronica at the post office earlier today," added Felix. "She mentioned that you were looking into Pits's suicide."

Cole clenched his teeth, unable to mask his frustration. Veronica had left town hours ago to investigate a cabin fire out on the land. He had repeatedly emphasized keeping the investigation close to her chest given its sensitive nature, but he knew she was resentful about the request for an autopsy.

"Sorry." Cole forced himself to be nice. "Our investigations aren't public knowledge. Veronica should know better."

Lorraine interrupted with a full carafe. They slid their empty cups toward her.

"It won't be decent by any means," she said flatly, pouring the coffee. "But with enough sugar and powdered cream, it's almost tolerable."

Both men stifled a laugh. "Remind me to start bringing a flask," said Cole.

Lorraine flashed her own from the pocket of her apron. "Never leave home without it."

Felix lowered his voice as Lorraine returned to the kitchen. "I hope I didn't make trouble for Veronica. I just felt a duty to help."

"It's . . . well, not your fault. Don't worry about it." Cole settled back into his chair to take weight off his aching knee. "People here get sensitive and rumors spread like cancer."

Cole pushed his coffee aside and dropped the thick file in front of him, flipping through it slowly. A few familiar names popped off the page, but in that moment, he was more concerned about his next conversation with Veronica rather than reading the contents.

Felix loosened his wool scarf, the suffocating heat in the room a stark contrast to the bitter cold outside. He propped his elbows up on the table. "All my notes are in there, and you'll find my handwriting more legible than most."

The previous social worker for the community, who was eighty pounds overweight and had a face marred by a life of chain-smoking and sunbed tanning, had left town without Cole even noticing. Outsiders filled most positions in these Arctic towns on short rotations. Burnout in the harsh conditions made for a revolving door of temporary residents. It made keeping track of people harder for the police.

"How long have you been in town?" asked Cole.

"Eight months next week. Nine months up in Pond Inlet before here. Overseas before that."

Although it would be preferable to have locals who spoke the language in these roles, the Inuit population had a low literacy rate, and few people graduated from the local high school in order to qualify for the positions. Southern transplants sought adventure, quick cash, or an escape from something worse than Arctic isolation. Teachers, nurses, police officers—few served more than two years before absconding. Cole stared out the window across the room into the darkness that obscured what should have been a view of the frozen surface of the harbor. He pondered whether the turbulent weather would pass over or coalesce into a full-blown blizzard and then made a mental note to check the forecast after he got back to the detachment.

"Were you close to her?" asked Felix, wrenching Cole back into the present moment.

Cole shook his head. "I mean, I knew her. I liked her. But I'm not close with anybody."

"Unfortunate," said Felix, analyzing the police officer in the same way Cole might have looked at his own suspects. "I mean, living like that can be a brutal existence."

Sipping on his coffee, Cole tried to hide his discomfort at the bitter taste. "It kind of comes with the job. She deserved better than what she got, that's all."

"Accepting that people sometimes take their own lives can be difficult," said Felix, staring at his own reflection in the blackness of the window. "We always want reasons, but sometimes we don't get closure."

"I don't blame myself. I just didn't see it coming."

"I did," confessed Felix.

The revelation caught Cole by surprise, and he focused entirely on the social worker. Lorraine unexpectedly shuffled toward them with a notepad in her hand. Both men went quiet. She brought an odor of fresh cigarette smoke with her to the table.

"Either of you eating?" she asked.

They exchanged glances before both shaking their heads at Lorraine.

"Neither of you are helping with my retirement savings," she said with a raspy laugh and a smirk. "Let me know if you change your mind."

Felix waited until she was out of earshot before speaking again.

"Hindsight is a critical lens. I'm sure you did all you could." He lowered his voice. "I am trained to spot the warning signs of something like this. Looking back, they were all there—risk-taking, substance abuse, mood swings. I'd only realized it after it was too late."

Cole nodded, suddenly filled with self-doubt, unsure if he could have prevented her death even if he had known.

"I'll have a word with Veronica discreetly," Cole said, shaking off the feeling. "In the meantime, I'd appreciate it if you kept the investigation to yourself."

"I'm a social worker in a small town," said Felix, pulling on his parka. "Other people's secrets are something I'm good at keeping."

Felix paused to don his hat and mitts, leaving his coffee untouched. Cole watched as he geared up for the cold weather.

"Can I ask you something?" inquired Felix, standing now with his hand on the back of the chair. "Do these types of investigations usually drag on?" Felix paused, choosing his wording carefully. "I only ask because her family has asked me about getting her body for the funeral."

Cole hesitated, considering the level of detail in his forthcoming answer. "Sometimes."

Felix nodded, waiting for him to elaborate, soon realizing nothing else was coming.

"She was a sweet girl in a hard world. Let me know if I can do anything else."

Back at the detachment, Cole sat at his desk, where a disorganized stack of unfinished occurrence reports loomed. The envelope containing the unread documents from the Carter lawsuit sat on top, a time bomb. A civil decision against him would likely leave him bankrupt and destroy whatever was left of his career, unless the administration moved to cut ties before then to avoid the embarrassment. Whispers of his ex-wife's scolding about procrastination and not taking responsibility echoed in his mind. He chided himself for not facing up to those possibilities like a man.

He changed desks to hide it all from his view and tugged a scratch pad free from a cluttered drawer. He needed something to take his mind off his impending doom. Sometimes getting all the evidence on paper helped to clarify a case in his mind, arranging the jigsaw puzzle pieces to form a border, hoping the finished edges would contain the chaos within.

Cole wrestled with every possible clue or question in the case and jotted them down. Minutes metastasized into an hour before he analyzed the list. If there was a common thread or possible alternative narrative, he couldn't see it clearly yet. A sinking feeling of uncertainty crept in, and Veronica's whispers mingled with his ex's familiar accusations. *Am I overthinking this?* No, the devil was in the details, he was sure of it.

When he rose for yet another cup of coffee to jump-start his fatigued mind, the shrill ring of the cordless phone grated on his last nerve. Cole zeroed in on the receiver across the room as it rang a second time.

"Maata is gone," said Ooloota Killiktee in a calm tone. "She's missing again."

Ooloota was an Inuit single mother in her mid-forties who worked at the post office. She had a handful of kids who were often in minor trouble, most notably her teenage daughter, Maata, whose behavioral issues had been escalating in recent months.

"When did you last see her?" asked Cole.

"Maybe three days. She took my purse. I need it back." Her voice was laced with desperation.

As Cole mulled over potential locations, his brain struggled to function through a fog of exhaustion. "Have you checked Sonnie's place, or over at Elisapee's house?"

"She's not there. I don't want her to get in trouble. I just need my purse."

"All right, I'll look around and get back to you," Cole assured her. The weight of yet another responsibility settled heavily on his shoulders as the call ended abruptly, without the customary goodbyes. Telephone etiquette was very different in the Northern communities, with little in the way of pleasantries or introductions. That had been a cultural adjustment since he arrived.

A bolt of inspiration hit Cole out of the blue when he recalled that Maata had been spending time around Pierre Jardin. His name had been etched onto the top of Cole's scratch pad, underlined with purpose. But then a glance at Pitseolala's file struck a chord within him that sent shivers down his spine: Weren't Maata and Pits good friends?

"Shit." Cole cursed himself for not making the connection earlier. The possibility of a copycat death emerged, ominous and palpable. Small-town suicides hit young people harder than most, and without proper infrastructure to deal with counseling, more fatalities were often the result. And when he considered that Pitseolala may have truly been murdered, the specter of a second killing loomed large in his mind. The urgency of the situation propelled Cole into action, but before he could throw on his parka, Veronica stepped through the front door in a gust of swirling snow.

CHAPTER 13

Maliktu couldn't recall the tent fire that disfigured him as a toddler. Fragmented, hazy snippets from the hospital lingered in his head—endless hallways, strangers in masks, and more pain than any child should ever have to bear. He'd often forget the extent of the burns on his face and torso until he encountered a repulsed expression at the local store or chanced upon his reflection. The bullies in his age group existed solely to refresh his memory, and his scar tissue served as a haunting reminder to everyone else in the community.

Uncertainty plagued him; there were too many gaps in his memory. His grandmother had shown him pictures of his face before the fire, and everyone else told ever-changing stories of the tragedy. Were any of his recollections real, or had his brain simply manufactured them based on what he'd been told? To the best of his knowledge, he was three years old when a kerosene lantern tipped over, setting the fabric of his parents' *tupiq* aflame in the middle of the night. Pitseolala, nine at the time, often recounted how their mother and sister had been overwhelmed, lungs destroyed by acrid smoke, bodies scorched by the hungry flames, wailing and screeching as they perished in the raging fire. His injured father carried both Maliktu and Pitseolala, trudging toward safety for hour after hour through the drifting snow and relentless wind, until he collapsed of smoke inhalation and ultimately died in a hospital.

The permafrost of the Arctic is too hard for tent pegs, so guide ropes must be tied to heavy stones. When their grandfather had taken them more than sixty miles to Tulukaat Island, where the ravens nested in huge groups, Pitseolala had shown Maliktu the circle of rocks where the tent had allegedly burned and the moss-filled crater where their father supposedly collapsed. A few weeks later, the location of her story shifted to only a stone's throw from their community, where they happened to be walking. Whenever she told him the tale, the details always varied—winter hunting expeditions or spring camping trips, sealskin or canvas tents. He was never sure which version he believed.

Perhaps his sister, like him, had also forgotten and filled her gaps with fiction to keep the wolves of confusion at bay. During sleepless nights, he would fixate on snow swirling under the streetlights outside his frosted window and question whether the tent story was even genuine. Perhaps it was a cabin, like the one he recently burned, or a vacant house, like the one that burned last summer near the southern edge of town. Its destruction was never his intention; he had learned to better control the fire since then.

The flames held the only nugget of truth in all those stories, leaving their unforgiving marks all over his body as tangible proof. In moments of solitude and loneliness, he closed his eyes and thought about the fire—so beautiful, so purifying, and oh so warm even on the coldest of nights. And whenever he wanted to rid himself of anything that troubled him, anything that conjured up his anger and frustration, he summoned those flames to repay the debt they owed him. And they never disappointed.

Inside the house where his sister died, Maliktu held the flickering lighter high above his head, his tired and bruised shoulder aching with the sustained effort. The temperature in the empty dwelling remained well below freezing without a working furnace, but its shelter was a welcome respite from the bitter wind. His earlier struggle on the compacted snow had left him bruised and battered, but he'd received worse beatings. He gingerly explored a loose tooth with his tongue, wiggling the insecure fang back and forth, tasting the metallic tang of blood in his mouth. He pressed his jaw closed, once, twice, exploring the threshold of pain. When he found it to be tolerable, he snapped the lighter shut and tipped his head back in relief, letting out a long exhale that crystallized in the meager light filtering through the adjacent window.

A strong gust shook the wooden bones of the building, causing it to shiver and groan. His heart skipped a beat at the sudden noise. Maliktu spun around and fumbled with the dead bolt behind him to lock it. The cruel kids who had assaulted him in the street had vanished, but he wasn't sure for how long. He thought of how he'd seen them through his fingers, such terrible creatures with hideous expressions. Anxiety gnawed at his mind before a chilling realization settled over him. Had the visions been increasing since he stopped taking the pills? Was he really grappling with monsters and ghosts, or the misguided products of his own malfunctioning imagination?

The sudden headlights of a passing vehicle threw sprawling shadows across the naked walls, shifting and morphing them into elusive shapes and forms, some good, some evil. His disoriented thoughts continued to spiral into uncertainty. He briefly considered checking the windows to see if the bullies still lurked outside but decided it was safer to stay out of sight.

Numbness clung to the boy's limbs after the long trek back across the sea ice from the stranded snowmobile. Pins and needles jabbed deep into his fingers and toes; he needed to move. He felt his way along the hallway, guided by the ambient glow from the back-door window, partially obscured by duct tape and cardboard. He shook his arms and legs violently to get his circulation flowing before shuffling into the kitchen, a reluctant swimmer preparing to dive into icy waters. Broken glass glittered faintly across the tile floor. A gut feeling told Maliktu that this was where his sister had died.

He stared up toward the ceiling, searching for some sign of where the rope had hung, but found only darkness. He shut his eyes and tried to absorb any remaining trace of his sister in the room. In the midst of his concentration, he recalled the ravenous flames of the shack licking at the night sky and longed for the comforting warmth of the fire on his scarred face. Opening his eyes, he pulled out his sister's lighter, eager to spark it up again, to see its flame reignited. His heartbeat relaxed at the sight of it, steady and even, as the oscillating light sent shadows dancing all around him. Grinning slightly and tenderly, he closed his eyes again, allowing the afterimage of the flame to linger on his retinas. A fragrance of woodsmoke, kerosene, and burning plastic embedded in the fabric of his parka flooded his senses. An eerie calm washed over him, finding solace in the presence of fire.

He reached into the pocket of his parka and fondled the handle of the flare gun for some kind of reassurance, some kind of protection against the melancholy. The children at school, from youngest to oldest, mocked his appearance. Some were afraid of it; others openly repulsed by it. He had no friends in this little community. And now that his sister was gone, he realized he was truly alone.

The wastebasket in the corner caught his eye. It overflowed with combustibles. He could torch the house like he did the shack, wipe all trace of this terrible place from the world. He imagined them all trapped inside, his whole school choking on the acrid smoke and screaming as their flesh burned as his had burned. Let them see what he could do, let them see his inferno, a fire large enough to bring the whole town running. Clicking the lighter open and closed like a boy possessed, he made his way to the cupboard beneath the sink. Tearing it open, he pulled out every bottle with a "flammable" warning and proceeded to empty them over the wastebasket. The chemical stench seared his throat and made his eyes water. Stepping back, he held the lighter at eye level, ready to spark the whole damned thing, his heartbeat fluttering with anticipation, the fire rising up within him, but as his thumb touched the flint wheel, a familiar voice cried out: "Stop!"

The sudden utterance startled him, and he turned abruptly, nearly losing his balance and fumbling with the lighter. It clattered to the floor and disappeared beneath the kitchen table. He dove after it, hands flailing, his fingers catching the edge and sending it scattering farther across the floor into a patch of light below the window. He leapt to his feet, arms shielding his face, bracing himself for another attack as he snatched up the lighter. When the assault didn't come, he lowered his hands and froze. He stared into the shadowy corner from where the shout originated.

"We're safe in here," a voice murmured. Maliktu recognized it immediately as that of his sister, but somehow altered, older, crackled and broken, as if transmitted through a faulty telephone line. How could she still be here, still be alive? A fleeting smile blessed his lips, then faded as he recalled their encounter at the seal hole, when he nearly drowned.

"No need to burn," said Pitseolala, her voice rising in volume and confidence. "They can't come in. I won't let them."

Maliktu clutched the lighter tightly inside his little fist. Pitseolala's pale face materialized from the gloom behind the door, emerging from the shadows like the sleek head of a bone-white beluga surfacing from the black depths of the moonlit waters. A miasma of decomposing meat and aged seal fat spread out through the room, causing him to recoil in disgust. Her skin appeared bloodless and translucent. One eye, cloudy and opaque, encircled in black eye shadow, peered out through her tangled tresses. This was not the sister he had known and loved, but an empty apparition, as if her image and her voice emanated from somewhere eons away.

He shut his eyes tight and tried to imagine his sister as she was in life, only to be confronted by the dreadful face from the seal hole—eyes blank, mouth agape, long black hair swirling in the icy void. Stepping backward, overwhelmed by the horrible memory, he felt lightheaded and gasped for air.

She retreated into the shadows, as if sensing the terror in her little brother. Her sudden movement snapped him back to reality. "There's no time for fear," she said. "I'm fading, falling apart." When she spoke, desperation flowed through her voice, a tone he'd known when she was alive and on the verge of tears, in moments of anger or sorrow.

Reluctantly opening his eyes, one at a time, Maliktu peered into the void behind the door. Pitseolala's presence permeated the room, swirling all around him, pressing against his skin. A nervous laugh escaped him at the unsettling thought of her not being dead. Tears of horror and grief streamed down his cheeks.

"All the other children he's taken," said Pitseolala, stammering out the words between anguished sobs. "They are all in here with me." She concluded with a deep moan, her voice doubling and tripling and quadrupling into a chorus of tormented children all keening through her gaping mouth. The cacophony rose to deafening levels, swarming Maliktu's senses with disorder and confusion. He dropped to his knees, hands pressed to his ears, unable to think, unable to shut out the sound.

Pitseolala emerged from the nothingness behind him and wrapped her arms around her brother in a loving embrace. The foul odor of the room transmuted into the scent of flowery perfume—a fragrance he used to hate but now sorely missed. The voices dissipated. Her long black hair wrapped tight around them, enshrouding brother and sister like a thick cocoon, leaving only their heads exposed.

"*Kuukutsi* needs you," she whispered into his ear. "He needs your fire to kill the devil." Her phantom breath felt hot and tangible on his skin. "Will you help him?"

There was no hesitation in the boy's mind; he knew in his gut what he must do. But when Maliktu parted his lips to respond, her fingers slipped into his mouth, prying it apart, forcing his jaws to their limits. Foul liquid from her rotting flesh ran down his throat, causing his eyes to well up and bulge. He gagged on the taste, icy and putrid, her entire hand now thrust into his gaping maw. At the moment he was certain he would vomit, her hand withdrew gracefully, presenting the loose tooth between her filthy, decomposing fingers. Warm blood pooled beneath his tongue and trickled down over his bottom lip. The straitjacket of black hair that once restricted him slithered away into the darkness, her presence dissipating like a memory unable to be recalled. The discarded tooth clattered on the frosted tile floor, ushering in an eerie silence in the vacant kitchen.

Maliktu left the house and stood outside in the snow. Days of ceaseless fatigue draped over his shoulders like a weighted blanket, further burdening his weary and aching limbs. The polar conditions had warmed up slightly since he'd abandoned the machine out on the sea ice, signaling a likely blizzard coming toward the community. Soft, plump snowflakes fell from an unseen cloud in the dark expanse above him. The distant, growling rumble of a snowmobile reverberated off the nearby houses, concealing both its location and its destination. He peered out toward the edge of town, where the darkness met the light, and resolved that if he was going to meet the policeman and aid his sister, he would first need to rest. With the source of his flame nestled in his pocket and the promise of an adult's help, he puffed out his chest in a gesture of bravery and clutched the knife in his pocket. Fear and heartache lingered, but it was anger that simmered in his rib cage.

If a devil had taken his sister from him, it had best prepare itself for war.

CHAPTER 14

Veronica stomped her feet on the well-worn mat to remove any remaining snow. A short blast of cold air ripped through the detachment via the open door. Shivers rippled down Cole's arms. Trudging into the office, she removed her winter gear and tossed it onto a nearby chair without acknowledging her partner's presence. Her snowmobile keys clattered across the tarnished surface of her desk, grating against the silence of the room.

"You check the weather for this evening?" she asked when she returned from the break room with a coffee in her hand. She struggled to see the surface of the bay ice through the frosted window. Her warm breath left a ghostly impression on the cold pane.

"My life has been depressing enough lately," he mumbled.

She ignored him. "Blizzard might hit full-on by the weekend if it doesn't veer south."

Cole wrestled with the delicate task of confronting her about leaking confidential info, unable to think of a decent way to do so.

"Supposed to be bad," she continued. "Gusting over a hundred."

"Felix dropped by." He threw the comment out there and paused, waiting for her reaction.

"The more I think about it, the more I'm certain that an autopsy is a terrible idea," she said flatly.

"We've been through this already," said Cole, sounding exasperated.

"Nothing is going to bring that family more peace than a funeral," she insisted.

"I know. But the more I think about this case, the more sure I am that we need to keep digging."

She locked eyes with him for the first time since entering the building. "For what? It doesn't take a detective to figure out what went down in that kitchen."

He let out a snort of nervous laughter. "You know exactly what I'm talking about."

"If you don't think she hung herself, then you don't know what it feels like to be a sixteen-year-old girl in Cape Dorset."

"I don't need to *feel* anything. I need facts. That's what *we* go by."

She laughed a little too loudly. It stunned him; he found himself stammering, fumbling for words.

"The *fact* is, people around here need closure," she said before he could muster a coherent sentence.

Gritting his teeth, he reminded himself that she spoke out of frustration, not malice. He inhaled deeply to gather himself. The ceiling lights seemed whiter than usual, more stark.

"You're *sure* someone else was involved?" she asked. "Is that facts, or your gut talking?" She gestured to the hefty manila envelope on his desk.

His cheeks flushed at her nod to the unopened package. He picked it up. His eyes narrowed in suspicion, and he wondered if she'd heard about the latest developments in the lawsuit. She'd obviously known about the disciplinary hearings and the reasons for his transfer. Gossip spread quickly among police officers, even to those at the edge of the world. She already knew how the failure of his intuition led to the Carter boy's death. He'd let that slip during the summer while they were camping out on the land, when they were still getting to know each other. He tossed the envelope into the nearby wastebasket in an effort to make it seem meaningless.

"You think I'm gonna fuck this up like I did with the kid in the river?"

"I think we need to stop talking now."

"You don't trust my judgment," he continued, his volume rising.

"That's not what I said. You're letting your emotions speak for you."

"But that's what you meant." Even as he spoke, Cole felt his self-doubt shifting into defensive anger, but he couldn't stop himself. He put a hand to his brow to shade his eyes from the glaring overheads. His mouth went bone-dry and he reached across his desk for a nonexistent coffee cup.

Veronica averted her gaze. "Do whatever you're gonna do. Just go back to work before you say something stupid."

Exhaustion and chronic stress had weakened his resolve, and his self-control ebbed away. The phone rang on the desk between them. Pressure increased behind his eyes at the noise, another migraine in the making. "Now I'm stupid?"

"Your words, not mine," she said, collecting items from her desk to relocate to one of the private offices.

The ringing persisted. He dragged his fingers roughly through his disheveled hair. A phantom belt tightened around his chest, making it difficult to breathe. "I was lucky enough to find someone to steer me away from the ditch at sixteen," he snarled. "She had nobody. The least I can give her case is the time and energy she deserved."

"Well, don't expect any applause from me," Veronica shot back, pointing at the ringing phone. "And you can take her family's calls from here on out."

"Fine." His voice escalated and his hands trembled. "But in the meantime, try not to broadcast our investigation to the whole fucking town."

She gathered up an armload of occurrence reports from the nearest desk. "It's not ours, it's yours," she said, loud enough for the prisoners in cells to hear, before stepping into the interview room and slamming the door behind her.

Righteous indignation swirled through him. *Fuck her.* The phone rang yet again. His headache spiked, a relentless throbbing in his skull. He picked up the receiver and jammed it back down repeatedly until the cradle cracked.

He needed to get outside.

Cole had almost cooled down enough to think about something else when he stopped outside Pierre Jardin's house. He blocked the bootlegger's expensive new Jeep Grand Cherokee in his driveway. Anything that couldn't fit as cargo on the daily scheduled planes came to town by freighter ship in the few summer months when the ocean wasn't frozen. Jardin brought the flashy vehicle up on the July barge, flaunting his illicit income to both community leaders and local law enforcement.

Opening the door for a moment, Cole poured the cold remains of his seventh coffee of the day on the snow. He wished he had something stronger to replace it. He killed the engine and held his breath, counting to ten to calm his nerves, his ears attuned to the steady roar of the gale outside. The wind had intensified since he left the detachment. He stepped out and confronted the elements, lumbering up the smooth walkway to the front door. Jardin didn't need to shovel it; the foot traffic of frequent customers kept the snow well compacted. Cole had known about his recent expansion from bootlegging into drugs before sales even began. Nothing stayed secret in this town for too long.

Without knocking, he pushed open the front door. Oppressive heat greeted him as he stepped into the darkened house. A blazing red-hot element on the stove cast the kitchen in a hellish glow. The smell of freshly burnt hashish suffused the room. Neglect was everywhere—overflowing garbage, dirty dishes on every surface, and an infant abandoned in a high chair. Despite having dried tomato sauce and noodles smeared all over its head and face, the child slept undisturbed. An electronic scale and a pile of weed sat on the table.

Navigating through the haze of thick smoke, Cole wet a dishrag at the sink and gently tended to the baby, discovering a discolored bruise on its forearm. The child stirred at the touch of the warm cloth but fell back to sleep, its head drooping to one side. No sounds of life except a muffled heavy metal tune droning from a stereo down the hall. A smoldering roach in the ashtray on the counter told him he wasn't alone with the baby.

Despondent rage, dense and suffocating, surged through Cole as he stared at the vulnerable child. More than just anger, this was decades of unresolved resentment rising from the depths of his own neglected childhood. Painful memories intertwined with images from the grotesque archive of victims' injuries stored on his hard drive. In that moment, he wanted to destroy everything around him. He wanted to cease to exist.

He stayed near the kitchen table with his eyes closed, listening to the muffled drums and bass line from the stereo down the hall, until he had composed himself enough to search the rest of the house. In the living room, an Inuit boy slumbered on the couch, old-school headphones covering his ears with a muted television flickering.

A toilet flushed down the hall. Jardin shuffled into the kitchen. Mid-thirties, shoulder-length hair, bare-chested in a robe and boxer briefs. The bootlegger barked out swear words as he tossed various containers and dishes around the countertop before finding his half-finished joint. Cole observed a crude skull etched into his left forearm to balance the older tattoo of an anchor on his right. A souvenir of his recent stint inside, he wagered. Jardin's abdomen was covered with a support bandage, his ribs broken from a snowmobile accident two weeks earlier. His latest girlfriend, Sheila, had been riding on the back of the vehicle and needed to be medically evacuated to the hospital with a broken femur. Cole didn't have enough evidence to prove a case of impaired driving.

"This place has really gone to shit since Sheila left," said Cole, announcing his presence.

Jardin glared at the unwelcome officer in his kitchen. Cole recognized that look of defiance; he'd seen it in other suspects over the years. None of those confrontations had ended without violence. A big part of him hoped this one wouldn't either, despite his current injuries.

"What the fuck are you doing in my house?" demanded Jardin, tossing the ashtray into the kitchen sink with a jarring clank. His scowl wavered when Cole picked up the bag of marijuana from the table.

"Is this yours?" asked Cole.

"You need a fucking warrant for that," he shot back.

"Oh, you're a lawyer now? I thought you were still a bootlegging, drug-peddling piece of shit."

Jardin gestured toward the teenager in the living room. "That's Noah's stash."

"How much do we have here?" asked Cole, hefting the bag as if to estimate its weight. "Three years, maybe four with your record."

Jardin cast an obvious glance at the gleaming knives on a distant rack. Before he could reach them, Cole rushed forward, seizing him by the throat and slamming him against the kitchen counter.

"You went for a blade. I don't think I need a warrant anymore."

Jardin squealed as his tender rib cage arched over the sharp edge of the counter.

"What about the scale and the baggies?" barked Cole. "Are they Noah's too?"

His throat was constricted, but the bootlegger managed a barely audible "yes." Cole leaned in with all his weight. The injured man moaned pitifully under the pressure.

"You're going back to jail," Cole smirked.

Jardin grabbed the arm that was choking him with both hands and wheezed loudly as the pressure intensified.

"What were you doing with Pitseolala on the night she died?" Cole loosened his grip just enough to let him answer.

"I don't have anything to do with that bitch," croaked Jardin.

The final word sparked a renewed rage in Cole. He leaned in again, harder this time. Jardin responded with a pitiful moan.

"Don't fucking lie to me; someone saw you with her."

Jardin's tone grew desperate. "I swear to God, I don't have nothing to do with her."

Cole eased up on the pressure to relieve his throbbing knee more than to grant Jardin any mercy. "What kind of vodka are you selling?"

"I ain't selling," he said between labored breaths.

Jardin's moaning escalated. He pushed at Cole's face with the heel of his hand when he felt his ribs cracking under his weight.

"Bullshit!" said Cole. He lifted a butter knife with a hash-burnt blade from the counter and held it up for Jardin to see. "You should be careful doing hot knives. It's really easy to burn yourself."

Cole tucked the blade into the hot coils of the burner under the watchful eye of Jardin.

"Russian Prince," Jardin spat out between sobs, pleading with his eyes. Cole released him and stepped backward. Jardin collapsed to the floor in an awkward heap. He groaned like a wounded animal.

"Then who's selling Absolut Vodka?" demanded Cole.

"It's gotta be the construction guys," cried Jardin, tears streaming. "They're the only ones selling liquor besides me."

Cole's thoughts drifted to Aiden, the construction worker Miller told him about, and the other migrants. He stuffed the bag of weed into his parka pocket and picked up the electronic scale. "I'm taking these for disposal. No charges. And we're not done talking about Pits."

"You re-broke my fucking ribs," screamed Jardin from the floor between coughing fits. The teenager, now awake, stood in the doorway of the living room, eyes darting back and forth between the two adults. Cole flashed him a friendly smile, then turned back to Jardin.

"You've got twenty-four hours to get rid of the liquor and weed. I'll be back tomorrow with a warrant."

"This is assault and robbery! I'm gonna sue!"

Cole walked back over and squatted beside Jardin, his bad knee protesting as it bent to take his weight. Half the misery and tragedy he'd seen up here came from substance abuse; he focused all his rage and frustration on the man making money from the suffering.

"If I find anything here tomorrow, I'll tell everyone in town that you got her drunk and told her to kill herself," said Cole. "You'll be dead by the fucking weekend."

Jardin put his head down and continued to whine about his ribs under his breath. Cole paused at the table on his way out and threw the wet rag he'd used to clean the baby at the fallen man's face. "You're lucky I don't arrest you for child abuse."

As Cole withdrew, a prolonged crash sounded from the far end of the hallway. His eyes shifted back and forth from the unlit corridor to the panicked face of Jardin on the floor.

"You can't go back there," stammered Jardin as Cole rushed into the hallway.

Undeterred, he stumbled forward, the music growing louder over the continued noise of breaking glass. Bitterly cold air and the smell of spilled vodka hit Cole as he rushed into the far bedroom. A panicked Inuit girl wearing only an oversize T-shirt and panties crouched on the top of the dresser next to a gaping window, its curtains fluttering inward.

Maata. He raised a hand toward her and started to say her name. Before he could make a sound, she flung herself out the window headfirst. A bewildered Cole stood amid a room strewn with shattered liquor bottles and thundering heavy metal from a nearby stereo while Jardin howled in the background.

Below, six feet down, the half-naked girl scrambled to her feet on a black sheet of ice and dashed off through ankle-deep snow into the surrounding darkness.

CHAPTER 15

A few blocks from his house, Cole reduced his speed when a pack of kids came into view on the icy road ahead. Children playing at all hours wasn't an unusual occurrence in Cape Dorset. They were often up all night, roaming the roads in packs, using conveniently placed snowdrifts to access rooftops and high windows for mischievous fun. Sometimes the cold streets were safer than home when their parents were drinking.

What time was it anyway? The clock in the truck had died weeks ago, and the constant darkness of the Arctic winter made keeping track of time feel pointless. After a long search for the runaway girl in the deteriorating weather, an exhausted Cole had thrown in the towel, leaving Veronica and a handful of volunteers to keep looking. Maata would likely freeze to death before they found her. He closed his eyes tight and opened them, trying to stay focused through the swirling snow in front of the headlights. Pitseolala's lifeless expression haunted him, her death clouding his mind, his adrenaline still pumping from the altercation with Jardin. The smell of the confiscated weed filled the cab of the truck, the scent swirling in the air from the exhaust of the dashboard vents.

The children stood in the road under the streetlight, a few feet apart in a semicircle. They took turns throwing rocks at the base of the pole with big windups and deep follow-throughs. Unfazed by his approach, they didn't move, so he made a wide, slow arc around them to the right. He was accustomed to having to do so with the local kids, who seemed oblivious to traffic. The situation appeared ordinary. Until he saw the dog.

It was huddled in a shadow behind the base of the light post. Tail between its legs, paws together, head down. Cole squinted hard, trying to comprehend what he was watching as he put the truck in park. The shaggy mutt stood in deep snow, tethered to the wooden pole with a thick length of chain. It had become entangled in the guide wires that supported the lamppost, leaving only a foot of slack for it to move.

Before he could reach for the door handle, one of the children, a boy about eight years old in a brown jacket, struck the dog in its side with a fist-sized stone. Unable to avoid it, the dog yelped loud enough for Cole to hear it through the glass and over the noise of the heater. He leapt out. His boots hit the ground as a second kid hit the dog with another rock. It screeched in pain.

"What the fuck is wrong with you!" he shouted, grabbing the nearest kid by the jacket, jerking one of his legs off the ground as a third child wound up and narrowly missed the dog's head. Cole held out his palm toward the children in protest. "Put the rocks down!"

None of the children obeyed his order. Instead, they stared at him with blank faces, frost-burnt cheeks, and snotty noses. The dog slunk behind the pole again, desperate for cover. Cole's face flushed; his eyes narrowed.

"Are you trying to fucking kill him?" he asked, his gaze flicking from child to child.

A wall of silent and confused expressions confronted him. They looked from the dog to the big man and back to the dog.

"Answer me!" he shouted. "What the hell are you doing?"

An Inuit boy in a stained green parka, with a mustache of mucus, piped up, "Throwing rocks at the dog."

His brain hurt. He wiped the dry corners of his mouth with the back of his free hand and held a deep, cold inhale in his lungs before letting it out slowly. Their heads were engulfed in crystal clouds with each frozen exhale. Their faces looked tired but mostly bored. Their eyes, dead.

"You're hurting the dog," he said, trying to reason with them. "Can't you see that?"

Silence. Blank looks, slack expressions.

His confusion shifted into rage. "Would you like me to chain you up and throw rocks at you?" he asked, shaking the boy he was still holding. His glare whipped from one child to another.

"No," said one of the children, all of them either scrunching their faces or shaking their heads.

He released the boy from his grip, sending him sprawling to the ground. As he stepped toward the nearest child to take the rock from his hand, he recognized the girl next to him. It took him a moment to realize she had recently visited the police detachment with her mother, who was selling sealskin mittens she had sewn. She stared right through Cole as if he were a ghost.

He looked to the windows of the houses around him for a possible witness, an adult who should have seen this madness and stepped in. There was nothing but darkness beyond the circle of the streetlamp and the truck's headlights. The oldest-looking boy, who couldn't have been more than twelve, stepped toward him. Cole instinctively rested his hand on his baton.

"Drop the rocks," he said. "Now!"

One boy in the back let the rock slip from his fingers and then the girl tossed hers weakly to the side. Slowly, reluctantly, the others followed suit, all staring at Cole, as if trying to anticipate his next move. His voice shook, blood warming his frosted cheeks.

"Get out of here!" He gripped his baton handle tight in the holster to steady himself. "Go on, go home!"

He waved them away with his free arm. The children turned and shuffled off, heads bowed in disappointment. They congregated beneath the outside light of a nearby house to watch what the officer would do next.

Cole moved toward the dog as it whimpered uncontrollably, approaching it slowly in a crouch with his fist extended for the animal to smell it. The dog hesitated but then sniffed his hand reluctantly. He held his fist there for a long time. He touched the dog's head gently and scratched at its neck.

"It's okay, boy." He dropped his voice to a whisper. "It's okay. I'm not gonna hurt you."

The ring that held the chain to the pole was encrusted with a thick layer of ice. He walked to the truck, glancing over at the children huddled together in the shadows beside the house. He pulled the bolt cutters from the tool bin in the bed of the truck. The dog started whining and barking. He clamped the cutters on the thick chain at the base of the pole and struggled to push the handles together. It wouldn't budge. The chain was too thick with ice. He went at it again, his neck muscles bulging, his back arched hard. He released the cutters and closed them. Wielding them like a baseball bat, he pounded away at the ice-covered chain in frustration. The chain bounced and shook, vibrating the supporting wires with a steady twang. One, two, three blows sent shattered ice spraying everywhere.

Without warning, the frightened dog leapt toward Cole with a snarl, coming at him from the side. He avoided the animal's advancing jaws by inches. He stumbled backward on the slippery stones as the dog bared its teeth and barked in a frenzy, continuing to lunge at him. Only the length of the chain kept him from being bitten. Cole fell hard against the rocks, striking his elbow on the frozen ground, a rocket of pain paralyzing his left arm. His bad knee buckled at an awkward sideways angle, and he hollered in agony. As he righted himself, the dog barked frantically, choking itself on the chain with each leap toward him. He crab-walked toward the truck and pulled himself to his feet using the rear bumper. He took a few tentative steps, easing weight onto his bad leg, surveying the extent of the damage. With each step, pain rippled through his torso. He opened the driver's side door, flinging in the bolt cutters first. He used the inner handle above the window to pull himself up into the front seat and slammed the door.

Cole screamed in frustration, pounding his fists like meaty hammers on the steering wheel. Agony seared his knee; his elbow was numb. He leaned back, grimacing as he tried to steady his shaking arms by gripping the wheel. The muffled sound of the barking dog filled his head. Heat flooded his face. The kids, still shuffling in the shadows nearby, were throwing hard chunks of snow at one another. In the darkness of the truck's cab, he screamed in rage and desperation until he couldn't scream anymore.

When the truck reached the end of the road, he stopped rubbing his knee and picked up the handheld radio. Someone would be able to track down the owner of the dog. Then, in a moment of clarity, he realized he had no idea who he was going to call. He looked at the broken clock. He didn't know what hour it was, or even what day it was. Insomnia and constant night calls had destroyed any sense of time he had left. When was the last night he slept more than a couple hours at a stretch? How did he even get here, to this street, to this town?

As he re-clipped the radio to its dashboard mount, Cole saw the children in the rearview mirror, circling the dog again. He watched them as they moved into the light, then he looked away. Their dead eyes and blank expressions flashed in his mind. Then Pitseolala's vacant eyes. Followed by the sleeping baby with the dirty face in the high chair. All lifeless, all empty. He thought of his childhood dog and imagined it being tortured with stones. Drawing breath became increasingly difficult, and he suddenly felt lightheaded. He stopped the truck. The children shuffled closer to the dog in the rearview. The animal was suffering. He had to do something. Anything.

Cole made a two-point turn on the narrow road and drove behind the semicircle of children. He left the engine running and slid gingerly out of the driver's side door with a painful grimace, leaving it ajar. It seemed colder outside than before and the wind had picked up; a specter made of snowflakes swirled in the light of the lamppost. The injured dog limped around behind the icy pole, desperate for cover as the children moved in. Cole clenched his teeth and hobbled forward, each step thrusting hot needles into his kneecap.

The children froze, stones in their hands, turning to look at Cole as he moved through their ranks toward the dog. He stopped where he had fallen on the icy rocks, making sure he was out of reach of the wounded dog's jaws. The canine raised its head slightly at the sight of the officer, its neck stiff with hackles raised along its arched spine. Its black upper lip lifted just enough to show a thin white strip of teeth beneath. Cole felt a moment of vulnerability with his back to the children and their stones. He closed his eyes, taking one last inhale, feeling the cold sting in his nasal passages.

In one fluid motion, he pulled the pistol from his holster, disengaged the safety, and fired three times. Two in the body, one in the head. Blood fanned out behind the fallen animal in a violet spray on the white snow. He closed his eyes again, but the outline of the animal was burned into his mind with the flash of the muzzle. He re-holstered his gun, opened his eyes, and hobbled back the way he came. All the way to the truck, through the crowd of stunned children, his gaze clung to the frozen ground. His ears still rang as he pulled the gearshift into drive.

CHAPTER 16

Cole limped back out into his kitchen. The frigid tiles stung his calloused feet. He had just shelved his groceries in his dimly lit pantry. He tried not to think about his failed attempts at eating better and getting back into fighting shape. Frozen pizzas, sugary-drink crystals, processed meats. Comfort food for the endless winter. His neck ached as he rolled his head from side to side, attempting to work out the knots acquired from lugging shopping bags in from the truck. His lower back ached and his knee throbbed. His elbow had swelled considerably, now too tender to touch.

The mountain of dishes in the sink made him cringe. *Tomorrow,* he promised himself for the third day in a row. He plucked a half-clean glass from the pile, wiped the lip on his fleece pants, and washed down two blue pills for the persistent pain. The image of the dead dog crept back into his mind, regret tearing at his gut. He shouldn't have killed the helpless creature in front of the children. He'd lost control. It was suffering, he reminded himself repeatedly. Trapped on a frozen chain, tortured, injured—nothing else he could've done. Later, he would have to get rid of the carcass. But for now, he needed a drink.

He collapsed on the couch, scotch in hand, cubes clinking against the glass. The half-empty bottle stood on the coffee table. Leaning back, he fixated on the ceiling until he found the strength to move. He fumbled to open his laptop. No new messages. Still no responses to anything he had sent. His fingers clacked on the keyboard, entering the search terms "Carter" and "Cole," only to close the browser and shut the laptop hard. *Not now.*

He dialed Rebecca's cell number, assuming she hadn't changed it. When she answered the phone, bustling noises and voices told him that she was out with friends on a city street, a landscape far removed from his reality. He couldn't see the clock from his position on the couch, but it was three hours earlier in Vancouver.

"Did you get Chloe's message?" she asked.

"No. Did she call here or my work?"

"She didn't say."

"I never got the message," he deflected, taking a slow drink, trying not to let her hear the ice rattling.

"She went down some steps on her bike. She had to go to the ER."

"Was she drunk?" he asked.

"Is that really your first concern?"

Strike one. He rubbed the thumb of his drink hand on his forehead. "Is she okay?"

"Why don't you call her back to find out?"

A large vehicle roared past on the other end of the line; a woman laughed in the background. He swallowed hard, struggling for a connection, something to keep the conversation alive.

"How are you?" he asked. "How's Lionel?"

"Please don't pretend you give a shit."

She knew he despised the man who'd taken her from him. *Strike two.*

"We haven't spoken in a while," he said, a poor attempt at nonchalance.

He took another steady, silent drink, waiting for her response.

"You stopped calling *me,* remember?"

Desperate to keep her on the line, he struggled to think of what to say next.

"I gotta go," she said. "Call Chloe."

Four seconds of silence passed; it felt like fifteen.

"It was my birthday nine days ago. I was really hoping to hear from you."

"You haven't changed, Elderick." She used to call him Cole, like all their friends did. Most of them were friends with only her now.

"What's that supposed to mean?"

"It means your daughter gets hurt and all you can think about is yourself."

She hung up. Gutted, he looked at the phone in his hand. His drink had disappeared, so he poured another while he replayed the conversation, noting anything he said that might have ruined it, for next time. If there even was a next time.

After pouring another drink, and emptying the last of the bottle, he dialed Chloe. His cheeks tingled, the buzz washing over him while he listened nervously to the phone ring. His thoughts drifted to an old box of red wine in the bottom cupboard. *How long did those things last before they spoiled?* Seven rings later, his call went to voicemail as usual. He hesitated at the beep but decided to leave a message.

"It's your father. I heard you had an accident and I hope you're okay. Your mother told me that you left me a message. . . . I'm not sure if you left it at my house or at my work. I am at home now, but I'll check the machine at work tomorrow."

He paused, realizing he was rambling.

"You can call me anytime, work or home, and I hope—"

Dial tone. He'd been cut off. His face fell. He tossed back the end of the scotch, the remaining ice crunching in his teeth. Hunched over the arm of the couch, he grasped for a dust-covered photo on the side table that had been turned down. Rebecca, hair pulled back, captured in a happier moment on the beach near their old summer place. Smiling, perhaps even laughing a little. A weekend when Chloe had stayed with her grandparents for a few days while they relaxed. Only fifteen years had passed since that moment, but it felt like a lifetime ago to Cole, sitting there in the empty house.

As he pulled the box of wine from the cupboard, a peculiar sound drew his attention upward. The building often creaked in the wind or shifted with temperature changes, but this particular noise from upstairs was something he hadn't heard since he'd lived there. A chill crept up his calves, settling in his knees. He was sure it was the sound of moaning, but all he could hear now was the gusting wind slamming against the house.

He limped to the bottom of his staircase. The tingling sensation elevated into his thighs, blossoming outward into his hips. Another moan, breathy and feeble, the faint whimper of a child, hung in the air. His pulse quickened. Hairs on his head stiffened and his mouth dried up. He breathed slowly, clenching and unclenching his fists with every breath to shake off the fog of the alcohol and pills.

He ascended the stairs as fast as he could manage. His bad knee ached with every step. Unsure of what to expect, he paused at the top, where he struggled to catch his breath. The bedroom light remained off, but he could discern the outline of the bed from where he stood. Home invasions were relatively commonplace in the territory. Many involved sexual assaults on sleeping women, but someone with a grudge who wanted to get even with a policeman wasn't beyond the realm of possibility. He instinctively reached for his gun, grasping empty air. He'd left it downstairs. With no other weapons in sight, he clenched his fists, tensing himself for a confrontation. He called out. No response. He moved toward the doorway, slipping his hand inside and flicking on the light.

The room was unoccupied. The wooden bed frame extended to the floor and the closet had no door—nowhere for anyone to hide. He moved to the window, fixated on his own ghostly reflection, and pressed his hands against their counterparts on the frosted glass. Outside, a lone pole lamp created a tidy circle of white in the sprawling darkness of the nameless street below. No one to be seen.

Behind him, the closet's coat hangers swayed as if touched by an unseen force. Their faint tinkling sent shivers up his spine, setting his already frayed nerves twitching. He spun around, eyes darting across the emptiness, desperate to discern a rational explanation. He held his breath and quickly assured himself that the breeze of his passing had set them in motion. Another chill swept through him, causing a flutter in his chest. There was something in the room with him—someone, he was sure of it. He could feel her. He swore he could smell her perfume. Bewildered, approaching panic, eyes locked on the only exit, he felt a primal fear flood his senses. He released his breath and willed her to appear in the empty doorway. He stared until he could no longer stand it and then whispered her name: "Pitseolala."

A snowmobile roared past the house, bringing him back to reality. He slumped on the unmade bed, feeling ridiculous and childish. A familiar urge to weep rose up within him but surfaced as a nervous chuckle and a dry cough. He went downstairs, his hand trailing along the rail, then checked the locks on the doors and windows. He felt silly for making certain but never hesitated in his task. Retrieving his gun, he stalked through the house, turning on lights to confront vacant rooms. *I'm hallucinating. It's the drugs, the lack of sleep.* With his pill bottles in hand, he picked up the cordless phone, unsure who to call but craving another human voice.

No dial tone—only an intermittent crackle with a faint hiss. "Hello?" he asked into the silence. Before he could hang up, a spectral drone emerged, emitting a vague melody he couldn't place. He hit the speakerphone button, and the weird music echoed throughout the kitchen. *Must be picking up the local radio signal,* he half convinced himself. Fumbling with the power button, he silenced the noise just as he realized it reminded him of a howling dog.

"Too much to drink," he muttered, leaning on the counter to steady himself, pushing the box of wine aside. Exhausted and unable to shake the melody from his mind, he shuffled back up the stairs to bed.

CHAPTER 17

Cole awoke sprawled on his back, gasping for air. The familiar hum of the baseboard heater dispelled any hopes that he was dreaming. He lay still at first, eyes shut, waiting for the paralysis to pass. A night terror, the Old Hag. Childhood fears seeped in, flooding his brain with cortisol. When he was growing up in Newfoundland, such nightmares were blamed on a demon in the shape of a hideous old woman who sat on a person's chest while they slept, but he hadn't suffered from being *hag-ridden* in years. Motionless, he endured his vulnerability for what felt like an eternity, a prisoner in his own body. The struggle for calm escalated into a desperate struggle for breath. With his brain starved of oxygen, unbridled panic took over.

His eyes snapped open to the dim glow of the bedside lamp. A grotesque revenant of Pitseolala squatted low on his chest, her body naked and decaying. Her tiny breasts were flattened against her bruised knees, her skin marred by discolored edema and blackened spider veins. Gaunt ribs protruded from her malnourished frame, and her filthy bare feet stung icy cold against his flushed skin.

She leaned closer, his ribs buckling under a weight far greater than she'd borne in life. Black orbs oozed tar-like tears down her pale cheeks. Anguish welled in his eyes as her bony fingers tightened around his neck. His carotid arteries swelled to the thickness of garden hoses. His torso spasmed with desperate efforts to draw even a single breath. His eyes bulged from the pressure building in his skull.

The fiendish doppelgänger studied his tortured labors with an almost comical frown. She bent forward until their faces were almost touching, just an inch apart. Stagnant, trapped air escaped her lifeless corpse, filling his sinuses with the fetid odor of rotten meat. Her long fingernails cut through the skin on the back of his neck, and his legs thrashed wildly in response. Black bile drooled out of her mouth, over her bottom lip, spattering onto his face and chest while blood-red sparks flickered deep within her eyes.

Cole's head surged forward, his attempts to scream thwarted by the dripping fluids that pooled in his mouth and nostrils. His legs stiffened, a sudden cramp burning in his calf. Pitseolala opened her mouth wider than humanly possible. Sheets of ancient ice, miles thick, cracked and rumbled, their grinding edges resonating from deep within her throat, reverberating to a deafening level. In the endless blackness of her eyes, he saw only his own death. Convulsions overtook him, his eyes rolling back, his bladder releasing; warm urine pooled on the mattress beneath him.

He burst upright, arms tangled in the wet sheets, screaming hysterically. His hands clutched at his cramping leg and his fulminating heart. Frantically reaching for his sidearm on the nightstand, he tumbled awkwardly out of bed. The alarm clock and bedside lamp smashed to the floor. Hyperventilating in the corner, he spun to face the shadows. His trembling hands cocked the gun and disarmed the safety. He waved the weapon back and forth across the moonlit room, desperately seeking any trace of an intruder.

But he was alone.

Gradually, the terror subsided and he confronted reality. The glow of the upended alarm clock bathed his aching and broken body in a soft red light. His boxer briefs were soaked through with piss and sweat. Cole lowered his pistol and wept in the dark until the tears ran dry.

Half an hour passed before he made his way downstairs. He downed a glass of spoiled red wine in a single breath. The blinking green light on the cordless phone illuminated a darkened corner of the kitchen. A slurred and incoherent message from Chloe. Calling back, he reached her voicemail again. He poured another wine, then another, pacing in the kitchen with the fabric of his mind in tatters.

Pissing my pants. Like a fucking child.

As he replayed Chloe's drunken message over and over, his thoughts drifted to the picture of Danny Carter he routinely kept in the breast pocket of his uniform. Cole closed his eyes and recalled staggering up the embankment of the icy river, unable to feel his legs, yet somehow walking across that crowded parking lot, carrying the waterlogged corpse of the little boy in his arms. That dramatic gesture had contaminated the crime scene, ultimately costing the prosecution their case against the real killer.

I let the boy down. I let Pits down. I let everyone down.

He fixated on the montage of photos on the refrigerator door, a mural of regrets and shame. Pictures of the wife who left him, the daughter who hated him, the mother who tortured him, and the father who abandoned him. He felt empty, worthless. The alcohol buzz only encouraged his self-loathing.

I've failed as a cop, a father, a husband, a son.

Cole closed his eyes again. Images flashed—the boy's floating corpse, Pitseolala's vacant stare, the canine in the muzzle flare, the dead-eyed children.

I killed the dog in front of the kids. What the hell was I thinking?

They'll report me. I'll die in jail.

Heat rushed up into his face. He stepped back. His thoughts drifted to the pending lawsuit and the potential end of his career.

I'll never get transferred out. I'll be stuck here forever.

Tears flowed, everything blurred. The glass slipped from his fingers, shattering against the tiles.

Open hands, breathe in. Close fists, breathe out.

It was far too late for that. The first punch collided with the center of the freezer door. Its impact rocked the appliance onto its hind legs. Tiny magnets exploded past him; pictures of his family swirled like dead leaves toward the floor. An anguished rage, primal and deep, erupted from the abyss within him. He unleashed a relentless barrage, each blow harder than the last, forming craters in the enameled surface of the door. The last strike landed with a horrifying crunch, pain rocketing up into his elbow. A shrill scream burst from his throat. Cole staggered backward, winded by the violent flurry. He collapsed with his aching fists unfurling like rusted claws, thick fluid swelling into his bruised hands. Rage dissipated, leaving only pain. An exhausted groan escaped his lips. His body surrendered; losing consciousness was a gift.

CHAPTER 18

The antiquated clock in the hospital room showed six in the morning. Cole slouched on the edge of the examination table, trying not to crinkle the sanitary paper beneath him. Unsightly bruises adorned both sets of knuckles and his left hand bore a nasty gash. His swollen hands throbbed at a steady rate, intensifying the nausea that gripped him. Gingerly, he cradled his wounded left while balancing an ice pack on top.

What have I done, he thought as he surveyed the damage, exhausted and disgusted. He hadn't fucked himself up this bad since Rebecca had served him with papers three years ago. Back then, a stiff right cross into supposedly unbreakable glass netted him a trip to the emergency room and sixteen stitches.

He picked up a travel magazine from the counter in an effort to distract himself from the pain. A muscle-bound tourist dove off a yacht into azure waters with a tropical archipelago in the background. Thailand, maybe Vietnam—both places Cole had never been. He laid it back down and hoped the bastard drowned.

Interrupting his self-pity, a visiting staff nurse entered the room—an unfamiliar face, a welcome reprieve from dealing with the permanent head, Janet. Cole glimpsed his reflection in a previously unnoticed mirror—pallid complexion, dark rings beneath his eyes, hair disheveled, and shirt wrinkled. His decrepit state deepened his misery.

"What happened?" the nurse asked, her clipboard poised for answers.

"I had an accident," he mumbled, angling away from her stare.

"What kind?"

"An accidental one."

Unamused but unfazed by his responses, the nurse settled in for a longer encounter than she clearly had hoped for. Her look of scrutiny reminded him of a mother scolding her child. He'd seen the same look on Rebecca's face whenever he'd gotten himself into pointless trouble.

"It would help me determine the nature and extent of the injuries," she clarified and turned to gather some medical supplies on the countertop.

"My fists met a very solid object at a high velocity," he said. Saliva clung, viscous, in the back of his throat, so he coughed repeatedly in a failed attempt to clear it.

"I hope that object deserved it." She leaned in to examine the lacerated hand. "Can you move your fingers for me?"

He squeezed his left hand into a fist. He clenched his teeth and waited for the pain to disperse. When relief didn't come quickly enough, he swore and then flashed her an apologetic look between grimaces. Tingling heat flooded his cheeks when the pain died down.

She gently pried his right hand away from his injured arm. "I can get this stitched up, but you should probably take some time off."

"I'd need to get someone flown in to cover for me first. It'll probably be healed by the time that gets arranged."

His comments fell on deaf ears; she continued making notes and preparing the tray for stitches.

"I'm sure it'll be fine," he added.

She raised an eyebrow and pointed her pen at the bruises on his knuckles. "Does that look, or feel, fine to you?"

The nurse prepared a rolling side table, urging him to rest his injured arm on top. She examined and stitched his wounds with quick precision, eliciting only restrained winces from him. She'd done this many times before, he told himself.

"Are you on any medication?" she asked when it was finished.

"Vicodin," he said. "And Oxaprozal. For my knee."

"Oxaprozin? The anti-inflammatory?"

He nodded. "While I'm here I wanted to ask you about something for exposure to tainted blood. A suspect spat blood in my face recently."

She positioned his battered hand palm down on the table and gently laid the disregarded ice pack on top.

"I'm also taking pills to sleep. Sominex, I think they're called. But I am ditching those; they're not working."

She flashed a disapproving frown. "You need to talk to your doctor. There might be contraindications with all those drugs at once. Not to mention the liquor."

He ignored her comments, distracted by the throbbing discomfort in his hand. He realized he still reeked of alcohol, despite brushing his gums raw before he left the house. He leaned back and tried to breathe more shallowly, but he knew the odor likely persisted.

"I can only give you a few painkillers until you see a doctor. And you should stop drinking."

She didn't make eye contact but let her words linger for him to absorb. Standing, she peeled off her latex gloves and picked up her clipboard to jot down more notes. When she finished, she sat again and confronted him at his level. "There's no cordial way to say this: You look like shit. You need time off, proper care for that hand, and some serious rest, especially to stay off that knee. I can write you a medical note or a formal email to your supervisor or whatever you'll need to make that happen."

"Thanks, but I'm good." Cole adjusted the ice pack, lifting it to peek at the bruises underneath. Pushing down the rising shame and fatigue, he sat up taller despite the pain. "I've got too much on my plate and there's no one to replace me."

She stared at him until they locked eyes. "We've been robbed twice this month. Both times they raided the medication locker and left with all our hand sanitizer."

He nodded, unsure where the conversation was going. Suffering and exhaustion deprived him of his usual witty remark or even an intelligent comment. "Did you want me to file a report?" he offered, unable to recall the incidents at that moment.

"They're drinking the sanitizer," she said, ignoring his question. "You know it, I know it. But the rest of the world—regular people, the media, politicians—I don't think they know what's really happening up here, or even if they do, they don't seem to care." She laid a consoling hand on his leg and squeezed, startling Cole out of his pain-addled stupor. "We're on the front lines of something awful, and burnout is more common than we like to admit." She articulated her last sentence slowly to make sure it sank in. "This job, this *place,* it will burn you alive if you let it."

Cole from five years ago might have cracked a joke to lighten the mood; now, overwhelmed with self-pity and exhaustion, all he could manage was the truth.

"I can't walk away," he mumbled.

"If you die tomorrow, they'll replace you in a week," she said. "Money, conscience, pride—whatever is keeping you here, you need to let it go."

"I know," admitted Cole, suddenly feeling vulnerable and confessional. "But my life is a mess, personally, professionally. I'm waiting for a transfer. I just need to survive until then, and I can find someplace better, someplace warm and peaceful."

A long silence stretched out between them. Cole buried his face in his hand and released a long, weary sigh before meeting her eyes again.

"You ever make a decision, as a nurse, one based on your gut, to later find out that you were dead wrong?"

"It happens, especially in jobs like ours." She paused, searching for the right words. "Everyone makes mistakes from time to time. But in the end, sometimes your gut is all you've got to go on."

Cole stumbled out of the examining room into the harsh light of the deserted hallway. The sudden glare hit him like a flashbulb in the dark. He squeezed the bridge of his nose with his good hand and struggled to recover. The few hours he'd spent passed out on the couch after peeling himself off the kitchen floor weren't deep enough to count as real sleep. No patients in the waiting room. No receptionist behind the desk, and the security booth sat vacant. Alone, as usual. A distant radio played a familiar tune; the name escaped him. His empty stomach rumbled. He couldn't remember the last time he'd eaten.

Cole shuffled toward the main doors but hesitated in the foyer when a feeling of dread seized him. He froze, staring back down the empty corridor, eyeballing the long rows of unlit doorways. A sour taste crept up the back of his mouth. He rubbed his hand against his leg to relieve the itch of his newly bandaged knuckles. Beneath the odors of bleach and pine-scented cleaners, a waft of familiar perfume drifted toward him, growing in strength. His breathing became erratic. Horrible thoughts of last night's ordeal drifted in. Was the smell of perfume present then? Was he remembering it only now? His hand drifted instinctively to clutch his holstered gun, but what good would it do against a persistent nightmare? He closed his eyes in an effort to suppress the anxiety. *Fear is just your mind throwing its own voice into the darkness*—his grandmother's words, not his. He steeled himself and spun around to face another empty corridor. The feeling, the smell, the dread—all dissolved as quickly as they came.

When he got behind the wheel of the truck, the engine was still cold. Veronica's voice sliced through the radio's crackle. Her message was curt but concise. A kid waited at the station claiming responsibility for the cabin fire—and he would speak only with Cole.

CHAPTER 19

Maliktu slumped into a worn-out plastic chair in the detachment's interview room. A steady ticking emanated from the baseboard heaters. The smell of the musty carpet reminded him of the waiting area outside the principal's office. Leaning heavily on the rickety table, he surveyed its dusty surface—a battered Bible with duct tape across the spine, five balled-up pieces of used tissue, and a three-year-old phone book. Behind him, a dented filing cabinet stood watch in the corner, and a rotary telephone rested on the floor near his feet, its frayed cord too short to reach the table. When Cole's voice cut through the silence outside the door, Maliktu drew up his hood, knees bouncing a mile a minute with anxious tension.

Cole entered wearing his full uniform and a grim expression. Steam drifted up from his mug; a steady flow of caffeine was the only thing keeping him upright. Maliktu's mouth felt parched and he regretted not asking for his own coffee when he had the chance. He noticed a thin yellow folder tucked under the policeman's arm.

Cole joined him at the table, slurping his too-hot coffee and scowling when he burned his lips. He began flipping through the file on the tabletop. Maliktu waited for the officer to break the silence, repeatedly tracing his forefinger down a long scar on his forearm. He'd hooked his arm on a nail when he had fallen between two oversize wooden crates while goofing around behind the post office last summer. Eleven stitches. He'd never seen so much blood aside from a butchered seal or caribou.

The stifling heat caused Maliktu to pull back his hood, revealing his face. He looked up at the policeman, who had finished browsing through the folder. Cole stared directly into his eyes and didn't flinch at the sight of his facial scars.

"My name's Elderick," murmured Cole, his voice ragged and slightly hoarse. "But most people call me Cole."

"*Kuukutsi,*" said Maliktu in a matter-of-fact tone.

Cole smiled at the familiar word and leaned in with his good arm to rest on the table. "That's what your sister used to call me. What does it mean?"

Maliktu hesitated, navigating between languages. He visualized the wall of barnyard animals in the school's library—an inadequate teaching guide for Arctic children—and tried to recall the English word.

"Pig," said Maliktu with uncertainty.

Cole erupted in laughter, leaning back and closing his eyes, welcoming a rare moment of humor. *How many times has Pits called me that?* He remembered how she always followed it up with a flurry of giggles, and he warmed at the joy it must have brought her to tease him without his knowing.

Maliktu, unable to resist, laughed along with him, but he was unsure why it was quite so funny.

"I've been called worse," Cole said, closing the file with a conspiratorial smile.

Maliktu pulled off his winter hat and used it to wipe the sweat from his hairline. He slid his bare hand across the condensation of the frosted window and rubbed the cool water over the back of his neck.

Cole scrutinized the hard contours of the boy's cheeks, the twisted flesh that had healed despite extensive burns. *A survivor,* thought Cole. He wondered if the boy would have already had the necessary surgeries and treatment to repair the damage to his skin had he grown up in the South with an affluent family.

"How'd you burn your face?" asked Cole before taking another sip of his coffee, more carefully this time.

Maliktu eyed him with suspicion, wrestling with issues of trust. "In a fire."

"Were you little when it happened?"

Maliktu raised his eyebrows high. "They died."

"Your parents?"

Maliktu lifted his eyebrows again, higher this time, eyes widened.

"Was it a house fire?"

Maliktu scrunched his face up tight in the Inuit manner of indicating a negative. "Tent."

Cole nodded, laying his good hand on the file. "We had a fire on the land recently. A big one."

The printer fired up in the main office beyond the closed door. Maliktu snapped his head toward the sound. When he returned his attention to Cole, the boy sized up the policeman, holding his breath as he did. He'd never seen a cop this close-up before. They were always speeding past him in the truck or arresting someone.

"What happened to your hand?" asked Maliktu, barely above a whisper.

"I fell."

Maliktu extended his arm and displayed the long scar for Cole.

"Is that from the fire?'

Maliktu scrunched his face again. "I fell too. Last year."

"Someone torched a cabin," Cole interjected, producing a printed photo that Veronica had taken. The image revealed the aftermath of the fire—a crumbling framework of charred black timbers against a canvas of white snow. Taken with a flashbulb in the dark, the picture looked haunting and unreal. "You know anything about that?"

Maliktu, avoiding eye contact, gouged away at the dirt under his fingernails. "I don't know."

"What don't you know?"

Maliktu offered a nonchalant shrug.

Cole understood the boy's pain and confusion; he remembered

being a child. His mother taken away. The beatings. So much violence. There were times when he wanted to burn the whole world down, including himself. An Inuit boy without parents, a murdered sister, bullied for his disfigurement, undoubtedly traumatized, if not from the tent fire, then from struggles that came later; there were no resources for these types of mental health issues in this town.

Crimes required punishment, but Cole had nothing but sympathy for the boy.

"I already know who lit the fire," he said.

Maliktu stopped picking at his nails and stared at him, trying to gauge if he was bluffing.

"In this country, you need to be twelve years old before they can charge you with a crime. Did you know that?"

Maliktu shook his head. His stomach roiled audibly, and he touched his abdomen.

"How old are *you*?" asked Cole.

"Ten," said Maliktu.

"So we can't charge you with burning down the cabin. You're too young."

Doubt crossed Maliktu's face. Unsure of the game being played, he hesitated, wondering if this was some kind of trick.

"The person who owns it is in prison. He's facing a murder charge down south. But there could've been someone inside; someone could have gotten hurt."

"No one was there," Maliktu blurted out. "Just me and my sister."

"Which sister?" asked Cole, unsure how many the boy had.

Maliktu stared through a gap in the window frost he had created with his hand, contemplating his response.

"Pitseolala," he whispered.

Deep creases formed, a sudden tension in Maliktu's face. Cole hesitated, giving the boy time to elaborate.

"She told me to come see you," Maliktu admitted. Cole shifted nervously in his seat, setting down his coffee cup.

"When did she tell you that?"

"Yesterday."

Cole, grappling with a maelstrom of emotions and questions, remained silent. Was this the product of a burgeoning mental illness? Or a child's malleable reality distorted by trauma? He proceeded with caution, trying to grasp exactly what Maliktu was telling him.

"When she *spoke* to you yesterday, was it like you were dreaming?"

"Maybe," responded Maliktu.

Cole stared down into the surface of the file on the table, lost in contemplation. When he looked up, a vision of the dead boy from the river flickered before him with a slack, lifeless expression. His blotchy skin hung wrinkled and waterlogged from his cheekbones, sloughing off in chunks. A soaked white T-shirt stretched across his frail torso, torn in places where his body had dragged along the shallow bottom with the current. The scent of decay and stagnant water filled the air. Cole tucked his head down and closed his eyes, afraid to face the manifestation of his nightmares.

When he opened them, Danny Carter was gone and Maliktu had returned, eyeing the officer with grave concern. Cole rubbed his hand across his face as if to wipe away the whole experience. As he did so, he noticed several dark red spots on the cover of the yellow folder.

"You're bleeding," said Maliktu, breaking the silence. He gestured to the policeman's hand. Cole glanced at the blood on his fingertips before taking a tissue from his pocket and pressing it to the weeping bandage on his knuckles.

A snowmobile engine droned past while Cole finished cleaning up the folder. He focused on his breathing and struggled to keep himself together through sheer force of will, dismissing the hallucination and focusing on the tangible form of Maliktu across the table.

"Did Pitseolala ever talk to you about her boyfriend?"

"No."

"Never?"

"Never."

Cole pursed his lips and nodded, satisfied the boy was being truthful.

Maliktu stared out the window, drawing row upon row of tiny *X*'s in the frost with his fingertip.

"She was at the fire," said Maliktu. "At the cabin."

Cole hesitated, unsure of how to handle the response. "You mean, you felt like she was there with you?"

"I saw her." Maliktu looked directly at Cole, his eyes filled with sadness and sincerity.

A chill ran up Cole's spine, taking him back to the health center, uncertain if the ghost of the dead girl had just drifted into the interview room. The compulsion to look over his shoulder was overwhelming, but he resisted.

"She liked the fire." Maliktu returned to drawing the *X*'s in the frost.

"How do you know?"

"I could see her smiling in the corner of my eye."

Cole wanted to lay a hand on the boy's shoulder but pulled back. He didn't want to admit that Pitseolala might somehow be reaching out to her little brother, and somehow reaching out to him. He couldn't. Not if he was going to hang on to the last dregs of his sanity.

"Sometimes when people lose people they love, their mind plays tricks on them. Things can seem real when they're not. Do you understand what I'm saying?"

Maliktu faced Cole again but remained silent.

Cole considered repeating his comments or perhaps wording them differently. He scanned the boy's face for some crack in his resolve, some doubt in his eyes.

"Do *you* see her?" asked Maliktu.

Cole contemplated the weight of the question, uncertain how to answer. He felt exhausted and frail in that moment, staring down at the bloody tissue in his hand.

"She told me that I had to help you catch the devil," continued Maliktu. "The one that killed her."

The hairs on Cole's neck stood stiff, his skin prickling with electricity at the mention of a devil. His thoughts skittered back to the cryptic comments of the drunken woman in the domestic situation, then to his night terror featuring Pitseolala on his chest. Ticking from the baseboard heaters seemed to increase in volume, and he felt a trickle of sweat careening down his back beneath the fabric of his shirt. A lifetime of hag dreams and terrible visions left him wondering if being *touched* wasn't somehow a curse, a plague of his bloodline, rather than a gift, as his grandmother had insisted. The creature on his chest last night certainly wasn't the Pitseolala he knew. A sudden memory of the blackened spider veins on her pale skin and the viscous tar flowing from her gaping eyes snapped him back into the interview room.

"Did she say anything else?" asked Cole, not knowing how to approach Maliktu given what he had just told him.

"She said she was running out of time." Maliktu hesitated, pondering the message from his sister. "I could smell her, bad at first, like she was dead. Then nice, like she used to smell."

"How did she used to smell?"

"Like flowers."

Cole felt the blood drain from his skull, the room closing in on him. His world slid off-kilter, vulnerable and groundless, as if he were falling backward in his chair. When he exhaled, unrecognizable noises drifted out of his mouth, inarticulate sounds. Without knowing what he was saying, he took a deep inhale and refocused, clearing his head of her. Cole hesitated to speak, unwilling to admit anything out loud for fear of making it all too real.

His voice sounded weak, almost inaudible, when he finally addressed the boy again. "I smell her perfume sometimes," said Cole. "Sometimes, I even feel like she's here."

A rap on the door startled Cole and he tipped the last of his coffee over on the table. He sopped it up as best he could with a bloody tissue, swearing all the while.

Maliktu watched in silence for a moment before turning his attention to a stray dog scampering outside the frosted window. The frantic whelp seemed to be engaged in a curious game with its own shadow on the icy road beneath the lamppost. The boy's eyes wandered to the eerie purple phosphorescence clinging along the edges of the nearby buildings, backlit by the glow of the moon on the horizon.

The knuckles rapped again, and Veronica's voice rang out through the door: "I found Maata."

"I'll be right there," said Cole, while unsuccessfully scanning for a place to discard the saturated tissue. He tossed it on the tabletop and made a mental note to clean up the mess later.

"Are you hungry?" he asked.

Maliktu nodded and Cole held up a finger to wait while he went to the detachment kitchenette to get the boy a meal. The prisoners were fed frozen prepackaged meals in plastic trays that were defrosted just before being eaten. Cole felt pretty sure the nutritional value of the meals was close to zero, but it was all he had to offer. While it rotated in the microwave oven, he splashed his face with cold water from the nearby tap, grateful there wasn't a mirror above the sink to remind him of his haggard appearance. His mind whirled in a maelstrom of lifelong doubts and fears, unable to hold on to a single one for more than a breath.

When he returned to the interview room with the hot meal and a plastic spoon, Maliktu began wolfing it down as soon as the utensil hit his fingers. *He probably hasn't eaten all day,* thought Cole.

"We can talk more after you're done," he said. "But there's something I need to do first."

CHAPTER 20

In the isolated North, there were no architectural firms. Plans for Arctic buildings were drawn up by so-called Southern experts who didn't understand, or had never considered, the unique requirements of living in such a harsh environment. Aesthetics always triumphed over function. For that reason, the concrete tombs known as the detachment cells remained swelteringly hot regardless of the season due to a flaw in the building's design.

Bodily fluids from countless prisoners lingered thick and heavy in the stagnant air of the windowless room. Cole sat on the concrete rectangle that passed for a bed. Across from him, the young girl, Maata, slumped on the floor against the wall, surrounded by a halo of profanity and crude drawings etched into the many layers of peeling paint. She hugged her knees to her chest. Her frostbitten feet soaked in a plastic tub of lukewarm water.

"The nurse will be here soon," said Cole, fussing with the bandage on his knuckles to relieve the itching beneath. He licked his thumb and attempted to clean a spot of dried blood from the back of his hand. "Then we can get you transferred to the health center; I left a message with your mother."

Maata released her legs and straightened up against the wall. She stared into oblivion. Her arms bore purple stains that matched the color of her haphazardly dyed hair. Cole studied the neat rows of thin white scars that peeked out from the neckline of her tank top. Since arriving in the territory, he had witnessed countless young girls engaging in self-harm, each one fighting a solitary war in secret.

"I need hotter water," she said, her voice slurred and fractured.

Veronica materialized in the doorway, shaking her head in disapproval. Maata's gaze flickered from one officer to the other, torn between focus and the brink of tears.

"If the water's too hot, it'll make it worse," Cole assured her, pulling Maata's attention away from Veronica's disdain. "This is better for frostbite."

Maata, frustrated, shifted her feet, causing water to spill over the edges of the container. Eyes closed tight, she clenched her jaw with her lips pulled back to reveal her teeth. Cole took note of the black-and-yellow enamel and receding gumline, which were not unusual for the region: There were no dentists in most Arctic communities, and dental hygiene at home was rare. Most Inuit kids also had high-sugar diets instead of the traditional high-fat, high-protein diet of their ancestors, so the number of decayed and missing teeth only increased as they got older.

"If Veronica hadn't found you, you might have lost your toes, running around in the snow dressed like that," remarked Cole grimly. "Or maybe even your feet."

She let out a frustrated snarl and coughed loudly before spitting toward the stainless-steel toilet in the center of the cell, missing her target by more than a foot.

"Or broke your neck jumping out that window," added Veronica, before switching to Inuktitut comments that Cole couldn't understand. Maata responded with a string of swear words, her eyes burning with hostility. Cole flashed Veronica a look of disapproval.

"I don't drink anymore," interjected Maata, staring at the floor, wiping sweat from her face with the back of her hand. "Not since I got pregnant."

The revelation hung heavy in the air. Veronica left the room with a huff of exasperation. The territory had the highest birth rate in the country, with the lowest birth weights and youngest mothers on average. Nearly half were single. He considered whether the odor of liquor might have been from the smashed vodka bottles on the dresser before her leap out the window but chose to abandon this thought.

"How far along is the baby?" he asked, trying to de-escalate things with a softer tone.

"Four months."

"Is it a boy or a girl?"

A shrug, indifferent.

"Who's the father?"

Tears welled in Maata's bloodshot eyes. The girl's breathing suddenly grew loud and fast. Cole realized he was on thin ice and decided to change the subject.

"You were friends with Pits," he said. "I used to see you guys together a lot."

"She left me behind," said Maata. A slight tremor moved across her face. "We were going to have our babies at the same time."

Cole's breath caught in his throat. *Pits was pregnant.* His mind whirled with possibilities and theories. Maata burst into a coughing fit nearly hard enough to break her ribs. He pushed himself to his feet, careful not to put too much weight on his bad knee, and limped out of the cell, leaving her to sob alone. As he reached the kitchenette next to the holding area, he paused, momentarily dazed by the sudden change in temperature and lighting. The room lurched and tilted like the listing deck of a ship in rough waters. He closed his eyes and leaned against the wall, trying to stabilize himself.

Cole returned to the cell with a paper cup filled with orange juice. They had stopped using plastic after a prisoner stomped on one and used the pieces to slash his wrists. Given his current situation, he couldn't afford to have that happen again on his watch. Maata had caught her breath and resumed staring at her frostbitten feet in the tub, with one hand resting unconsciously on her belly.

"Who was the father of *her* baby?" he asked after a long silence, an involuntary rise in pitch betraying the intensity of his emotions.

No response.

"If she was knocked up, I need to know, Maata."

The girl nodded reluctantly. She shifted her feet in the water and whimpered from the resulting pain.

"Who was the father?" he repeated.

Another fit of hacking coughs engulfed her small frame for almost a minute. The barking sounded deep and wet, a testament to the hours spent running from house to house half naked in the harsh cold. Cole lowered his voice, speaking tenderly. "She's gone, so it doesn't have to be a secret anymore."

"I didn't know she was pregnant until my mother asked her. My mom just knows stuff, she can feel it. When I asked Pits who from, she wouldn't say."

"Any idea who it might be?" asked Cole. "Jardin, maybe?"

"She fucking hated Jardin. And she knew I loved him—she wouldn't do that to me."

In obvious pain, Maata pounded her head into the concrete wall, groaning with each impact. Cole hesitated on the brink of intervention, processing their conversation. He realized that Maata and Pitseolala were of similar build and height. Pudlat might have mistaken one for the other when he saw Jardin.

"The nurse is here!" shouted Veronica from the main area. "And the kid bolted after he ate."

Cole, barely processing Maliktu's sudden departure, refocused as Maata's voice cut through his frenetic thoughts.

"Satanasi," the girl whispered, her gaze fixed on her swollen feet, a calm settling over her. She repeated the name again in a hushed tone. The unfamiliar name lingered in the air like an intruder, troubling Cole. "It was him, I think."

"Who is that?" Cole leaned in, desperate for answers. "Her boyfriend?"

"He gave her the baby," she said, before being overcome with sobs and covering her face with her hands.

Cole stood on the edge of yet another mystery, watching Maata's despair for a few breaths before stepping out of the cell. He slid the thick door closed as quietly as he could.

Cole hunched over his desk with his fingers poised above the keyboard. Stacks of unfinished paperwork surrounded him—open cases, occurrence reports, time sheets. The envelope from the Carter lawsuit had been pulled from the wastebasket but remained unopened on his desk, refusing to disappear on its own. So much to do, so little focus. The revelation about Pitseolala's pregnancy had wedged itself in his mind like a knife between the ribs. The identity of the potential father could be crucial to the case. Maliktu had left before Cole got a chance to talk further about his sister's life. The boy's disconcerting comments about Pitseolala's perfume and Pitseolala being at the shack fire had left him shaken and insecure. Instead of transcribing his notes from the interview with Curtis Reynolds, he found himself staring at the blinking cursor on his screen for far too long.

As a procedural formality, he entered the teacher's name and date of birth into the national law enforcement database. The CPIC system allowed him to search for criminal records, including details of past convictions, pending charges, and outstanding warrants. The internet in the North was notoriously slow and unreliable, a continual annoyance for Cole. The vast geography and poor infrastructure rendered it almost unusable at times.

Janet, the head nurse, had departed for the health center with Maata in her custody. Cole had avoided eye contact, given how their last conversation had ended. The tension between them during her short visit to the detachment was unmistakable. By the time he returned to his desk, the CPIC search had finally concluded. He printed out the sheet and was beginning to place it in the file when the results caught his eye.

Rather than the clean record Cole was expecting for a schoolteacher, Reynolds had two prior charges from three years ago under section 151 of the Criminal Code—sexual interference with a person under sixteen. Upon closer examination, he saw that both counts had been marked "withdrawn." Cole promptly typed the teacher's name into a search engine. A slew of news links appeared on the screen. He had faced accusations of sexual relations with two students at a private school in Montreal where he taught: both females, both around Pitseolala's age. Cole had seen fabricated allegations before, but he'd also seen real victims intimidated into recanting accusations after they were made. What was he dealing with here?

The prosecutor had apparently dropped the charges due to a lack of evidence, and Reynolds was supposedly exonerated. But the newspaper accounts were short on details due to confidentiality agreements and the court's publication ban. If the allegations were true and he'd done it again, Pitseolala's pregnancy would have been a ticking time bomb for the teacher.

Cole wrapped his head around a new theory of the case. A close friendship may have started innocently, but it could have escalated into a full-blown affair. A vulnerable and troubled but attractive young woman. A tall, good-looking man in a position of trust. Reynolds's wife and daughter lived in another province. The disclosure of such a relationship and the unborn child would not only destroy his career and his marriage but could also lead to more criminal charges. A man in that position couldn't afford to let the truth come out.

Cole's mind wandered as he considered the possibilities. Reynolds might have asked her to get an abortion, but that would have been complicated to arrange without the secret coming out, and she may not have agreed to the procedure. Pitseolala's reluctance, or refusal, could have led to a volatile situation. She might even have threatened him or tried to blackmail him. He knew this was wild speculation, but plausible for a smart girl with nothing to lose. Reynolds would have been left with no choice but to silence her permanently.

CHAPTER 21

The police truck rumbled to a halt in the crowded parking lot. The temperature gauge on the dashboard read –29 degrees with the windchill. Beneath the glow of the security light, a pack of Inuit teens dressed in multicolored parkas clustered on the front steps of the store, white clouds of exhaled smoke and frozen breath hovering above them. All around the dilapidated building, the compacted snow was littered with scattered trash, dog shit, and discarded cigarette butts. Simmering resentment had left Cole and Veronica trapped in the silence of the vehicle on the ride to the report of a disturbance; few words had been exchanged between them since their argument. Mercifully for both of them, it had been a short drive.

From behind the wheel, Cole surveyed the crowd outside the store, which was partially obscured by blowing snow and the frosted windshield. A stray dog, its tail between its legs, weaved through the vehicles and people before nearly being run over by a passing snowmobile. Jagged memories of the chained dog he shot slunk out of the shadows of his mind—the flash of the muzzle, the blood sprayed on the snow, its twitching body dying beneath the streetlight. His breathing difficulties intensified in the suffocating dry heat from the dashboard vents. A sudden realization struck him. He still hadn't disposed of the dog's body.

He wondered if anyone had heard the gunshots. He worried that the children had told their parents. Everyone in town owned at least a single rifle, and random gunfire was not that uncommon. But if an adult had actually seen him shoot the dog, it would have been a very different story.

The days of dog teams had vanished, and few attempted to resurrect the tradition. By the 1960s, the demise of the nomadic Inuit lifestyle and the rise in popularity of the snowmobile had all but ended the use of sled dogs as a means of transportation. The culling of these dogs by the police and local authorities in the 1950s and '60s due to rampant canine disease and to curb stray dogs attacking children, as well as a lack of available veterinary care, reduced the population to near extinction. Conspiracy theories gained prominence in the 1990s that the real goal was to shackle the traditionally nomadic Inuit to sedentary lives where they could be managed and assimilated. Two official inquiries, both lengthy and expensive, discredited those myths, but the specter of a "dog slaughter" persisted, and an unsettling undercurrent threatened to surface at any provocation. Cole knew that a policeman shooting a dog for any reason could ignite a powder keg.

Veronica touched his arm, interrupting his thoughts. Her exasperated tone cut through the friction between them. "Are we ever gonna talk about your hands?"

Cole remained quiet and focused on a growing web of fractures in the windshield. "I fell on the ice last night outside my place," he said after a long pause. "The night nurse patched me up."

"A fall on the ice?" she asked, her voice dripping with skepticism. "Or a tussle with Jardin?"

She studied his face as if she were grilling a suspect. Dread gripped him when he realized his clandestine visit to the bootlegger was no longer secret.

"He called," she informed him. "Left a message, said you assaulted him."

"I never hit him," he said, still refusing to make eye contact. *I only squeezed his broken ribs and choked him when he reached for a knife.* He would stick to that version of events if Jardin decided to make an official complaint. "I went by to talk and found a baby covered in filth and sitting alone in a roomful of smoke."

She sank into a defeated slouch at the mention of the baby and released a frustrated exhale through her nostrils. "Piece of shit. Sheila can't come back to find her kid in foster care. Social services better fly that damn child over to the hospital so she can take proper care of it."

"I already called Iqaluit," he said. "They've informed her and they're dealing with it."

She raised her eyebrows in silent acknowledgment.

"I'll erase his message when I get back," she added.

A truce, perhaps, but no apologies from either. During his brief time in the North, he noticed that people up here weren't very keen on holding grudges. The hostile landscape of the Arctic required cooperation for mutual survival; bad blood could get everyone killed. Yet his relationship with Veronica seemed to be in steady decline over the past few weeks. It left him wondering how things became so toxic so quickly.

Stepping out into the cold, they confronted the unforgiving climate. The wind, having momentarily relented, left the air feeling crisp. Knowing the lull wouldn't last, they hurried toward the entrance as fast as Cole's leg would allow. The store manager often cranked classical music or opera arias at top volume in a feeble attempt to drive away loitering kids. Today was no different. Mumbled greetings emanated from beneath numerous hoods as the officers passed through the gauntlet of smokers. He clutched the makeshift rebar handle and wrestled the outer door open. The heated space between the sets of doors was crammed with huddled bodies seeking refuge from the cold. He squeezed through into the grocery store, where he and Veronica regrouped by the first cash register. The cashier, a petite Inuit teen, had a large hematoma above her right eye. Such bruises were all too common on women's faces in the community. He noted the injury, but before he could ask Veronica about the girl, he was interrupted by Cyril Higdon, the store's manager.

"Get these fucking thieves outta my store," shouted Higdon. He pronounced "thieves" as "teeves" in his thick Newfoundland accent. He pointed to a group of people clustered near the end of the last checkout aisle. Five women and two men, all Inuit save for the preacher. A dozen board games lay scattered on the floor. Other customers kept their distance, continuing to shop or gathering at the fringes to watch the unfolding drama.

Cole didn't recognize any of them except the reverend, Avon Desmond. A corpulent figure in his fifties, with a thin mustache and dyed black hair, he reeked of fraudulence. His face and name adorned posters littered all over town during the month leading up to the arrival of this religious group. Based out of Florida, they had been touring around the Arctic spreading their own brand of "hellfire and healing" evangelism, collecting donations from anyone who wished their relatives languishing in hell moved to a better location. They also specialized in "curing" ailments with a laying on of hands. All of it disgusted Cole, who'd seen enough religious abuse and scandal in his own upbringing to make him wary of this particular ilk.

Cyril, now backed by the officers, confronted the evangelicals in his bright green apron. He was accompanied by a young Inuit boy wearing a matching bib and black winter gloves used for stocking the freezer section.

"Children in this town are using these Ouija boards to contact the devil," proclaimed Desmond, pointing his Bible at the approaching manager. He spoke with the booming voice of a man who had spent his life at the pulpit. "The Dark Lord is commanding them through the spirit world to commit sin."

Cole noticed that most of Desmond's crew were wearing name tags on their parkas. It was common for the Inuit in certain communities to take biblical names—Ezekiel, Methuselah, Jedediah. He had even met a boy named Judas once. But an Inuit suffix was often added to Christian names to make them flow better in Inuktitut—Lucassie, Markoosie, Pauloosie.

"Well, the devil works in fuckin' mysterious ways," said Cyril to Desmond. "Because we haven't sold one board since we got 'em."

Cole held up a hand toward the manager to calm him.

"Adultery, suicide, drug abuse!" interrupted the preacher, white paste evident at the corners of his lips, his gaze flitting from face to face among the passing shoppers as they rolled their grocery carts by him. "They cannot ask for salvation themselves once they are dead. All of these innocents will be cast into the bowels of hell when they die."

The tension among the employees working the cash registers was palpable whenever the preacher spoke. The church group brought comfort and solace to some people in town, but for many, it intensified fear and anxiety.

Cole matched him with a loud, authoritative voice: "If you want to buy the games and burn them, or bury them, or whatever you've got planned, go ahead. But you can't take them without paying."

Cyril nodded at every word and his mouth lit up with a broad smile. He folded his arms high across his chest. Desmond was clearly agitated by Cole's remarks, his face contorting into a grimace. His lips were trembling. The church group began whispering among themselves, presumably reciting some kind of prayer. Their calm features and closed eyes were in sharp contrast to the countenance of their animated leader.

Observing the rising anxiety in the preacher's demeanor, Veronica spoke in Inuktitut to the group in a calmer but equally authoritative voice. Cole assumed she was translating for the benefit of those who spoke little or no English. Sometimes Veronica would repeat what he said; at other times she would have full conversations he couldn't understand. But he trusted her to do the talking for unilingual elders and those with limited English skills; he had no other choice.

"They should not be for sale at all," said Desmond in the same tone he likely used for his sermons, making sure his comments were heard by the other patrons of the store. "We are here doing God's work." With the last line, he raised his Bible high above his head, causing everyone around to look up at it, as if waiting for the gesture to mean something more.

"You can either buy them or leave them," Cole said. "But you can't take them."

"We are not going until they are removed from the shelves." He repeated himself in Inuktitut at top volume, lowering the book. Since the early days of contact with indigenous cultures, religious missionaries looking to convert wayward souls had to learn the language to communicate with the local people and gain their trust. This preacher was no different.

Cole pulled Veronica aside and whispered into her ear. "Keep them calm while I talk to Cyril and see if we can't resolve this another way." Veronica nodded, then stepped forward to speak with the group.

Cole guided Cyril into the cereal aisle, out of earshot. "Can't you just take the games off the shelf and tell this clown you're getting rid of them?"

"And who's gonna pay for that?" asked Cyril. "It certainly ain't coming out of my bank account."

"Just stash them in your office until they leave town. You can put them back on the shelves when they're gone."

"I'm still trying to recover from the poison meat fiasco." A month earlier, a rumor started that the meat at the Northern Store was poisoned after a local girl died of a burst appendix. The majority of the community refused to purchase any from the store, even after it was reduced on clearance. "I had to throw out a hundred and sixty-eight pounds of chicken. You know what that cost me?"

"These con artists are only in town for three more days until they move on to Igloolik. So let's just defuse this, and all will go back to normal once they leave. Okay?"

"One condition," said Cyril. "I don't want them coming back in the store."

"Deal," said Cole, firmly shaking Cyril's hand. "I'll speak to them."

Cole walked back out to the group. Veronica was looking through her notepad, ignoring Desmond, who was in the middle of a hand-holding silent prayer with his brethren.

"Reverend," said Cole, loud enough to break the concentration of the group. "The manager has agreed to take the games off the shelves. But you can't have them. He's gonna send the games back to the manufacturer in the South."

Desmond nodded, apparently satisfied. "We will continue to do the Lord's work," he announced to all the customers within earshot. "We will keep praying for the souls of the children of this community."

"That's great," said Cole, smiling. "But I think your work here in the Northern Store is done." He invited the preacher to walk toward the door with an outstretched arm. "Let's talk more about that outside." Desmond moved past the officers, his group shuffling along behind him.

"Three more fucking days," whispered Cole to Veronica as they neared the front door.

Veronica barely concealed her amusement as they stepped out into the night. "This is your religion, not mine."

The gaggle of smokers on the frozen steps had swelled to twice its former size. A dozen more gathered in the crowded parking lot to listen to Desmond's frenzied sermon from atop the back of a parked snowmobile. During the short time the officers were in the building, the cab of the police truck had gone frigid. Cole started the engine and let it idle; pulling away cold was never good for a vehicle's lifespan. Fighting the chill, Veronica cranked up the dashboard heater and slipped a notepad from her chest pocket. Cole hunched over the steering wheel in an attempt to relieve the fist-sized knots in the muscles of his back, most of them impossible to alleviate.

He checked his damaged hand and winced at the touch. The rearview mirror reflected his exhausted face. He stared into his own eyes, trying to push back the darkness threatening to consume him. As he tried to ignore the pain, Cole wondered how long the pills would last before they ran out, and how long he could do his job without them. Veronica finished her notes and tucked the pad back into her pocket.

"I can't stop looking at that nasty hand of yours," she said matter-of-factly before gloving up once more.

"Only four stitches," he confessed, shifting into drive. "But it fucking hurts like hell."

Veronica muttered something under her breath as Desmond and his crew piled into a nearby van. She pulled up her collar tight against the cold. Cole rolled out of the parking lot and headed back toward the police station.

"Maata said Pits's new boyfriend was named Satanasi," said Cole. "You know that guy?"

"Not personally." Veronica offered him a muted chuckle. "Satanasi is what people around here call the devil."

He mulled over this revelation in grim silence for the rest of the drive, wondering if Maata's words held some literal or metaphorical truth.

When the truck pulled into the parking lot of the detachment, the door to the storage shack swung ominously open in the wind. Cole leapt out without turning off the ignition. His boots hit the ground and a sharp pain exploded inside his bad knee, forcing him to lean against the front of the vehicle while Veronica rushed toward the shed.

"She's gone," shouted Veronica. "Pitseolala's gone."

CHAPTER 22

Cole cursed himself for leaving his leather gloves in the truck. He fumbled with the cold steel of the padlock; its shackle was completely severed, a narrow bite in the steel indicating that it was likely done with bolt cutters. Turning it over and over gingerly in his freezing hands, he cursed in disbelief. *Who would have the balls to steal a corpse from the police?* He resisted the urge to smash the damaged lock through the passenger window of the truck.

Scanning the icy ground near the door, Cole searched for other evidence. Forensics in these isolated Arctic towns were often futile given the harsh weather, isolation, and lack of investigative tools. Drifting snow outside the shack had buried any potential footprints, cigarette butts, or tire marks. A tightness gripped his chest, and he wanted to scream in frustration. He tossed the now-useless lock aside and joined Veronica inside.

A single bulb hanging from an exposed rafter cast deep shadows that closed in around Cole, darkening his thoughts. He surveyed the workbench where he and Miller had laid out Pitseolala's body. The sight of the empty tabletop caused the tightness in his chest to increase. His windpipe constricted; his lungs felt smaller. Veronica, who had squatted down next to the table, shined her flashlight beam across the floor beneath it.

"Nothing," she said, frustration rising in her voice as she stood up.

Cole paced back and forth in the cramped shed before sweeping his injured hand across a low shelf, sending a stack of old paint cans and tins of nails to the floor in a violent spasm. Afterward, he leaned against the back wall with his head bowed in exhaustion and spent anger, the sound of the crashing items still reverberating through the confined space.

"Right under our fucking noses," yelled Cole in disgust, trying to contain his growing rage by taking another couple of deep breaths with his eyes closed. When he opened them, he found Veronica staring at him, hesitating to say anything, as if waiting to see if his outburst was over. He relaxed his shoulders and let his arms dangle loose to show her he was calm and collected once again.

"What the hell would anyone want with a dead body?" she asked.

"Maybe to hide something," said Cole. "Maybe to send a message?"

"Hide what?" asked Veronica. "Message to who?"

"Whatever it is, I'm gonna find out." He shoved his frozen hands into the fleece-lined pockets of his uniform and straightened up, gearing into action. "We couldn't have been gone from the detachment more than an hour. Someone had to have seen something."

"Leona and Titus across the street are usually home all day," said Veronica, making a beeline for the exit. "I'll do a knock and talk, see if they witnessed anything."

After she closed the door behind her, Cole stared at the vacant tabletop, a bottomless pit opening up inside his chest, all hopes of solving the case tumbling down into it. He wanted to vomit. His stomach churned with nothing inside but endless amounts of black coffee. Bolt cutters weren't something a civilian would normally have, and you couldn't just buy a pair at the local store. Then a particular thought struck him as relevant: *I know where someone would have access to them.*

Whenever a winter storm approached, the wind would die down, the mercury would rise, and the ravens, like the forerunner birds of his grandmother's tales, would soar in high circles. Cole had likened it to the receding of water before a tidal wave crashes ashore. Foreboding calm settled over the community that evening, so thick in the air that it was almost tangible, ominous even to the most casual of observers.

He arrived at the construction site on the western edge of town. The night sky on the drive over, once a sea of stars, yielded to the blinding halogen floodlights encircling the worksite. Above the skeletal structures of the unfinished duplexes, swirling snow reflected the intensity of the lights against the darkness of space, creating a spiraling void above it all. Cole imagined he was looking up into the depths of a black hole.

A young Inuit man in winter overalls and thermal boots opened the chain-link gate at the entrance for his truck. Dozens of men scurried to and fro wielding power tools and operating machinery, a frozen ant nest of activity. The crew onsite was a mixed bag of races, ages, and sizes; everyone was bundled up in survival suits and safety gear to allow them to work outside in the frigid conditions.

The town's population had increased exponentially in recent decades. The birth rate of the territory was more than double the national average, and most people lived in public housing. Half of the inhabitants collected welfare as their main source of income, and the unemployment rate was the highest in the country, so homeownership was rare among the Inuit people. More government infrastructure to support its people also meant more Southern workers being flown in to provide technical and administrative support, erect buildings, and run programs. Because the government failed year after year to provide adequate housing for the rising influx of Southern employees and the mushrooming Indigenous population, new building projects were a constant in the territory.

He sat in the warm truck amid the construction chaos, eyeing the crowd for someone in charge. When no one fit the bill, he opened his door to flag down a passing worker, as his driver's side window couldn't be lowered without the risk of it freezing open. After a quick exchange with a reluctant laborer, he learned that the foreman was in a work trailer at the back of the lot.

Karl Öysti sat behind a cluttered desk, his obese body practically engulfing his overtaxed office chair. Cole didn't bother to sort out whether he was a contractor or an employee. He called himself the foreman, so that was that. He had dark-ringed eyes and three chins concealing any possible trace of his neck. Dirty salt-and-pepper hair jutted haphazardly from under his black knitted cap. Piles of invoices, work orders, and assorted documents covered his desk, all topped with an open bag of cheese puffs and three cans of soda acting as paperweights.

The man remained high on Cole's list of people in town who would likely die of a heart attack before his time in Cape Dorset ended. There were no ambulances or paramedics, only the police. Cole had given CPR to seven people in town already. Only four of them survived. He wondered how he would manage to find a pulse through Öysti's thick layers of fat, let alone do chest compressions.

Öysti held up a finger for the officer to wait a moment as he growled orders into the handheld radio in what Cole assumed was Finnish. Somewhere outside, a dog barked in the distance, followed by the revving of a forklift engine. Cole scanned the room while he waited. The small trailer office reminded him of submarines he had seen in old films—dim light filling the cramped space, the scents of sweat and diesel exhaust heavy in the stagnant air, unfamiliar mechanical noises reverberating off the metal walls. The baseboard heaters were cranked, creating a space that felt hotter than a greenhouse in summer. Cole couldn't help but notice the damp, V-shaped sweat stain on the front of Öysti's gray T-shirt as he hung up the phone.

The fat man grabbed a cigarette from the nearby ashtray and raised his eyebrows to the officer while taking a long drag. The dry air left Cole's lungs feeling constricted and his throat parched, causing his first words to come out hoarse: "I know your people like saunas, but it's sweltering in here."

A deep cackle morphed into a hacking cough that took nearly a minute for Öysti to recover from.

"I hate the fucking winter," said Öysti. "And I don't pay the power bills."

He leaned back for another drag. A thin wisp of smoke drifted up to the ceiling.

"Is this about the beating the other night at the workers' residence?" he asked, reaching into the half-empty bag of cheese puffs, removing a large fistful, and then letting them fall into a pile on the papers in front of him.

Cole ignored his question. "Does anyone onsite have access to bolt cutters?"

"What's this about?" asked Öysti. His tone implied that he wasn't sharing any information unless he was sure it wouldn't get him in trouble.

"Someone stole something from the police shed," said Cole. "They cut their way in."

"Oh," said Öysti, his eyes widening slightly. "When?"

"Earlier today," said Cole. "Anyone take any tools offsite since this morning?"

Öysti laughed. "The workers steal anything that will fit in their suitcases so they can resell it when they go south, and the locals . . . they treat this place like a fucking buffet." He raised a handful of puffs to his mouth. "I can't keep tools on this site."

"They took something important," said Cole, growing impatient. A bead of sweat rolled down his forehead and he wiped it away with the back of his busted hand. "Otherwise I wouldn't be here."

"I'm a foreman, not a tool boss." Öysti scooped up a can of soda and took a deep swig. He flashed Cole a condescending look that made him want to slap it from his bloated face.

"What do you know about this big skinhead named Aiden?" said Cole, glancing out the window toward the yard.

"Ah, so it is about the beating," said Öysti with a satisfied grin. "You two can sort that shit out in person. He's manning the chop saw on the second floor of the first duplex."

Cole trudged across the bustling worksite, his boots squeaking on the compacted snow, barely audible over the hum of activity. He ventured into the duplex structure, encountering an unfinished staircase leading to the second floor. The shrill whir of a circular saw fired up as Aiden, spotlighted under an industrial work lamp, came into view. Cole sized him up immediately—shaved head, a wolf tattoo surrounded in runic symbols peeking out from the neck of his parka, and death's-head skulls on the backs of both hands. They clocked in at the same height, but Aiden tipped the scales about two weight classes higher.

He reminded Cole of a regular felon whom he would often cross paths with during one of his first postings in Alberta. That thug remained polite and friendly at the beginning of every arrest, but once the cuffs came out, he would always initiate a fight. Younger Cole hit the gym three times a week and sparred with active fighters to keep sharp. He would have tackled anyone, anytime. Those days were long gone. He knew he wouldn't last a round with a hoodlum like the one in front of him.

Aiden lifted his head as the saw powered down after a series of cuts. Cole raised a hand to get the big man's attention. At the sight of the uniform, Aiden froze—but only for a moment. Cole had no sooner stepped forward to introduce himself than Aiden sprinted toward the edge of the second floor and leapt through a narrow gap between support beams. Cole stood beside the power saw to catch his breath before stumbling toward the ledge to inspect the ground below. Expecting to see Aiden in a heap with broken limbs, he instead watched the fleeing suspect pull himself out of a waist-deep snowbank.

Cole stumbled down the stairs, but by the time he reached the yard, Aiden had vanished. He swore in frustration until a worker in bright orange coveralls pointed toward a chain-link fence at the far end of the worksite. He hobbled toward his truck as fast as his leg would allow. Aiden had barely crested the top of the fence when Cole put the vehicle in drive.

A forklift backing up hindered his exit from the compound. He pounded on the horn. After losing crucial seconds, he maneuvered the truck around the diesel rig and raced through the gate.

Spotting Aiden in the distance, he accelerated around the outer fence and headed toward him but soon realized he was approaching too fast for a crucial turn. Slamming on the brakes, Cole locked the truck into a long skid on the icy road that sent him drifting past the turnoff. When the vehicle came to rest, the back wheels were firmly lodged in a snow-filled ditch. Enraged at his own stupidity, he floored the accelerator while heaving the steering wheel back and forth, alternating between drive and reverse. Despite his best efforts, he succeeded only in making the vehicle more immovable.

He reached for the radio but hesitated before calling Veronica for help. She had finished her shift and was likely sitting in her warm apartment. He'd have to confess to going after Aiden alone and then admit to letting a suspect escape by foolishly jamming the truck into a snowbank. Granted, Aiden had limited options now that he had fled from the police. As an outsider, he had nowhere to hide, and the nearest community was at least a two-day ride by snowmobile. He wasn't going anywhere anytime soon, so getting in touch with Miller seemed like a much better option to Cole.

While he waited for Miller to answer on the handheld radio, Cole made a mental note to alert the police in the surrounding detachments to be on the lookout for a stranger of Aiden's description, should he manage to get that far. With no immediate response on the radio, Cole knew he couldn't afford to wait until the bitter cold set in. He bundled up and resigned himself to the long walk of shame to Miller's place.

CHAPTER 23

All the lights were out in the house where Pitseolala had died. Yellow police tape barricading the front entrance fluttered violently in the wind. People were superstitious about a place where there had been a violent death; no one would want to live in a residence where a young girl had once been found hanging. Plywood sheets had already been nailed over the lower windows to protect them from vandals. Empty and lifeless, it would likely remain vacant for a long time.

Cole awoke in the driveway to the distant growl of a passing snowmobile. The engine had been off when he'd fallen asleep. He attempted to clear his head with a long, slow exhale that filled the cold interior of the vehicle. *How long have I been out?*

After the long walk to Miller's house, they shared half a bottle of whiskey and several beers before using the winch on Miller's all-terrain vehicle to free the police truck. *What time did he pull me out of the ditch?* Cole asked himself. *Two, or three in the morning?* The dashboard's broken clock offered him no assistance, and his wristwatch was buried under layers of clothing.

Once fully alert, he recalled the moment when he'd stopped at the abandoned house on his way home from Miller's. Through the frosted glass of the passenger window, he could see that a snowdrift had formed on the steel staircase of the empty residence. Grim thoughts of the last time he climbed those steps seeped into his mind. *Was that a week ago already?* A sour taste crept into the back of his throat as he thought of what he'd found inside that fateful night. *Or was it yesterday?*

Cole started the engine and cranked the heater; cool air blasted from the dashboard vents as it warmed up. Snow swirled in the low beams of the vehicle; the unlit street beyond them lay deserted save for a pulsing red dot that approached in the darkness. It took a moment for Cole to recognize it as a burning cigarette. An unidentified man with a large, fur-trimmed hood came into view. The stranger trudged toward the police truck, head down against the gusting crosswind, wading through a large drift that had formed in the road. *Someone should have plowed that by now,* Cole thought, adding it to the long list of necessary tasks that people should have been doing in this town. His injured hand ached with the cold, so he gingerly rubbed it warm, careful to avoid the cut on his knuckles.

Why did I come back here? he asked himself. Later, in his logbook, he would record that this had been a routine check for vandalism, but deep down he knew the truth. A wave of guilt washed over him as he prepared to pull away. He ran his tongue over his upper teeth and back across the bottom ones. He needed badly to brush them, and he desperately wanted another drink even more. He debated going back home to accomplish both, but at that moment it seemed so far away. Everything did. Cole pushed the button to lock the doors and turned off the headlights. There would be no hag dreams in the driver's seat, and no piss-stained sheets or bloodstained floors if he slept in the truck, only the soft rumble of the engine and the gentle rocking of the cab in the gusting wind as he closed his eyes.

The following shift saw Cole and Veronica parked out front of the Kullu family house. The curtains remained drawn and the porch unlit. All the houses on that stretch looked the same, distinguished only by the varying debris in their yards and the makes of snowmobiles in their unplowed driveways. Most of the homes in Cape Dorset were not privately owned, and many were shoddily built during the rushed construction deadlines of the short summer.

"Seems like there's nobody home," said Cole, his foot on the brake.

Veronica held up a hand to wait, her eyes fixed on the house. She pulled on her fur hat and leather gloves. "He's probably carving out back."

Reluctantly, Cole slid the gearshift into park and donned his winter gear as well. He winced as he struggled to pull his glove on over his bandages.

"I'm no doctor," she said, "but it looks broken."

Ignoring the pain, he rotated his arm as if searching for fractures through the layers of fabric and flesh. "It's just bruised."

"You need to get some spikes for your boots," Veronica said with a hint of sarcasm and pointed toward her feet, clearly mocking his lie about falling on the ice. "Like mine."

Cole grunted affirmatively. He hated lying to everyone, telling them that he fell, almost as much as he hated losing control in the first place. He was moving to get out of the truck when Veronica laid a hand on his arm, stopping him from turning off the ignition.

"Did you get *any* sleep last night?" His partner stared at him with concern in her eyes. For a moment, he wondered if she somehow knew about his visit to the construction site and his misadventures with the police truck. Cole made a weak attempt at a reassuring smile. "A little."

"What's keeping you up lately? Kids again, or ravens on your roof?"

Local children were often seen roaming the streets at night making a racket; they particularly enjoyed tormenting police officers with gravel thrown at their homes during the wee hours. And the dark corvids had a strange habit of hopping around on the metal roofs of Northern homes at all hours. He didn't dare tell her about the late-night drinks with Miller or anything leading up to them, especially after his run-in with Jardin the bootlegger that went less than smoothly. He reminded himself for the third time to warn the other detachments and run Aiden's particulars through the federal databases to check for outstanding warrants and a criminal record.

"You ever woken up and you can't breathe, like someone or something's on your chest? Then you can't move. Awake, but still asleep. And you feel like there's someone else in the room." Cole realized he was gripping the wheel too tightly and released it. "I used to have those dreams a lot when I was younger."

"I heard an elder talk about dreams like that once. I can't remember the word for it in Inuktitut."

Cole waited for more, but Veronica just stared, expressionless, out the front windshield without saying a word. She jabbed a finger at the radio. "This shit has to stop."

From the speakers came a voice droning in Inuktitut at a volume so low that Cole had forgotten the radio was playing. The lone local "station" consisted of a pile of compact discs and cassette tapes located in a closet in the community center with a low-watt transmitter setup. It was manned for only several hours a day. Programming was in Inuktitut, but everyone in town listened to it for the music whether they spoke the language or not.

"They don't need to be playing this stuff," Veronica continued, turning it up.

"What is it?" asked Cole, concentrating on the language he didn't understand drifting through the speakers.

Veronica's face tightened. "Bible stuff. They've been playing it for days because of that group visiting. End-of-the-world shit."

"Revelations?"

"Yeah, that's the one. Winding up all the crazy listeners for us in time for the full moon."

Cole turned off the radio and shuddered at the thought of the future calls they were bound to receive. The two shared a long silence, steeling themselves to face the cold climate outside the vehicle and the grieving family who was going to learn about the theft of Pitseolala's corpse.

The high-pitched wail of an electric grinder filled the air around the two officers when they stepped out of the truck. Veronica halted near the front corner of the Kullu house.

"Ghost house," she whispered, pointing for Cole's benefit across to the derelict neighboring residence that had been boarded up years earlier. He trudged up beside her for a better look. His gaze followed the length of his partner's arm toward the snowdrift in front of the abandoned building. "It never used to drift there before, not until the woman who lived there died," she said, emphasizing the last word.

On several occasions, Cole had heard both Inuit and non-Inuit locals swear up and down that the drifting snow was somehow drawn to the derelict house. They claimed that the snow collected there more than anywhere on the street, right under the picture window where the former owner was shot and killed ten years earlier. Cole had pulled the police file out of curiosity. According to the report, the victim was shot in the bathroom and then dragged herself to the back bedroom, where she survived long enough to die on a medical evacuation plane en route to Iqaluit. But Cole never bothered to point that out to anyone who mentioned the cursed snowdrift.

"Shit," said Cole, turning to Veronica with a deadpan expression. "If snowdrifts are any indication, I think this whole town might be haunted."

The two officers walked around to the back of the Kullu house, tracing the snaking extension cords through the layers of snow. As they turned the corner, a makeshift shack came into view—a small framework of two-by-fours covered in contractor's plastic held in place with heavy staples. A dim light inside projected the silhouette of an old man hunched over against the outer covering. The grinder's screech intensified as Cole and Veronica approached. Veronica pulled back the plastic curtain covering the door. The elder, Pingwatsiak, sat on a stacked pair of overturned milk crates. He wore thick work gloves and a heavy parka stained with seal blood. Veronica waved her arms until she got the elder's attention. Pingwatsiak turned off the noisy machine and removed his protective earphones and tattered Bruins ball cap before he beckoned the officers farther inside and out of the bitter wind.

Veronica greeted the elder in Inuktitut. The old man pulled down the scarf that protected his mouth and nose from stone dust and made a vague sound that Cole didn't quite catch. He then laid the grinder down on the frozen ground beside him and pushed the fluorescent work light away from his stone carving to better illuminate the room. Cole examined the piece of soapstone sitting on the table-sized crate in front of the elder. Made from serpentine soapstone, consisting of a dark green mineral mottled like a snake's skin, the carving depicted a polar bear roughly the size of a large house cat. Upon closer examination, Cole could discern distorted human faces swirling within the animal's hide. He had seen numerous carvings like this one since his arrival in Cape Dorset. Known as transformation pieces, these works of art depicted the ability of a shaman to change shape and take the forms of animals.

He used to think that these large and complex soapstone carvings were an ancient tradition. Veronica had a good laugh at that idea: "You really think we carried around big, heavy carvings on our sleds when we were roaming the land hunting for food?"

The Inuit were originally a nomadic people. Prior to the arrival of European traders, all their utensils, tools, and weapons were furnished from stone and animal parts. It wasn't until the 1600s that the Inuit began to carve small animals in ivory to trade with whalers for necessities like guns, booze, and tobacco. This artistic culture gained momentum in the 1950s, when the government actively encouraged handicrafts, stone carving, and printmaking as sources of income for the Inuit, going so far as to bring instructors, tools, and materials to remote communities and create markets for the artworks in Southern Canada.

Veronica said something to the old man in Inuktitut and the elder raised his eyebrows high in response. She stepped forward and picked up the heavy piece of serpentine to admire it.

"This one is really nice," said Veronica to Cole before handing the carving to him. "He's famous, you know."

"Oh, I know," Cole said, hefting the piece. He offered a smile to the old man. "Tell him I think it's beautiful."

Veronica translated and the elder nodded at Cole in appreciation. Cole set the carving down on the pedestal as close to its original position as he could manage. Veronica spoke to Pingwatsiak at length in Inuktitut and he listened attentively before providing a very short response. He shoved his hat into his pocket and pushed past the two officers toward the exit.

"I told him about her body going missing," explained Veronica with a confused expression. "He said he already knows and wants us to come inside."

CHAPTER 24

Maliktu Kullu awoke on a makeshift mattress in the bottom of his closet. The dark cupboard served as a solitary refuge in his grandparents' overcrowded house. He rubbed the sleep from his eyes, detecting faint traces of kerosene and charred wood on his unwashed fingertips. Instinctively, he reached for the pocket of his jeans, finding the familiar shape of his sister's lighter through the denim. Keeping it with him brought a strange solace he didn't quite understand.

A sudden craving for a cigarette brought him bolt upright on his bed. He pushed his tongue into the gaping space where his tooth used to be. The familiar droning of his grandfather's grinder outside grated on his nerves. Normally, he wouldn't have minded the noise, but waking up with a stiff neck and a headache had left him irritable. Harrowing visions of a nightmare persisted in his mind. He had dreamt of jumping from ice floe to ice floe across the expanse of water behind the house. Pitseolala used to spend whole afternoons in late spring with him, leaping from one ice pan to the next, chasing each other to the far side of the harbor, all the while avoiding the frigid water beneath them. But in his dream, there was no sunshine, no Pitseolala, and no ice floes. Instead, the dark surface of the ocean teemed with bobbing corpses in the pallid moonlight. Naked bodies of dead children, from newborns through teens, covered the vast surface of the black water, thousands upon thousands of them as far as the eye could see. They all floated face up, their rotting flesh illuminated in the moon's glow, their once-delicate features distorted and bloated. Each one moaned in agony when his heavy boots landed on their chests with every leap, until a cacophony of such tortured voices filled his sleeping head, forcing him awake.

He pulled back the tattered blanket covering the closet door. The streetlight leaked in through the edges of the curtained window, illuminating the mattress where Pitseolala once slept. Maliktu wished he could have carried the bed with him to the hunting shack and burned it with her belongings. He averted his eyes from it in frustration and pulled his soiled T-shirt over his head; the smell of smoke in the fabric sent rousing shivers through his body.

Out in the unlit hallway, the house lay quiet, save for mumbling voices and canned laughter from a television commercial in the living room. Passing his grandparents' room, he paused at the sound of heavy breathing from within. Mercifully, his grandmother had finally fallen asleep after a restless night of crying out for his sister's return. He stepped inside the room, his bare feet creaking on the cold tile floor. He stood at the foot of the bed, flicking his lighter over and over in the darkness. The image of her prone body illuminated with every flash of the flint.

The grinder slowed to a halt outside, and his grandmother groaned and rolled onto her side. Maliktu slipped out and down to the living room, where his uncle and his girlfriend slept together on a battered couch. Their two children, both under eight years old, slept on a small mattress in the corner, huddled together, facing the wall. The occupants of the house were always in a state of flux. On the flickering television screen, a pale little girl talked with a boy her age on a playground in the snow. Both of them spoke a language Maliktu didn't understand, and he couldn't read the subtitles, so he didn't linger.

Yesterday, there had been talk of a funeral for Pitseolala and arguments with his grandparents over his refusal to attend. Three muffled voices sounded from the back porch as someone entered the house. In an attempt to avoid another confrontation, he quietly donned his winter clothes and stepped out the front door into the darkness of the morning.

Pingwatsiak's wife slumped on a mattress with her back against the wall. She coughed repeatedly into a tattered cloth. Her face appeared ghastly in the feeble light of the bedside lamp. Cole picked up his pace so he wouldn't startle her in the doorway. The old woman's hacking intensified as he continued down the hall, following the elder. He paused at what had to be the children's room. Veronica and Pingwatsiak kept going, conversing in Inuktitut as they walked into the kitchen. He leaned in and felt around for the light switch.

Two bare mattresses lay on the floor in separate corners, single blankets thrown haphazardly over each of them. Random fist-sized holes had been punched in the drywall at various intervals. Scribblings and drawings made with a permanent marker covered the walls up to the reach of a small child's arm. A couple of cinderblocks with a length of wood placed across as a shelf leaned against the far wall. It was piled with unfolded clothes up to his waist. The other wall, above one mattress, was decorated with girlish posters of teen heartthrobs ripped from magazines. Above the second mattress, tiny scraps of paper were held up by pins and electrical tape—remnants of pictures that had been hastily torn down. Pitseolala's bed, he knew.

A cluster of perforations in the drywall near the pillow, clearly made by the stabbing of a knife, caught his eye. He ran his fingers over the jagged cuts, feeling the anger and frustration beneath his fingertips. Cole lifted her mattress, hoping for a hidden diary, but found only two used condoms and some soiled clothing. The uplifted edge fell to the floor, and he closed his eyes. He felt his jaw clenching involuntarily again, his throat closing up. *Open hands, breathe in. Close fists, breathe out.*

He drew back the blanket that was nailed across the closet as a curtain. Winter clothing, both boys' and girls', of mixed sizes, hung from plastic hangers. Squatting carefully to avoid hurting his bad knee, he examined the makeshift foam mattress on the closet floor. A pair of boys' briefs, a tattered hunting magazine, and a broken plastic handgun. The musty smell of urine filled his nostrils. It was barely big enough for the boy. *He must sleep in the fetal position to fit in here.* He doubted that the boy would switch to Pitseolala's now-unused mattress. *Too painful,* he thought. He rose, slowly, using the doorframe as an aid. He had seen enough; it was time to join the others.

The two police officers and the elder sat at the kitchen table. The room smelled of iron and ocean, blood and saltwater.

A hunk of seal flesh the size of Cole's microwave thawed on a piece of cardboard in the center of the floor next to an axe likely used to chop it up. A long smear of blood on the linoleum revealed that it had been dragged there from the front porch. The chunk of meat was brownish crimson, with a thick layer of fat stained bright red by its spilled blood. Memories of the last time he ate seal, camping with his father as a child on the south coast of Newfoundland, came flooding back. He recalled boiling up a big feed in a large aluminum pot over a small keyhole fire on the rocky beach. He had been offered seal meat many times since moving to Cape Dorset, but he could never bring himself to eat it raw like the Inuit. The thought of trichinosis weighed heavily on his mind, and on his stomach. Even after living here in the Arctic, it still felt like the coldest he had ever been was on that trip with his father.

How old was I on that trip? And why weren't my brother and sister with us? Or were they? He wasn't sure if it was the fading of memory with age that prevented him from remembering the details, or if those memories were simply collateral damage from years of trying to forget all the misery he had endured as a child.

Veronica brought Cole up to speed on the conversation with

Pingwatsiak. Unable to speak English, the elder prepared his cup of tea while the officers spoke and then waited for Veronica to start speaking to him in Inuktitut again.

"Apparently, someone called yesterday to tell the family that the body was ready for pickup from the police shed, but they had to come quickly. So he called one of his sons, who took her body away by snowmobile on his *qamutiq*."

"What the fuck?" asked Cole, dumbstruck. He tried to gather himself. "The caller, did they say who they were?"

"His wife answered. Her English isn't very good. She didn't recognize his voice, but she was sure he was *Qallunaaq*. The caller never identified himself."

Cole felt the tension in his neck tighten, and he rolled his head back in an effort to relieve the pain. Nothing made any sense, and he wasn't even sure what questions to ask.

"His son said the lock was already cut when they showed up," Veronica continued. "They are bringing her by truck to the church this afternoon for the funeral. They apparently made an announcement on the radio earlier this morning."

"Jesus Christ," said Cole. "What the fuck is going on?"

"I have no idea," said Veronica. Her flabbergasted expression mirrored her partner's.

The elder said something in Inuktitut and Cole heard Maliktu's name among the foreign words. The elder's face seemed to shift from sorrow to sore disappointment at the mention of the boy.

"Where is Maliktu now?" asked Cole, looking at the elder.

"He doesn't know," said Veronica without translating the question. "He's apparently stopped going to school. He's refused to attend the funeral and has been avoiding everyone since Pits died. He also stopped taking his medication."

"What kind of medication?"

"As far as I can understand, it sounds like he's been diagnosed with some kind of mental illness. Hearing voices, seeing things. Pingwatsiak says his marijuana use has been making it worse."

Maliktu's grandfather and Veronica launched into a long discourse in Inuktitut. Near the end of the conversation, the elder palmed his chest gently several times. Veronica turned to Cole with the translation.

"Maliktu is bullied quite a bit by other kids, but he is a good boy. He always helps his grandparents, but the elder says he is getting too old to care for him. He's got problems with his lungs and his wife is getting weak with age."

Cole was unsure of what was being translated and what Veronica was omitting or adding based on her prior knowledge of Maliktu's home life or on her deeming something to be irrelevant. This was always a concern for Cole when working with interpreters in the community, but he trusted her judgment. Before Cole could ask another question, the old man spoke again.

"He wants to know if it's necessary to discuss the phone call with his wife. She has only been crying and sleeping since Pits died. He doesn't want to disturb her if we don't have to."

Cole responded by shaking his head, first to his partner and then more emphatically to the old man. Pingwatsiak, satisfied, pushed his chair back and shuffled across the kitchen to attend to the boiling kettle. Veronica leaned in toward Cole, her eyes wide and serious.

"Please tell me I don't have to ask for her body back. Don't make me go through that."

Cole stood up and stared down into the tabletop for several breaths. The idea of disrupting the funeral disturbed him. And he knew the autopsy request would likely be rejected by his superiors regardless. The whole case seemed like a distant dream at that moment. Lingering doubts swelled to massive proportions in his mind. The caller story made no sense. Perhaps the family fabricated the call to force the funeral, or perhaps someone in the community cut the lock and made the call to let them have one. Or maybe someone out there really was trying to cover up a murder. His mind seemed incapable of making sense of anything anymore. His legs felt wobbly, his balance unsteady. The only thing he was certain of was that he needed to lie down. He needed time and space to think, and more important, he needed rest.

Looking her in the eye, Cole shook his head decisively. "I'll be in the truck. Let him know they can keep her body."

Cole sat in the driver's seat of the truck, head thrown back, eyes sealed against the hot air blasting from the dashboard vents. Had he made the right decision to let them keep Pitseolala's body? He didn't have an answer, so he focused on the stillness and the quiet hum of the engine instead. He was asleep in minutes.

He awoke to the sound of Veronica climbing into the passenger seat. He twisted his head and hunched his shoulders to relieve the discomfort of sleeping at an awkward angle. She held out something toward him. It was a weathered piece of driftwood, slightly larger than his thumb, carved in the rough shape of a seal. The surface was stained a faded red. He fondled the talisman, rubbing its smoothness between his fingers.

"What's this for?"

"It's for your *uqumangirniq*."

"My what?"

"I blanked on the word, so I asked the elder. I told him you were having those nightmares, and he gave me this for you."

"A wooden seal?"

"That's an *aarnguaq*. A very old one. Ping said you can wither away from those types of dreams. He said you can't prevent the evil spirits from attacking your soul, your *tarniq,* because you are asleep, but this will help protect you."

He turned the seal-shaped token over in his hands, pondering its age and wondering if anyone had ever died from a hag dream.

"And you believe all this stuff?"

Veronica broke into an unexpected laugh. "When I can't sleep, I take pills."

Despite his weariness, he found the will inside himself to smile. He tucked the talisman into his breast pocket, wedged between his wedding ring and the photograph of Danny Carter.

Another charm certainly couldn't hurt.

CHAPTER 25

Cole stared at the pixelated image of Curtis Reynolds on the security monitor. Pitseolala's teacher sat alone in the interview room, leaning forward on the table, his little man bun bobbing whenever he took a sip from his coffee. He checked his watch repeatedly, likely wondering what was taking Cole so long. He had left the room nearly ten minutes earlier, telling Reynolds that he needed to print something out. The truth was he wanted to make him sweat a little.

He had even turned up the heat in the cramped room. He didn't do this out of cruelty, though Cole had to admit to a visceral dislike for the man and a consequent lack of concern for his discomfort. He wanted to see how he reacted under pressure, as well as push him off-center before questioning him.

When Cole returned, Reynolds appeared nervous and agitated, slumped in his chair, oppressed by the heat and the stale air, which now carried an unmistakable tang of fear sweat.

"I was beginning to think you weren't coming back," he said.

Cole ignored his remark and placed a digital recorder on the table between them without activating it. Reynolds eyed the device with obvious suspicion.

"We have some new information in Pitseolala's case. I was hoping you might be able to shed some light on it."

Reynolds's mouth twitched briefly into a shape that wasn't quite a smile. "Okay."

"The last time we spoke, you said that you didn't have much of a relationship with Pitseolala."

"That's true. When she came to class, which wasn't very often, she rarely spoke."

"What about outside of class?"

Reynolds immediately became wary, hesitating before he spoke again.

"What are you suggesting?"

"I'm not suggesting anything. I'm just curious."

"What is this all about?" He eyed him suspiciously.

"We have reason to believe that Pitseolala may have been pregnant at the time of her death."

Surprise flashed across Reynolds's face. "What? I didn't know anything about that. I mean, that's not something she ever confided in me about."

"Did she ever confide in you about other things?"

Reynolds paused before answering, making hard eye contact with Cole. "I'm not sure I'm comfortable with where this is headed."

"I know about your prior charges in Montreal."

"I think I'm done here." Reynolds slid his coffee to the center of the table and pushed his chair back.

Cole made a conscious effort not to come to any conclusions based on Reynolds's comments and body language. After the Carter case, he no longer trusted his gut; there had to be hard evidence or a confession. If he was wrong, the fallout would destroy this man's life and livelihood merely by allegation. He had to tread carefully.

"Now I understand why you didn't want to speak with me at the school."

"Those girls lied," snapped Reynolds. "They fabricated the whole thing out of some perverse fantasy and ruined my fucking life. It almost destroyed my marriage and my career before it got thrown out."

"Having the charges dropped isn't the same thing as being found innocent. I've got a young pregnant girl whose teacher was previously charged with sex crimes against his students. And I believe she—and her baby—were murdered."

Reynolds's eyes went wide, blood draining from his face. "I think I need to talk to my lawyer."

The truth was that Cole had no hard evidence to hold Reynolds. He didn't have reasonable grounds to charge him with any crime. His only hope was to provoke or frighten him into a confession or, at the very least, get him to reveal information that might incriminate him.

"You're not under arrest. You don't have to talk to me. You can leave. You can call a lawyer when you get home. I just wanted to have a follow-up chat. Unless, of course, you wanted to give a statement."

"I won't be making any statements," said Reynolds.

"Let me tell you what I know." Cole sat down and relaxed his tone. "Pitseolala's friend told me she had a secret boyfriend."

"And you think that person is me?" Reynolds looked incredulous.

"I didn't, but then I found out about Montreal. Homeroom teacher sleeps with students. Both girls similar in age to Pits. What should I think?"

"I'm not saying anything else."

"Where were you on the night Pitseolala died?" asked Cole.

"I've been at home alone every night this week."

"With your wife and daughter living in another province, you must get lonely there."

Reynolds glared at him.

"Do you own any bolt cutters?"

"Bolt cutters? No. I don't have any tools up here."

Cole paused before asking the next question, the only one that mattered. They had no forensic samples from the fetus, but Reynolds had no way of knowing that.

"It would be helpful if we could exclude you as the father. Would you be willing to give a DNA sample?"

Reynolds refused.

"If you're not the father, why not submit to the test?"

"This is just like last time. You're not trying to help me and anything I do to help you just makes it easier for you to fuck me over. I am so fucking done with this shit. I'm out of here." Reynolds stood up abruptly. "And I am going to talk to my lawyer and then we're going to sue your sorry ass."

He quickly left the interview room, slamming the door on his way out.

With the slam still echoing in his ears, Cole whispered to himself: "You'll have to get in line."

CHAPTER 26

A hand-carved wooden Jesus on the cross hung, crooked, above the homemade altar. The Savior's face had been crudely repainted with colors that didn't quite match the skin tone of the rest of his body. The grotesque paint job reminded Cole of a drunken drag queen he had once arrested in Alberta. He smirked at the random memory from a lifetime ago, all but forgotten.

He stood at the back of the room, near the door, leaning against the wall to relieve his aching knee, leaving the limited seating for family and locals as they streamed in out of the cold to await the arrival of the body. The stagnant air of the overheated church mingled with the scents of pine cleaner and cheap incense. No windows meant no airflow. The furnace had been cranked since the minister arrived to unlock the doors hours before, and the sweat of the congregation now flowed freely. Cole shivered despite the suffocating heat. A miasma of stale alcohol filled the room as the crowd grew, many of them coming down from a binge after last night's community dance.

Oblivious to the sadness that surrounded them, a couple of toddlers rolled around laughing in the main aisle. Both were malnourished with dirty hands, their lips and the skin around their mouths stained bright colors from eating too much candy. He felt nauseous watching them play. He could understand why Maliktu refused to come. This was not where he wanted to be either.

Cole swallowed hard and dropped his gaze to the pew in front of him. Cigarette burns riddled the back of the bench. He ran his index finger slowly along the wood, connecting the black dots. His eyes focused on the stitches on his injured knuckles. He'd been clean since breakfast. No coffee, no booze, no pills. He'd traded it all for constant pain and a withdrawal headache.

A shout from the doorway alerted the crowd to the arrival of the body. Cole stepped outside into the bitter cold. The rusted remains of an abandoned snowmobile, stripped of any useful parts, lay discarded just outside the main door. He shoved his hands deeper into the pockets of his parka and shuffled away from the church with the rest of the crowd. He counted his steps as he walked; seventy-five to the cemetery on the hill behind the dilapidated chapel. There was no fence around the burial ground; the Inuit had no need for such barriers in a place where land was communally owned. Dozens of simple white crosses were scattered seemingly haphazardly about the graveyard, many half buried by the drifting snow. Since he arrived in Cape Dorset, he hadn't seen anyone visit the area, outside of funerals.

They stopped walking. He looked away from the open grave and noticed a small wooden cross—a name and dates scrawled in permanent marker with crude hearts drawn at either end. He calculated the time between the dates. Six months old. His nostrils flared as he breathed in, the cold air stinging his sinuses. The moon, almost full, came into view from behind cloud cover. He billowed icy crystals with a long exhale.

Cole had arrived for this posting during the summer. He had seen the cemetery when it wasn't blanketed in white. Beneath the snow, each grave was cribbed with pieces of thick timber and a sheet of Plexiglas screwed over the wooden frame. Inside the makeshift display cases lay random favorite objects from the lives of the deceased: empty packs of cigarettes, plastic flowers, children's toys. Wind-weathered stuffed animals wrapped in plastic were duct-taped to several of the crosses.

He walked among the graves while he waited for the ceremony to start, treading lightly over the snow to avoid breaking through the hard surface. Most of the people buried beneath his feet hadn't reached their tenth birthday. Some hadn't had a chance to learn to crawl. Accidents, murders, suicides, illnesses. Dying of old age was rare in Cape Dorset.

An odor he couldn't place drifted past him. *Was it the same flowery scent Pitseolala wore on the night he found her body?* He rubbed a gloved hand under his nose and shuddered before realizing it was a woman's perfume from the crowd carried on the wind.

He returned to Pitseolala's gravesite and stood between two elderly Inuit men. Both were smoking, heads down with their parka hoods pulled up and their backs to the wind. Everyone around him was finishing the cigarettes they had lit before leaving the chapel. Twilight had peaked five minutes prior, so the funeral procession all had headlights on. Several snowmobiles and four-wheel ATVs followed behind them, a handful of people clinging to each machine. Pitseolala's plywood coffin lay in the back of a banged-up pickup truck. Two of her male relatives sat on either side of the casket, holding on to the sides of the truck bed to keep from tumbling out onto the uneven road. Neither wore a hooded parka, instead tucking their heads down behind the cab to protect themselves from the wind. A chill came over Cole as he watched them approach the grave. He shook his arms and shuffled his feet to get the circulation flowing, surveying the crowd as he moved.

All the mourners were Inuit except for him, the local minister, a couple schoolteachers, and Felix Bauer, the social worker, who chatted nearby with Pitseolala's aunt. Veronica had remained at the detachment to make a court appearance in Iqaluit by telephone. He hated going to court, especially doing it remotely on a landline and spending the bulk of the day tethered to his desk and kept on hold, but he envied her excuse for not attending. Funerals made him increasingly uncomfortable in recent years, perhaps because he was getting older and had been to so many of them. Each one felt more like a dress rehearsal for his own.

As the truck pulled up and the men gathered to haul the casket out, the minster took a sheet of paper from his parka and unfolded it.

"And now a reading from the Book of Job," said the minister, pausing to allow the man beside him to roughly translate his words into Inuktitut for the mourners. He had barely finished the first line when the wailing started. This was Cole's fifth funeral in Cape Dorset, and the keening began at roughly the same time every time. A visiting nurse had once told him that this style of mourning was "an Inuit thing." He wasn't sure if that was true, but he'd certainly seen nothing like it anywhere else he'd been.

"Ah, would that these words of mine were written down, inscribed on some monument with iron chisel and engraving tool, cut into the rock forever," said the minister, followed by the Inuk layman's translation.

Cole looked out across the vast expanse of uninhabited land beyond the graveyard. There was no vegetation this far north, nothing living beneath the snow. The landscape reminded him of the stony cliffs back home, near his grandfather's burial site. His grandmother had told him spooky stories at night over the many times he stayed with her as a child. Wailing banshees, eerie lights in the woods, ghostly doppelgängers that foretold a person's death. He was reminded of her tales as the keening of the mourners stirred the dogs on the nearby sea ice to howl along in unison. The clamor rose in pitch and volume, and his pulse pounded in his ears.

"This I know: that my Avenger lives, and he, the Last, will take his stand on earth. After my awakening, he will set me close to him, and from my flesh, I shall look on God."

Cole looked up, brooding, toward the ancient, rocky hillside, where a shadowy figure caught his eye in the fading twilight. As quickly as he saw the silhouette against the moonlit snow, it disappeared. His mind was playing tricks on him again. He twisted his phantom wedding ring as his injured hand tingled with pins and needles. A band constricted around his torso; his teeth clenched. This was more than a hangover.

The minister continued, his voice rising, practically shouting over the din of the mourners and the bracing wind.

"He whom I shall see will take my part: These eyes will gaze on him and find him not aloof!"

Panic overwhelmed Cole at the sight of the plywood coffin being moved out over the grave by a series of men holding attached ropes. He suddenly imagined her alive in the box, her fingernails snapping and bleeding as she clawed at the inside of the lid, mourners unable to hear her pounding and screaming over the keening of the family members and the incessant shouting of the minister. *Open hands, breathe in. Close fists, breathe out.* He turned toward the truck and jostled through the crowd, squinting as his vision blurred, clenching and unclenching his hands as he struggled to breathe. *Keep it together. Just get to the vehicle.* Staggering over the uneven ground through shin-deep snow, he fled the graveyard.

Cole pulled himself into the cab and slammed the door behind him, cutting off the unholy sounds. He gripped the steering wheel with both hands, knuckles whitening, and leaned his forehead against it. *I should have reported it as a murder.* Taking off his hat, he balled it up and squeezed it in his fists. *I should have taken a medical leave when I hurt my knee.* He needed to get his breath under control. *There'd be an emergency response team here to replace me.* He needed to slow his breathing, slow his heart rate, stop the panic. He needed to be somewhere else. Anywhere else.

A rapid knocking on the window broke his train of thought and snapped him out of his spiral. Felix's face appeared through the frosted pane on the passenger side. Cole pulled himself together, replacing his hat on his head. He took two deep breaths before he unlocked the doors and motioned for Felix to get in.

"Much obliged," said Felix, opening the door and taking the passenger seat. "I saw you heading out and was hoping to catch a ride back to work."

Cole steadied himself and then forced himself to speak as he started the engine. "You leaving early too?"

Felix acknowledged with a nod. He removed his gloves and

warmed his hands on the dashboard vents. "Not to be disrespectful, but I've had enough wailing and potential frostbite for one day."

"Agreed," said Cole. He yanked the gearshift into drive and the two men rode away from the cemetery in silence until they passed the old hotel. The once-beautiful mural of Inuit art had faded and cracked before being covered in graffiti by the local kids.

"I wonder if things'll ever get better here," said Cole, thinking aloud.

"Before the white man came, the average lifespan was less than thirty-five," said Felix. "They were nomads, living day-to-day on the brink of extinction. I'm not sure it was ever good, despite what the academics would have us believe."

Cole didn't respond. When he first arrived in the North, he used to hang out in the evenings with professional non-Inuit who were there on short contracts or visiting the town—doctors, lawyers, nurses, tradespeople. Conversations inevitably descended into a verbal tailspin of war stories of their negative experiences in the North, particularly after a few drinks, each trying to outdo the other with tales of institutional dysfunction, deteriorating social ills, and witnessed atrocities. No one in the South would believe any of them unless they had spent time up here. It was a secret fraternity of tragedy that he'd never wanted to be a part of. Here, in the truck, Cole was unwilling to get into a debate with a stranger about the merits and history of the Inuit. He'd given that up long ago; it wasn't his place to judge or speculate about a culture that wasn't his. He'd decided to leave that to reporters and professors who had never been here.

The truck rounded the turn toward the school and passed the usual crowd loitering in front of the Northern Store. His mind drifted back to the funeral and the oration of the preacher.

"You believe in God?" Cole asked without taking his eyes off the lone headlight of an oncoming snowmobile.

"I spent my life working and volunteering in war zones and disaster areas. Afghanistan, Congo, Louisiana after Katrina, Haiti after the big quake. I think a man has to be godless once he experiences places like those. It's too hard to reconcile any kind of loving God with what you see there. And here."

Cole slowed the truck to allow a group of pedestrians to cross the road toward the elementary school. He switched on his high beams again once the people passed.

"Do you?" asked Felix.

Cole shook his head. "But I think it might help to right now."

They rolled to a gentle stop outside the town hall, where Felix's office was located. Felix readjusted his winter gear before stepping out. He paused with his glove on the door handle. There was an odd expression on his face that Cole found hard to read.

"You sticking around for the holidays?" Felix asked.

"Yeah." Cole nodded. "I'll be here."

"No family to visit?"

Cole snorted derisively before he could catch himself. "Not this year."

"I'm heading out this weekend on a flight south. Weather permitting. Heading someplace hot for a little while."

"Good," said Cole, shifting the vehicle into park and taking his foot off the brake. "Think of the rest of us when you're down there."

Felix turned to leave again, hesitating a second time. "How goes your investigation into Pitseolala's suicide?"

"Well, there won't be an autopsy with her body under six feet of permafrost. So, I'd say not great."

"Did you find anything of use in my file?"

"To be honest, I haven't read it in full," he lied, not wanting to get into a discussion about what he'd seen in the file. He flashed Felix a sad smile before looking back at the road. Nothing but swirling snow in the glow of the headlights. In truth, he'd pored over the report a dozen times, searching for a clue to her death that simply wasn't there. Reviewing Felix's file had brought him no closer to understanding why Pitseolala might have taken her life. It merely brought the anger and frustration over her death back to the surface. Perhaps the autopsy being canceled was a sign that it really was time to let it go. "I just skimmed through it a couple times," he said.

Felix adopted a serious expression and spoke in a softer voice. "Is everything all right?"

Cole tightened his grip on the steering wheel. A sudden gust of wind rocked the vehicle. "What do you mean?"

Felix hesitated, gesturing at Cole's injured hand before locking eyes with him. "I saw the look on your face when you were leaving the funeral." He paused again, as if searching for the right words. "You looked . . . distressed."

After a long silence, Cole replied, "Have you been talking to Veronica about what's going on between us?"

"Not at all." Felix looked away, adjusted his mitts, and glanced at his watch before looking back at Cole. "I just spend all day talking to people who are going through tough times. So I know what that looks like."

"Yeah," Cole mumbled, unable to think of anything else to say without saying too much, which he really wasn't up for. Especially with a stranger.

Felix offered him a warm smile. "It may be a cliché, but it really can help to talk about it, whatever it is, with someone. Hell, sometimes it's enough just to have a little company. Why don't you pop by my place for supper and a drink after you close up shop?"

"Thanks for the offer," said Cole, intending to decline. He thought about going back to his ugly, soulless house for another shitty meal, remembering that he'd poured the remainder of his liquor down the drain in a moment of misguided clarity. He nodded slowly. "I'll swing by."

"It's the house tucked right behind the health center. Anytime after six."

He waited until Felix crossed the parking lot and opened the door of his building, watching the interior light bleed out into the darkness in the brief moment it was ajar before he pulled away.

Maliktu perched on the steep embankment in the soft gloaming light. Snow filled his left boot from an earlier misstep that sunk him up to his thigh. The climb had taken him less than an hour but felt like years. From up on the hillside, everyone down in the cemetery looked insignificant. He tucked himself into a crevasse between two halves of a split boulder that was twice his height to escape the wind. This was one of his hiding places, where he could nestle himself away from the world, far from the town and the harshness of reality. His grandfather had once explained how water would seep into a crack in a rock and the expanding ice could push even the strongest stone apart. Maliktu rubbed a fur mitten along the rugged surface of the corridor through the boulder and closed his eyes, imagining instead that an angry giant had split the rock with a blow from the edge of his huge hand. He pulled one of Pitseolala's cigarettes from the pocket of his parka and sparked it up. The music from the hills was constant now. It swelled up inside him. The darkness between the stars above him mirrored the darkness he felt in his heart without his sister, and only fire could keep it at bay. He could sense Pitseolala behind him, watching, waiting, and he knew there was something out on the horizon he couldn't quite discern, something big, something ferocious, much larger than a giant, large enough to swallow a whole town. All through his body he felt the changes in the atmosphere, the subtle shifts in pressure and temperature. A storm was coming for them all.

CHAPTER 27

Maliktu had passed the building a thousand times without consciously noticing its foreboding presence. Unseen and unremarkable, it blended into the background of the neighborhood. A relic of the early 1950s, clad in wooden clapboard, the little house sported a faded and forgettable shade of green. Since its construction more than half a century ago, it likely housed a revolving door of transient inhabitants year after year. An equally ancient Ford truck lay dormant in the driveway, hemmed in by a winter's worth of snow. All the curtains were drawn so tight that no light could slip between the fabric and the frames. The shadows around the edges of the house seemed somehow blacker than the night itself.

To the casual observer, it looked vacant, but Maliktu knew in his heart that something very dark and dangerous lurked within its walls. He stood alone, staring at the house from across the deserted street. His eerie music drifted to him gently from the surrounding mountains, whispering its sad and discordant refrain. Schools had emptied an hour ago, and Cape Dorset hunkered down in preparation for the coming blizzard, yet he remained outdoors despite the threat. If he had any reservations that this place housed the person who killed his sister, they were canceled out by the hazy outline of a familiar figure in the shadows across the street. Pitseolala appeared as a flickering shape, gray on black, almost invisible unless one was really looking for her. She waited, motionless except for the bottom edge of her *amauti,* which flapped silently in the wind. She stood at the corner of the house, waiting for him to join her.

Earlier, Maliktu sat in his own house while the rest of the family mourned at the funeral. Cold and weary, he had had enough of watching the burial from high up on the snowy hillside and wandered down to warm up before they returned home. Drawn by a strange urge to his living room window, he pressed his face to the glass, cupping his hands around his eyes to shut out the background light. The icy pane stung his bare hands and numbed the tip of his nose. Holding his breath to keep from fogging up the glass, he saw her silhouette across the street, beckoning him. He obliged, dashing to the porch, throwing on his snow pants, and donning his hand-me-down parka. Tearing open the front entryway, his boots clomping on the icy steps, he began a long chase across town, following her apparition, which led him to this mysterious house.

He had forgotten his gloves in the mad rush to get outside and so he pulled his hands up inside the arms of his parka. Frigid air rushed up his open sleeves; the skin of his arms burned from the bitter cold. A passing sewage truck barreled down the road between Maliktu and his sister. Because the hamlet had no underground pipes, trucks pumped toilet waste out of every home in the hamlet, day and night, making children wary of the icy roads. The massive tanker's rumble deafened Maliktu, who snapped his eyes shut against the rushing air, remembering his friend Qavavau, who was struck and killed two winters ago.

When he opened his eyes, the vehicle was already halfway down the hill, and Pitseolala had vanished into the night. Desperation drove him to sprint toward the spot where she last stood, yelling out her name, hoping it would carry to her on the wind that whipped past him. Each step through powdery snow proved treacherous, and he sank to his waist three times before reaching the rear of the house.

A faint light emanated from a small window at the top of the snowdrift built up against the rear of the building. Climbing the packed slope with determined kicks, Maliktu caught a glimpse of his sister through frosted glass before she drifted out of view. Ice clung to her hair, and a lifeless flap of skin dangled from her cheek.

For agonizing minutes, he stood frozen by the window, desperate to see her again. Numbness crept into his feet and hands. It was now or never, just moments left before he succumbed to the relentless elements. He wedged his deadened fingertips into the edge of the frame and jerked repeatedly. Frozen solid, it wouldn't budge. Brushing away the snow, he hammered on the icy frame with his elbow, but it still wouldn't give. Locked, he decided. Leaning back, he braced himself on the slope and kicked at the glass until it shattered. He reached through the shards and unlocked the frame.

Maliktu sparked up his lighter, its flame flickering in the howling wind that whipped flurries around the room. Floor-to-ceiling wooden shelves held an array of dry goods, cleaning products, and liquor bottles. He realized that he was standing in the sealift room of the house, surrounded by the owner's provisions brought in during the summer months before the sea passage was choked with ice. He felt a sense of security only the warmth of the house could provide. Snapping off the lighter, he climbed up onto the nearest shelf, using boxes of detergent to block the wind coming through the fractured glass.

In the darkness, he groped with his still-numb fingertips until he found a doorframe. His heavy boots clomped on the hardwood floor, echoing through the silent house. Mindful of the possibility of an occupant taking a mid-afternoon nap motivated by the constant darkness of winter, he stepped out of his boots, holding his breath as he carried them across the room.

His leg muscles tightened, ready to sprint back to the broken window at the slightest provocation. Hairs lifted on the unburned portions of his neck and arms as a pungent odor enveloped him. Amid the musk, the unexpected scent of perfumed flowers cut through the air. Before he could process the aroma, a giggle erupted from the shadows—a familiar sound that once went unnoticed but now sent chills down his spine, setting his nerves on edge.

He relit his lighter with his hands trembling, further shaking the wavering flame as he pursued the source of the laughter toward a door adjacent to the kitchen. The adjoining room appeared empty save for the furniture. He scanned for any hint of his sister's presence but found himself alone. Perhaps she had brought him to the place she wanted and then returned to whatever strange plane she inhabited now.

Relief at her absence washed over him. Despite his deep affection for her, memories of their last encounter flashed in his mind, and he cringed at her disfigured appearance and the unholy sounds that had erupted from her throat. He placed his boots in the center of the room for a moment, his forearm aching from their weight. He rotated his wrist in circles to relieve the tension. Fumbling in the dark, he discovered an electric heater and squatted down to warm his frozen fingertips. Holding his lighter aloft, he identified a bed, a chest of drawers, a nightstand with a stereo and a lamp, along with a closet door in the corner. His mind raced with questions. Why here? What was he looking for?

He noticed a dark green soapstone carving on the dresser, a sculpture reminiscent of the work of his grandfather. The figurine portrayed the transformation of a great shaman into a multitude of beasts all at once. Its face half man, half raven. The legs and claws of a bear. A body that swirled in metamorphosis. An object gleamed in the light of his flame, hung on a thin chain from the raised arm of the shaman. Even in the near dark, Pitseolala's cross was unmistakable. The realization struck him—this was why she had brought him here.

Without warning, snow crunched on the steps outside under the weight of shuffling feet. Maliktu jerked his head toward the sound. A banging noise followed, loud and frantic. His thoughts drifted to imagined visions of her killer trying to break down the door. His limbs seized and his brain threw itself into overdrive. Closing his eyes, he hoped and wished for the noise to fade away.

And soon it stopped, only to be replaced by muffled voices. Maliktu opened his eyes, realizing that it was men, not a monster, who lurked on the threshold. Panic set in as he considered his predicament. He didn't dare run back to the sealift room to climb out the window he had smashed; there wasn't time. The front door opened and closed with a slam. The voices moved inside the house. Maliktu scanned the bedroom quickly before diving under the mattress. He held his breath and waited while the unknown men moved into the kitchen. He couldn't hear what they were saying through the walls of the bedroom, but he knew that they might discover him at any moment.

Maliktu curled into a fetal position beneath the bed. The kitchen light flicked on. From under the bedroom door, a crisp line of light seeped through the gap between the duvet and the floorboards, illuminating the cramped space. The voices outside intensified, now audible but still unrecognizable. He drew a deep breath through his nose, holding it, in an effort to control his racing heartbeat. All the noises inside him—the rapid thump of his pulse, the grinding of his teeth, the rumbling of his guts—seemed deafening in the heightened anxiety of the moment. As his brain whirled, he heard the sound of breathing but realized that he was still holding his own. He felt a hot breath on the back of his neck as the pungent stench of decaying flesh enveloped him.

CHAPTER 28

Beneath the dim light of a single bulb, Felix struggled with the dead bolt of his frozen front door. He used his aluminum key chain to chip away at the ice over the keyhole that had built up since he had left for work that morning.

Cole, with Pitseolala's file tucked under his arm, shifted his weight onto his good leg. The snow crunched and squeaked under his feet as he repositioned himself on the doorstep. Too much time bearing weight on his bad leg in the cold brought continuous dull pain to his compromised knee. He had arrived at Felix's house five minutes ago to find the social worker locked out. The bitter cold made it feel like an hour had passed. Fine crystals of exhalation from the two men sparkled in the light before drifting away on the crisp breeze.

"You need help with that?" asked Cole. "I've got lock deicer in my truck."

"No, it's like this every day," replied Felix. "It'll just take a sec."

Cole wasn't sure how many more seconds his aching joints could handle. A distant snowmobile engine droned past, echoing off the neighboring buildings. He distracted himself from the pain by surveying the landscape around him. A dozen chimneys sent smoke drifting up above the town lights. In the gloom, he could barely make out the familiar shape of a polar bear pelt stretched out on a wooden frame leaning against the house next door. Bears rarely came into the community unless they were starving or lured by the scent of a rotting carcass discarded illegally at the local dump. The sight of the hanging pelt reminded Cole of the danger a live bear on the loose in a small community could pose.

Felix gave a celebratory exclamation as the dead bolt turned. He opened the door, flooding the front step with light and a rush of warm air.

"Come in, come in," said Felix, holding the door for Cole. They shuffled inside to escape from the cold. Felix removed his fogged-up eyeglasses, and both placed their parkas near the electric porch heater.

"Sorry for the wait," said Felix, with an undercurrent of anger in his voice. "I was hoping to get home before you arrived to start cooking supper."

"No worries," mumbled Cole, struggling to untie his frozen bootlaces yet again. He cursed the police force for not issuing boots that could be easily slipped on and off.

"I'll make us some tea," said Felix, heading for the kitchen and flicking on lights as he went. "Or would you prefer some coffee?"

Despite the bland and generic exterior of the house, the interior had the hygge of a Scandinavian cottage. Bright white walls, furs draped over scattered furniture, unlit candles, and artwork created a warm and cozy atmosphere. Unlike the newer homes in the community, including Cole's own dwelling, the older ones built during the bygone days of fur trading and missionaries always had a quirky layout and a quaint charm, and were often made with sturdier materials and better craftsmanship. He eyed a pile of pallets next to an antique woodstove that supplemented the oil furnace. Such stoves were rare in the territory, given that they lived so far above the tree line. He was tinged with jealousy as he considered his own spartan house.

"Tea is fine, thanks," said Cole, removing his gloves and hat. "You've got a really nice place."

"Thank you," said Felix, pulling down little boxes from the cupboard. "What kind would you like? I've got pu-erh, Darjeeling, and Lapsang souchong."

"On second thought, I'll have coffee. As long as it is coffee flavored."

Felix laughed, revealing his pristine white teeth. "Instant okay?"

Cole nodded.

"Make yourself at home," said Felix. He hesitated before grabbing the kettle and rubbed his forearms with his palms. "Strange. It's a lot colder in here than it usually is."

Cole laid Pitseolala's file on the table. "Anything's better than outside."

Felix set the kettle on the electric range to boil before adding more pallet scraps to the woodstove. Cole noticed three masks hanging on the living room wall. One was rust colored with deep-set eyes and a crooked nose with several small leather pouches tied into its long gray hair. The second looked African in origin to Cole—a bald face with delicate feminine features, hand-carved from what appeared to be mahogany, with jagged teeth and wooden hoop earrings. Ritual markings lined its cheeks and forehead, its eyes exaggerated and bulging, almond-shaped with lids half closed. A third false face was more devilish and colorful, an open, angry mouth with large curled horns.

"You like masks," said Cole, with an intonation that made it half a statement, half a question.

"I try to pick one up in every country I visit. Those three are from my ex, who knows I have a thing for masks and apparently still has a thing for me."

"Divorced?"

"In a fashion, yes." He walked over to stand next to Cole. "We used to travel extensively. Got married in Haiti, more symbolic than official. When we separated, we stopped communicating, but every so often I'd get another mask addressed to me from a different place. I have about six more from her in storage down south."

"Could be worse. My ex just sends me bills and papers to sign."

Felix let out a laugh. He pointed to each mask, identifying them as he went. "That one's a *Mwana Pwo* from Angola. That's Navajo from the States. And that one is a Krampus from Germany. I've also got an Iroquois false face and a copper mid-century African one from a very remote region in the bathroom."

Another mask on the far wall grabbed Cole's attention. It didn't fit in with the others. A bone-white plaster cast of a young girl's face, eyes closed, expression tranquil. Felix noticed Cole's interest and walked over to admire it with him.

"Beautiful, isn't she? I found her at an antique store in Paris."

Cole stayed silent, taken in by the girl's expression. Calm, serene. Her lips tight, edges upturned as if she were smiling at a pleasant thought.

"She's the most kissed woman in the world," said Felix.

Cole looked toward his host, skeptical and curious for more details. Felix carefully took the mask from the wall.

"They call her *L'Inconnue de la Seine*." Felix held it for Cole to get a closer look. "*Parlez-vous français?*"

"Languages are not my strong suit," said Cole. "Unfortunately."

"It means 'the unknown woman of the Seine.' Sixteen when she was pulled out of the river at the Quai du Louvre in the 1880s. She had thrown herself into the water to die and no one claimed her body. The story goes that they were so taken by her beauty at the morgue that they made a plaster cast of her face. Copies were made, then more and more. Before long, every fashionable person in Paris had her death mask on their wall."

While Cole examined the smooth, flawless skin of the dead girl, his thoughts drifted to the Carter boy he'd carried up that steep embankment. The child's bloated and discolored face, his gaping mouth and lifeless eyes, forever etched into his brain. He wiped a hand across his lips as if to erase the bad taste that memory had left.

"I've pulled bodies before. They don't look that healthy when they come out."

Felix replaced the death mask on its hooks. "I have a confession to make," he said. "I did an internet search on you after we met. I read about the poor boy in Alberta. Very tragic."

The kettle in the kitchen mercifully whistled. Cole seized the distraction to change topics. "So who kissed her?"

Felix laughed abruptly, moving to the stove. "In the sixties, a Norwegian toy maker created the first CPR dummy. He used her face for the prototype. They've been using it ever since."

Cole followed, taking a seat at the kitchen table.

"I may have made out with her once. Back in my depot days."

Awkward laughter filled the space between them. Felix moved the wailing kettle to a cold element. He picked up a chef's knife and stared at the kitchen tiles.

"There's water on the floor," said Felix with a perplexed look before crossing the room to activate the record player. Moody jazz filled the room. "I hope the refrigerator isn't leaking." He grabbed a roll of paper towels and wadded up a handful, using it beneath his foot to mop up the unexplained spillage.

"You said you traveled a lot," said Cole. "Any warm spots I should consider for my retirement?"

"Sadly, I spent most of my time outside this country in destinations with government travel advisories. They were all unbearably hot, so when I did go somewhere less dangerous for pleasure, it was usually someplace cold—Russia, Greenland, Iceland."

"You really got around. I'm envious. I've never been off the continent."

"I never spend more than a year in one place if I can avoid it. The Portuguese have a word for which there is no English equivalent—*saudade*. It means nostalgia, a longing for something you once had. Whenever people ask me, I tell them my *saudade* keeps me moving."

"You speak Portuguese too?"

"No, but I lived there for a time, ninety-four to ninety-five." A wistful expression came over Felix's face, as if he'd thought of a fond memory from that period.

"So, what are you longing for that keeps you traveling?"

"Something I can never have back." There was something in Felix's tone, a sadness perhaps. Cole instinctively shifted gears to avoid pressing the topic. His voice lifted.

"You got any family down south for Christmas?"

"No. I'm pretty much alone. My parents are both gone. I had a sister, but she died a long time ago."

"I'm sorry."

"Don't be." Felix poured the contents of the kettle into two cups, one with a tea bag and one with instant coffee, before bringing them over to join Cole. "We were both very young at the time. She fell from a train bridge while we were walking home from school."

Cole felt the weight of the statement bearing down on both of them as they sat at the table. He struggled for something to say that would be meaningful and appropriate. "I can't imagine losing a sibling like that, as a kid, I mean."

"You strike me as an only child," said Felix.

"No. Younger brother, older sister."

"Was your father a policeman as well?"

"No, he drank full-time. My brother was a cop for a while, but we don't talk much anymore."

"Where is he now, your father?"

"Somewhere in hell, I assume."

"That's a shame. Family is important."

"That's what people keep telling me."

"When was the last time you spoke with your brother?"

"I think it was last Christmas." Cole's position in the chair was growing stiff and uncomfortable with the personal interrogation, however friendly, and he shifted his weight unconsciously. The tinkling piano and meandering saxophone coming from the stereo grated on his nerves, like Muzak whenever he was on hold with the head office. "What's this song?"

"Lee Morgan, 'Ill Wind.' It's one of my favorites."

Cole laid both hands on the thick file in front of him when Felix stood to scrub carrots that were sitting in a bowl in the sink. The bruises on his bad hand captured his attention for a moment. Black, yellow, and blue. Blood still trapped beneath his fingernails. He tucked it beneath the table to avoid looking at it. He lifted his good hand to his bruised elbow. It still felt tender, even to the slightest touch.

"Do you like it?" Felix asked, not bothering to lift his gaze from the task at hand.

"Honestly?"

Felix gave a subtle nod, agreeing to hear the unfiltered truth.

"Not particularly," said Cole.

"That's another shame. Have you ever really listened to jazz?"

"I'm more of a rock 'n' roll kind of guy."

"Well, I'll put on some Coltrane. It's difficult to dislike."

Cole offered a smirk. "I'll see what I can do."

"I have the album in my bedroom. Just a moment." Felix dried his hands as he moved away from the kitchen counter and disappeared into the bedroom. Cole stared down into his cup, wiping the undissolved granules of instant coffee from his front teeth with his tongue. A familiar static hummed from his belt radio, the volume previously muted. He adjusted the knob and unclasped the handheld receiver from his shoulder.

"Cole," he gruffly acknowledged. "Go ahead."

"You free?" asked Veronica, who was manning the lines for the evening.

The two officers took turns to give each other a reprieve from constantly being on call. "We got a dispatch on the main line I can't handle alone. Over."

Cole groaned audibly, frustration mingling with the realization that a home-cooked meal and a round of drinks were slipping away. "What's up?"

"Atsiaq residence. Unwanted people in his house. Looks like the full moon madness is starting early."

Not a crisis, but something he couldn't justifiably send her out for alone. "All right. Gimme five. I'll meet you at the station and we can head down together."

"All right. Over and out."

Felix reappeared from the bedroom with an unusual sense of urgency. His face had taken on an ashen pallor, his eyes darting around the room as if seeking an unseen presence.

"You okay?" asked Cole.

"Yeah," replied Felix unconvincingly. "I'm fine."

"You look like you saw a ghost."

Felix's eyes met Cole's with a flicker of shock. A desperate chuckle escaped, and the tension in his face dissolved. "I haven't been getting much sleep lately. I think the winter is finally getting to me."

"Welcome to my world," muttered Cole. "And it's only December."

Felix gave him a distracted nod.

Looks like we both have our demons, thought Cole.

"I just got a call from Veronica and I gotta roll," said Cole, standing to gather up his gloves and hat. "Drunk and disorderly at someone's residence."

Relief washed over Felix's face, his distraction evident to Cole. "That's okay. I'm not feeling so well anyway."

"Rain check?"

"Sure, maybe when I get back from my holiday." Felix gestured to the file on the kitchen table. "Are you sure you're done with my reports?"

Cole nodded. A heavy sigh escaped as he planted his hat back on and headed for the door.

"No more loose ends to tie up?" asked Felix as Cole sat down in the foyer to put his boots on. He laced up in silence as he contemplated the question. Felix didn't press him for an answer but waited patiently in the doorway.

"I think any loose ends got buried this afternoon."

CHAPTER 29

Maliktu lay on his back beneath the bed with his eyes closed as Pitseolala's warm breath drifted across his cheek. Her exhale carried the foul odor of death and decay. A faint gurgle bubbled up from her throat, and his teeth clenched at the sound. With trepidation, he opened his eyes, fumbling for his lighter, keeping the flame close to the floor, away from the flammable underbelly of the box spring. He wondered, *Is this what it feels like to be buried alive?*

His vision adjusted to the low light as he listened for the indistinct voices from the kitchen. Unfamiliar music played from somewhere in the house. He rolled over toward his sister. Deep within her eyes, red sparks flickered; her pupils dilated beyond human limits. He could see that her skin had turned a mottled gray, and bloating had pushed putrefying gases into her face, where pus-filled blisters threatened to explode.

Before Maliktu could scream, she pressed the tips of her ice-cold fingers over his lips to silence him. The taste of rotting meat slipped into his throat and he fought the urge to retch. Her filthy mouth spread into a wide rictus, and he could see his own terrified face reflected in the blackness of her lifeless eyes. His sister's teeth appeared rotten and stained with blood. Without warning, the flame seared his thumb, and the lighter flickered out. He rolled away, shutting his eyes tight with his back to his sister, whimpering at the thought of her rotting corpse behind him until he could take no more.

Clawing at the hardwood floor, he dragged himself out from under the bed and put his boots on. Backing himself up against the bedroom wall, he stared at the underside of the mattress in the faint light, expecting her to come crawling out after him. He put his hand behind the cross, lifting it up to look at it, debating whether to snatch it away. The sound of a whistling kettle jerked his head toward the kitchen. He scanned the room for an escape and found none. Footsteps on the kitchen tiles clacked to a crescendo as they approached the bedroom. Maliktu dropped the cross, letting it swing from the shaman's arm. He glanced toward the underside of the bed, unable to bear the sight of his sister's corpse in that coffin-sized space again, and so he threw himself inside the closet.

Crouching low, he hid as far back in the wardrobe as he could manage without making noise and peeked through the slight opening. The bedroom door swung open and the light snapped on. The shadow of a man slid across the floor as he retrieved a vinyl record from the rack beside the nightstand, then stopped in front of the chest of drawers. Both of them watched as the cross still swung, sparkling in the light as it rotated on the chain.

Felix caught the cross between his fingers and stopped its movement. He dropped to one knee, bending down to look under the bed. He put his fingers into a puddle of melted snow, rubbing the liquid between them before standing up. He tilted his head, chin upward, and sniffed the air like a wolf sensing something unusual in the night air. The static of a handheld radio erupted from the kitchen. Felix snapped his head toward the sound. He swung back to face the bedroom, surveying every object as if to catch them moving. His eyes lingered on the hanging cross and then on the closet door for almost longer than Maliktu could endure, his expression dazed and bewildered.

When he left, Maliktu crawled out and tiptoed back over to the hanging cross. *Now or never,* he realized. He lifted the necklace gently from the carving with trembling hands while the voices resumed conversation in the kitchen. Unable to open the clasp, he forced the chain over his head. He slipped the cross beneath the neckline of his shirt and pressed the cold crucifix against his scarred skin. Despite his fear, grief overwhelmed him at the memory of her wearing it.

A chair scraped across the kitchen floor. The voices of the two men moved in the direction of the front door. Maliktu waited with bated breath until the door opened and then slammed shut. Silence persisted. He breathed a deep sigh of relief and headed for the bedroom door assuming both men had left.

As he reached for the doorknob, footsteps pounded toward him. He dashed back into the closet. Felix exploded into the room and headed straight for the cross. He looked at the empty space where it had hung, his eyes welling with disbelief in the mirror above the dresser. He spun around to face the room, hatred in every inch of his body language.

"Do you think you're scaring me?" Felix shouted before dropping down on all fours to look under the bed again. He strode out of the room, only to return a moment later with a kitchen knife in his hand. His expression bordered on deranged, his mouth twitching uncontrollably.

"You think I'm afraid of you, *you little bitch*?" A deep, cackling laughter filled the room. Standing taller, Felix wielded the knife, swinging it outward in various directions at his unseen adversary.

He went to the drawer in the nightstand and frantically pulled out an object wrapped in white satin about the size of a small dinner plate. Working feverishly, he sat on the bed and unwrapped the contents—an oval mask covered in black velvet barely big enough to conceal a human face. It had no discernible features other than two eyeholes. Placing the knife on the bed beside him, he picked up the mask, securing it behind his head with two thin bands of ebony ribbon. As soon as it covered his face, Felix's posture relaxed and his hands dropped calmly to his sides. His voice deepened when he spoke again, words flowing out sedated and drawling, like a man who had too much to drink. Felix's speech seemed clipped and twisted, running together at times as if he were speaking backward and forward all at once, crackling at times like the shifting of spring ice. Initially, Maliktu thought the words were muffled by the mask, but when he listened closely, it became clear that it was a language unlike any he had ever heard. Picking up the knife from the bed, Felix turned toward the closet, his movements graceful and fluid, like a dancer in slow motion, droning those same ungodly words over and over and over.

As the ceaseless incantation rose in volume, his sister's face appeared from the shadows beside Maliktu, her mouth gaped wide as if to devour her brother's head, her foul stench rising in the cramped space, burning Maliktu's eyes and nostrils. Pitseolala's hot breath exhaled into his ear. A guttural sound erupted from her mouth, and in sheer terror Maliktu heaved himself to his feet, smashing through the hanging clothes and slamming his full body weight into the half-closed door.

The closet burst open, and the door struck Felix squarely in the face. The man sprawled backward onto the floor, the knife slipping from his fingers, clattering away across the hardwood beneath the bed frame. Maliktu sprinted as fast as his legs would allow toward the front entry, slamming into the kitchen table and knocking over a chair. His heavy boots pounded the living room carpet while loud curses and infernal shrieks sounded far behind him. He reached the porch in less than a breath.

Maliktu fumbled with the dead bolt and yanked the outer door wide open. A blast of cold air and swirling snow ripped through the porch. His front foot had no sooner crunched on the snow of the front steps than he was yanked back onto the porch by the hood of his parka. The boy instinctively grabbed for the doorframe and twisted his torso around, spiraling down inside the oversize coat. His body slipped free like a snake from its own skin, sending Felix crashing backward into the wall of the foyer, crushing a shoe rack in the process and bringing down a host of winter gear on top of him. Maliktu snatched the dropped parka from the floor between them and seized the opportunity to escape. He ran down the steps into the night, hurling himself forward. The music from the hills exploded in his skull, driving him faster and faster as it peaked in intensity and volume. As he ran farther down the block, in the corner of his eye, ten steps to his left, he saw that his sister ran alongside him. Looking back to check if Felix was pursuing them, he watched as her impossibly long black hair billowed and flowed behind her as far as he could see.

They ran through the deserted streets, dashing between buildings to complicate their route, unsure if they were being followed. As they passed the old hotel, the boy dove headfirst through a narrow gap under the building. He kept low, raising his head only enough to peek over the drift toward the frozen seashore.

Maliktu could hear his own name being shouted over and over. The voice rose and fell on the swirling air currents, echoing off the landscape around them. He was alone again, sisterless, but sheltered beneath the structure. Only fear kept him from thinking about how cold his body truly was. He was considering fleeing again toward his own house when a tall figure emerged from the shadow of a nearby residence and entered the clearing in front of him. Felix wore a bright red parka, and even from Maliktu's hiding place, the boy could see the cool glint of a long blade dangling from the madman's hand. Realizing he was nearly frozen and still clutching his winter coat in a death grip, Maliktu pulled on his parka in the cramped space. In the process, he banged his elbow on an insulated pipe hanging under the house. Stinging pins and needles exploded up his forearm on impact, but he clamped his mouth shut before a noise could escape to avoid alerting the looming figure. A gust of wind brought a huge whiteout across the space between the buildings, bringing visibility down to zero. And when it cleared, Felix was nowhere to be seen. Something much darker had taken his place.

A grotesque *amautalik* lurched through the knee-deep snow beneath the light of the lamppost. Its gaping mouth revealed a jumble of bony fangs, and even at that distance, the stench of rotten walrus meat wafted from its breath. A black tangle of scraggly hair, interwoven with tiny bones, covered the *amautalik*'s swollen head, while a sinewy necklace of infant skulls dangled from its stout neck. He watched in horror as its corpulent body shifted beneath the rancid layers of animal pelts as it stumbled past.

Maliktu backed away from his vantage point, the sound of his heartbeat thumping in his ears. The beast flashed its claws in the air, clicking its bony nails together. That hellish sound forced him to imagine the *amautalik* tearing him out from under the building, using those skeletal fingers to pluck out his tender eyes. The mere thought of such a death caused him to cover his face, peeking through his ice-cold fingers for further danger. As if reading his mind, the creature twisted its head in the direction of his hiding place and sniffed the air for prey. Aroused by his scent, the *amautalik* abruptly altered its course toward him. Maliktu reached into his neckline and squeezed the cross tight in his little fist while he stared in terror at the hideous ogre drawing near.

Before he could flee, two hands slid over his eyes and his world went dark. Pitseolala's voice whispered in his ear: "You were born in a fire. Only fire can save you."

When she removed her fingers, the creature was gone.

And so was she.

CHAPTER 30

An "unwanted person in a dwelling" usually meant the police showing up and persuading a drunkard to leave a residence. The worst-case scenario was a catch and release—arrest someone, a couple of people at most, and provide them with food and lodging in cells until they were sober in the morning. Cole had performed such arrests countless times since he'd been stationed in Cape Dorset. But tonight, as he sat in the truck outside the residence mentally preparing to face the situation, a chill rippled up through his torso.

He reflexively reached for the heater, knowing full well that the setting was already cranked to high. The sound of Inuktitut talk radio droned at a low volume from the vehicle's speakers. Through the sheers on the front windows of the residence, silhouettes shifted back and forth at a steady rhythm while the light trembled behind them. The projected shadows seemed out of place, almost unsettling. This didn't feel like any house party he'd broken up before. Cole shook off his apprehension and gripped the bottom of the steering wheel with both hands to steady the tremor in his arms. Still, something felt wrong. He blamed it on his tired mind; his exhaustion had given everything he went through a dreamlike quality as of late. Nevertheless, his thoughts unconsciously drifted to the pump-action shotgun strapped in behind him.

Next to him in the passenger seat, Veronica surveyed the house with the same trepidation evident on her face. Half a dozen people shuffled aimlessly in front of the Atsiaq residence. With heads down, hoods up, and cigarettes randomly flaring, the crowd milled about in an effort to stay warm. Cole thought that the mob resembled a swarm of fireflies, an insect he hadn't seen since moving to the Arctic hinterlands. The front door to the house gaped wide open, bathing the movements of the people out front in a soft light, stretching their shadows across the snowy front yard toward the idling truck.

"I got Aiden's date of birth from the foreman and ran him through the system like you asked," said Veronica. "He jumped bail on a prior aggravated assault and a bunch of other shit back in March. So at least we know why he ran." She paused as if considering whether or not to say something else. "And that he likely wasn't involved with Pits's suicide like you thought."

Cole chose not to take that last remark as a personal dig at him. He wasn't in the mood for another argument. "He won't get far. If he doesn't turn himself in before we find him."

Cole could feel Veronica staring at him while he focused on the house.

"Were you ever going to tell me about getting the truck stuck?"

Cole huffed in surprise. Miller must have let it slip, or someone saw the truck wedged in the ditch last night. "Probably not," he said without looking at her, then stepped out of the vehicle.

Atsiaq Peter came to greet the officers. He was grossly underdressed for the weather. Wearing only a Metallica T-shirt and tight jeans, he shimmied back and forth in the cold with his hands shoved in his pockets. The man shivered uncontrollably, even though he had been outside only as long as it took him to scuttle across the icy driveway to the police truck from the neighbor's house. He fired off a few sentences in Inuktitut to Veronica before addressing Cole directly in English. As he spoke, his eyes bulged beneath his lopsided crew cut.

"Get them the fuck out of my house, man. They're crazy."

"Who is?" asked Veronica.

"Churchies from outta town. *They got my son.*"

"What do you mean, they *got* him?" asked Cole.

Atsiaq gesticulated erratically as he explained the situation, rambling at a breakneck pace: "Ottokie was pissed about something stupid and he told the teacher at school he was gonna kill himself like Pits. The teacher called the house so I tried to talk to him about it but my sister freaked out and she talked to those church guys and now they're taking over my fucking place."

The two officers exchanged glances, sharing their perplexed looks. "What are they doing exactly?" asked Veronica.

"Killing demons and shit, I don't fucking know. But they've got Ottokie in there and won't let him go."

"Does your sister live here with you?" asked Cole, wanting to clarify if the church crew were guests the sister invited into the home. *That will complicate things,* he thought.

"No, man." He pointed beyond the house next door. "She lives up there."

"All right, we'll check it out," said Cole. "Head next door and get warm. We'll deal with it."

Atsiaq raised his eyebrows in affirmation and dashed back to the neighbor's place with his hands still jammed in his jeans. Cole and Veronica marched side by side through the crowd to the front door.

The heat inside the Atsiaq residence was suffocating, even with the front door open. The stench of body odor hung thick and dirty in the air. Cole and Veronica had to push through another throng of onlookers on the porch to make their way into the living room. A dozen people stood in the house's main area with nearly a dozen more kneeling and sitting wherever they could. *It's like a house party without any booze or music,* thought Cole.

A figure dressed all in black stood in the center of the room with his back to the officers. Aloft in one hand was a thick book; the other hand was splayed across the forehead of a young man sitting on a kitchen chair. The boy couldn't have been much older than fourteen. Two middle-aged men held him in place with joint locks on his arms. The teen's eyes were squeezed tight, his face half covered by Avon Desmond's palm and contorted in a grimace. With his head back, the preacher shouted toward the ceiling.

"Oh Lord, grant this young man liberty from the evil spirit that possesses him," he bellowed. "Grant me authority over the demons that plague him!"

Cole was about to intervene when movement in the room beyond caught his attention. A man and woman convulsed beside each other on the linoleum in the kitchen. Encircled by observers, the pair writhed as if being electrocuted, yelling gibberish as they thrashed about. The minister's booming voice brought Cole's attention back to the living room.

"I beg, Saint Michael the Archangel, that you give me the victory of Christ against evil. Put me under the shadow of your protective wings and with your sword defeat God's enemy who wishes to destroy this child."

Desmond stepped in closer to Ottokie and made the sign of the cross before laying his palm on his forehead. Around the teen and the preacher, people knelt on the floor with their hands clasped in prayer and eyes closed, raising their interlocked hands to the heavens.

"I cast you out, unclean spirit, along with every Satanic power of the enemy, every specter from hell, and all your fell companions, in the name of our Lord Jesus Christ. For he has stripped you of your powers and laid waste your kingdom. He has cast you forth into the outer darkness, where everlasting ruin awaits you and your abettors."

Cole stepped forward, treading carefully through the congregation members kneeling on the floor. When he grabbed the arm of the minister, the preacher opened his mouth to speak but stopped.

A murmur of confusion swept through the room. The minister wet his lips and lowered his voice to speak directly to Cole. He looked over Cole's shoulder to where Veronica stood by the entrance keeping an eye on the situation should anyone else intervene.

"Jesus has given me authority over the unclean spirit inside this boy," said the preacher, pushing the top corner of his Bible into the chest of the officer ever so slightly.

"The only authority here is mine," said Cole, pushing the book aside. "You need to take this elsewhere and let this kid go."

"His aunt has requested our help." The minister tipped his head toward the kitchen, presumably in the direction of the woman he was speaking about. But Cole didn't take his eyes off the preacher. He released his grip on Desmond's arm, resting his hand on his holstered gun. "His father doesn't want your help. And he doesn't want you in this house."

"This child is being driven to sin by the forces of darkness," said Desmond, half to Cole, half to the onlookers. "He must be saved!"

Cole looked down at the boy. His eyes were open, tears flowing.

"Let him go," Cole said, directing the two men holding a crying Ottokie in the chair to release him. They hesitated, looking to Desmond for confirmation.

Cole raised his voice: "Now!"

The men released the teen and stepped back. Ottokie leapt up from the chair and slipped between Cole and the reverend, pushing through the crowd toward the exit.

Cole raised his voice and turned to address the people in the room with a slow and deliberate tone. He paused, choosing his words carefully.

"If you do not live here, you need to leave now. If you do not leave, you will be arrested."

Behind him, Veronica repeated the order in Inuktitut with the same tone and authority as her partner.

The minister interrupted the translation: "We are not leaving!"

Cole leaned in toward the reverend and dropped his voice to a whisper.

"If you don't tell these people to leave, I will take you into custody. Only you. And you will rot in a cell with the drunks and the crazies until the blizzard is over." He pulled back and glared at the preacher. "Am I making myself clear?"

The minister's breathing deepened and his expression intensified, a kettle roiling to a boil. His eyes were dull and glazed, his mouth slack-jawed like a dead fish. He stepped backward with a finger pointed an inch from Cole's face.

"Anyone who tries to interfere with the work of God is in league with the devil!"

The preacher shouted louder in Inuktitut and the people in the room followed his lead. A man kneeling next to Cole let out a moan that startled everyone, his face contorting in hideous rigor. A woman on the couch screamed, her head falling backward and her eyes rolling up into her head, lost in what appeared to be a fever dream. Cole, distracted by the commotion, had allowed the reverend to step out of arm's reach. When Cole attempted to grab him again, the minister whipped around to face him. Lukewarm liquid sprayed into Cole's face.

"Agents of the devil are among us!" shouted Desmond.

The voice scraped nails across the chalkboard of Cole's mind. Disoriented by the spray, Cole wiped the fluid from his face with a gloved hand, blinking rapidly to regain his vision. He spat once, then twice, to rid his mouth of whatever it was he'd ingested.

"Agents of the devil are among us!" he repeated.

He focused on Desmond, who wielded a squeeze bottle of holy water, swinging it around in the air, casting streams of liquid in all directions as he spoke in tongues, spraying the assembled worshippers. Like gas to a bonfire, the spurting water and chanting in gibberish sent the faithful into a frenzy. They rose to their feet and joined their leader in rambling unintelligibly at a high volume. Cole's fur hat was snatched from his head; a pull on his jacket caused him to lose his balance. He stumbled into a man next to him and ended up falling on his bad knee; considerable pain shot up into his hip. Instinctively, he clutched his gun to keep it from prying hands. At the edge of his vision, he saw Veronica standing by the entrance to the living room, hands resting on her belt, seemingly unfazed by the developing scuffle. He had no time to consider her inaction. They surrounded him, blocking out the light from the scattered lamps around the room, plunging him deeper into blackness.

The heat of the bodies pressed against him overwhelmed him and his thoughts swirled into a maelstrom. A set of bony fingers clawed at his face. Multiple sets of hands molested him, grabbing at his uniform. He threw a hard elbow out to the right, nearly losing his balance again and ending up face down on the floor. Handicapped by having one hand glued to his holstered pistol, he thrashed and spun, lost in the sea of bodies. The preacher's voice continued to rise above the commotion in a frenzied oration.

Through the gloom and the surging crowd, the room tilted and spun. He struggled to get a hand free to wipe the sweat from his eyes. Dizziness overtook him as he pushed with his forearm against the man in front of him. Acrid smoke inexplicably flooded his lungs, and the taste of ash filled his mouth, causing him to choke and gag. He clutched his throat and shut his eyes. In the blackness of his mind's eye, an image appeared, a face emerging from the nothingness, as clear as if it were right in front of him. It was a vision of himself engulfed in flames. His uniform blazed as he flailed his arms. He saw his own face blackened, the flesh of his forehead and cheeks bubbling from the intense heat with dark blood pouring from his eyes. The pain overpowered him as he watched himself burn, his entire body being consumed by the flames.

Boom!

Boom!

Boom!

Three earsplitting cracks broke the spell, and the majority of the crowd dropped to the floor, sprawling for cover and cringing in confusion. Cole's ears still rang from the sudden noise, but the room had fallen deathly silent. The taste of ash in his throat, the vision of the flames—all gone. He turned around in slow motion on his good knee, his shoulders hunched to his ears from the sudden noise. Veronica stood in the doorway, her gun drawn and sweeping the room, a panicked look on her face. Behind her, frantic onlookers poured out into the street, their heavy boots rumbling down the wooden steps. Cole looked down; his pistol was out of the holster and gripped in his hand, smoke drifting up to his face from the barrel. Below it, three bullet holes marred the linoleum floor beside his left boot. He tried to speak, stuttering and stammering.

"Jesus Christ," he mumbled.

Cole stood with considerable difficulty and re-holstered his gun. He locked eyes with Veronica, who still held her firearm aloft, appearing panicked. He had no recollection of drawing his weapon, let alone firing it. Cole nodded slowly and raised a palm toward her to let her know that things were back under control, despite being unsure himself. She put away her gun with hesitation and Cole turned around to face the preacher.

Desmond held the bottle of holy water at his side in one hand and his Bible in the other, his stance and expression defiant. "You shall burn in the fires of hell for this!"

Cole licked his chapped lips and drew in a deep breath. When he exhaled, his left jab hit the preacher dead center on his chin, sending him sprawling over the chair that once contained Atsiaq's son. Cole wiped the remaining holy water from his face with the sleeve of his parka and reached for his handcuffs. The fallen man lay stiff as a corpse, his arms locked straight above his head, out cold. Everyone who remained in the room fell silent with wide eyes and nervous expressions while backing off to give Cole room.

Cole rolled the unconscious man over onto his belly. He whispered in the preacher's ear when the second handcuff closed with a satisfying click: "I'm already there."

CHAPTER 31

Cole tore off his black leather gloves and threw them on the bench. The cement of exhaustion set in his veins, fusing his ligaments, weighing down his limbs. He continued to wrestle with the haunting vision of himself on fire and his lack of memory of discharging the gun. Firing his weapon under any circumstance required an incident report; he needed to file it promptly with an ironclad explanation. But he didn't have one.

His body slumped against the porch wall, and he dragged a limp hand down his face. *I shouldn't have hit the preacher.* He closed his eyes, imagining he was already nestled in bed. *But damn, it felt good.* His boots came off after two separate struggles with a breather in between. Outside, the storm grew in intensity and a violent gust shifted the wooden frame of his house with a resounding crack. Cole stood up and promptly swore when he planted his socked foot in a puddle of cold water. *Fuck's sake.*

The entryway light flickered on. A thin pool of water had spread across the floor with his coat heaped in the center, where the accumulated snow had melted. Cole bent down and lifted his dropped parka. Sweat had begun to cool on his back, causing him to shiver as he straightened up. He hung the wet coat on a wooden peg above the heater. Shuffling feet on the crunchy snow and a series of barking coughs erupted from outside the front door. He looked through the peephole in the door, but it was frosted over. Another loud cough came from outside, followed by a series of knocks. Cole laid a hand on his holstered pistol and opened the door with caution.

Maliktu stood on the doorstep wearing only a parka, no hat or mitts. The boy hunched over, trembling, arms wrapped around himself to keep warm. His expression was one of utter exhaustion. Cole stepped out onto the landing, scanning around for any sign of trouble, before whisking the boy into the warmth of the house.

Maliktu sat wrapped in a blanket on the couch with a hot water bottle clutched to his chest. An empty bowl of instant noodles lay on the coffee table in front of him. Cole, still nursing heartburn from too many coffees earlier, stood in the doorway of the living room. His untouched meal remained on the kitchen counter.

"I called your grandfather and your aunt, but no one is answering. Neither is Veronica. I'll try to get ahold of someone in your family, but in the meantime, you can stay put and warm up. It's not safe to be driving around out there right now."

The boy nodded, avoiding eye contact with Cole. His demeanor had improved since coming in from the cold. Cole approached the couch and sat on the far arm.

"You can't be wandering around in the middle of winter without—"

"She was in the alley," said Maliktu, quietly but with distress evident in his voice.

"Who was?"

"My sister." Maliktu pointed from beneath the blanket toward the corner of the room. "I saw her, out there, through my window."

Frustrated, Cole sighed and his shoulders slumped. "As much as you want her to—*we* want her to—she's not coming back."

"I followed her to a house. She went inside, so I smashed the window."

Cole narrowed his eyes. "You broke into a house?"

Maliktu didn't answer.

Cole covered his face and breathed into his hands. "*Fuck,*" he whispered before dropping his arms to his sides. "Did you take anything?"

Biting his lips, Maliktu nodded. As the blanket dropped from his shoulders, he was shirtless and shivering, but not from the temperature. Cole opened his mouth to speak, pausing as he saw the extensive burn scars across the boy's chest for the first time, realizing the severity of his injuries.

"Are you still cold?" Cole stepped to the thermostat on the wall and turned up the heat. Maliktu pulled the blanket over his shoulders again, looking up at Cole.

"The man chased me out. He fell in the doorway."

"What man? What house?"

"The green house behind the health center."

Cole's face shifted from confusion to frustration to anger. "Don't lie to me. I was just at Felix's house. No one broke in while I was there."

"Felix," repeated Maliktu, crying. "Is that his name?"

His exhausted mind struggled to understand the boy's question. Concerned, but unsure what to believe. "Did you follow me there?"

Maliktu slumped forward on the couch, sobbing.

"What did you take from—" Cole stopped, dumbstruck, pointing at what the boy held in his hand. *The cross.*

"Where did you get that?"

Maliktu spoke without lifting his head. "He had a knife. He came after me."

"Enough bullshit." He grabbed the boy by the shoulders. "When did she give it to you?"

Tears flowed down Maliktu's scarred cheeks; his eyes widened. Cole's posture relaxed when he realized he was scaring the boy. He sat down next to Maliktu, reaching out to touch the hanging cross dangling from the boy's fingers. "I've been looking for this," said Cole. He rubbed his thumb across its surface. "Everywhere," he whispered.

"It was hanging on a carving in his bedroom." Maliktu handed the necklace to Cole. The tears were coming in a steady stream; the boy sobbed uncontrollably, shivering more than before. He pulled the blanket tight around the boy, and Maliktu clutched him in a desperate hug. He cradled the back of the boy's head in his hand. Maliktu sobbed until he had exhausted himself; then, leaning back, he wiped the remaining tears away with the edge of the blanket.

"Do you think she's in hell?" asked Maliktu through his tears.

"Pitseolala?" asked Cole. "No, I think she's in heaven."

"Do you believe in heaven?"

Cole made a split-second decision to tell the truth. "No, not really. Do you?"

Maliktu shook his head. "Then where is she?"

"I don't know where she is, but I know it's not in hell."

"I think she might be in hell," said Maliktu.

"Do you think she killed herself?"

"A lot of people are talking about hell. She says a devil killed her."

"I don't believe in devils."

"What do you believe in?"

His voice was weak and fading as he spoke. "I don't know anymore," said Cole.

While the boy slept on the couch, Cole sat at the kitchen table and looked at the calendar hanging by the sink. A red circle around today's date indicated a full moon. In the window overlooking the barren tundra, his reflection stared back at him against the darkness outside. *Maybe Pits gave it to Maliktu. A gift before dying.* His gaze drifted to the boy's parka hanging on the coatrack. He desperately wanted to believe Maliktu. *Or maybe Pits gave it to Felix. A gift for trying to help her.* An old man had once given him a cheap pocket knife for not charging him for driving impaired. Cole politely refused, but the man's wife forced it on him, pressing it into his hand while talking fast in Inuktitut. Cole spun the phantom ring on his third finger as he closed his eyes and listened to sounds around him—the rumble of the wind, the windows rattling, the furnace humming. He picked up the cordless phone from the base unit, nervously swirling his thumb above the numbers to call Felix. *And what would I say? Um, did a deformed Inuit boy break into your house?* He laid the phone down on the table.

Felix's résumé lay on top of a pile of papers. He had forgotten to put it back in the file before he'd returned it. He slid it across the table toward himself. Volunteering for disaster relief after Katrina and down in Haiti, working for NGOs in Sudan, Congo, and Afghanistan, social work in the Balkans, then in the Northwest Territories, and then three different communities in this territory. Never more than a year in one place. He opened his laptop. He typed "Felix Bauer" into the search engine. A personal trainer in the United States, a historical figure from the 1700s, a physicist at Cambridge. But no world-traveling social workers. He left a message with the detachment in Pond Inlet requesting any information they might have on Felix from when he was working there. He thought about how strange Felix seemed when he'd come out of his bedroom; perhaps he'd discovered the cross was missing.

Then it hit him, jumping from the page as if in bold.

Master's Degree in Social Work. 1995.

His superior officer when Cole was a rookie always told him to start at the beginning and work your way forward. Cole deleted Felix's name from the search engine and plugged in the name of the university where Felix earned the degree. He wrapped the necklace slowly around his fingers while the web page loaded. He checked the time in the corner of the screen. It was late afternoon in the school's time zone. He clicked the contact link and dialed the number for the registrar's office on his home phone. An older woman answered. He considered telling her that he was a police officer and that he needed information about a suspect, but people, especially those in administrative positions, tended to clam up at the first whiff of law enforcement. The moment he heard her voice, he decided to lie.

"Hi, my name is Felix Bauer," said Cole, holding the résumé in his hand like a script. "I graduated in the mid-nineties from your school with a master's degree in social work and an undergraduate degree in anthropology."

"Yes?"

"Well, I'm working up north now, way up in the Arctic, for the territorial government, and my new boss is being a real pain in the ass."

"How can I help you?"

"I showed him my framed degree, but he wants an actual copy of my certificate for his records."

"Well, that's easy enough to do. You can fill out the form online and send in a request with a check or money order."

Cole hesitated.

"Well, that's the problem, you see. I did that, and they told me it was never processed."

"When did you send it in?"

"Oh, it's been months ago now and my boss has been harassing me, saying I could lose my job. I spoke to someone on the phone from the student registry."

"That would be this office. Do you recall who you spoke with?"

"As I said, it was months ago. I don't recall."

"Okay. Well, let me take a look. You know your student number?"

Cole laughed theatrically. "Student number? That was so many years ago. I'm lucky if I can remember my phone number."

"Hold on." Fingers typed on a keyboard. "I don't see any record of your transcript request, Mr. Bauer."

"Well, I sent it in. Can I do it with you now over the phone?"

More typing. "I can't seem to find you in my system. Is Bauer spelled B-a-u-e-r?"

"Yes, ma'am."

"Would it be under any other name?"

"No, ma'am. It shouldn't be."

"Well, that's strange." Long pause. "Your degree isn't coming up in the database at all. And when I widen the search terms for different years, I don't see a Felix Bauer enrolled in any programs here from 1990 onward."

A cold chill ran down Cole's spine as a flush of blood warmed his face.

"Thanks for your time."

"Sorry I couldn't be of more—"

Cole ended the call. He stared down at the résumé in his lap before picking up the cross again, playing with the chain in his fingers. If he thought about it too long, too hard, he would find holes in the narrative, questions unanswered, and alternative theories. But in the end, it was his gut that told him everything he needed to know.

Then he remembered what Maliktu had said about seeing Pitseolala in the alley. He walked to the picture window, the phone still clutched in his hand, and pulled back the curtain to reveal the prologue of an epic blizzard crashing down upon the town, a pre-storm before things got worse. There was no one in his alley.

He shut the curtain and, in the moment before he turned around, he felt a presence behind him. He smiled, a slight smirk, almost imperceptible. Even though he wasn't afraid to turn around, he knew he didn't need to. He already knew it was her.

An hour later, Cole hunched forward in the unlit shower with his palms against the wall. A night-light plugged into the razor outlet near the sink provided the only illumination in the bathroom. The scalding water pelted down on the aching muscles of his neck and shoulders. Having the lights out always made it difficult to tell if he was truly clean, but the lack of visual stimuli eased his constant headaches.

After, he tossed back two painkillers before sweeping up the broken glass on the kitchen floor and tossing it in the bin. The dried blood spatters on the tiles took much longer to mop up. He threw the piss-soaked sheets from the bed in the washing machine and laid out fresh sheets on the couch to sleep. The thought of returning to the bedroom offered no comfort to his overloaded mind. The room, the mattress, all of it was cursed by the hag dream as far as he was concerned. He'd given Maliktu the guest bed after four failed calls to the family. In the morning, he'd drop the boy off at home once the weather cleared a bit. Then he would bring the cross and his discoveries to Veronica to formulate a plan.

Cole microwaved a frozen dinner he had pilfered from the detachment. Watching it revolve, he tried not to think about the maelstrom of shit surrounding him. The meal went down quickly, bland but filling. He tried not to think about how much time had already been subtracted from his overall lifespan by his diet. Sober and literally clean, he lay on the couch in his underwear in the darkness. Even if he had wanted to worry about something, he couldn't have. In his mind, there was only calm before the storm.

CHAPTER 32

Cole parted with Maliktu the next morning when he dropped him with his grandparents. During the night, the boy had slid from the guest mattress onto the floor, pulling the blankets down with him. Cole found him cocooned inside the bottom of the closet. Seeing him there brought Cole, who considered himself incapable of feeling anymore, a flicker of happiness, an ember from a fire he thought extinguished.

When Cole arrived at the detachment that morning, he was surprised to find Veronica's personal snowmobile idling out front. Visibility had dropped considerably overnight, cloaking everything in a veil of whiteness. He banged his ice-laden boots on the outer doorframe and shook the excess snow from his clothing before entering. Inside the warmth of the detachment, Veronica tidied up her workspace with a determined expression. She wore her civilian attire instead of her usual uniform.

"We need to talk," declared Cole.

"There's something I need to show you first," replied Veronica with a single-minded composure that unsettled Cole. Placing a stack of files on the photocopier, she retrieved her keys from the entrance counter. "It's outside."

"It can wait." Cole held up Pitseolala's cross, letting the necklace dangle beneath it.

Ignoring the gesture, Veronica slid her arm into her parka sleeve. "I really don't think what I have *can* wait."

"I found Pits's crucifix," said Cole, his tone thick with gravity and urgency. "And I know who killed her."

"Pits killed Pits. End of story," Veronica scoffed, seemingly unconcerned. Zipping up her coat, she gathered her beaver mitts and knitted cap. "You're gonna want to see this; it's out in the truck."

Patience worn thin, Cole stepped forward aggressively, thrusting the necklace toward her face. "Maliktu broke into Felix's house last night and found this hanging from a carving in his bedroom."

Veronica laughed incredulously. "The social worker? Maybe she gave it to him before she died. Did you try asking him that?"

"He's not a social worker. I checked."

"What are you talking about? He's been here for over eight months. He's got a government office."

Cole stuffed the necklace back into his pocket. "I called the university where he got his degree and pretended to be him. They said he never went there."

Veronica's bewilderment was on full display. "You impersonated him?"

"He never spends more than a year in one place," he continued. "He's been doing this type of work all over the globe. He told me that. The detachment in Pond Inlet messaged back this morning. Felix was the social worker for a young girl who committed suicide. They suspected foul play. He offered to help them using his file on her. Sound familiar?"

"That's all the evidence you have?" Veronica's sudden laughter set Cole back on his heels. Her voice went up an octave. "I am beginning to understand how you fucked up the Carter case."

Cole winced as if he'd been jabbed in the face. His tone turned indignant. "I was cleared by the disciplinary committee. Carter is just going after the goddamn money because he can't get his son back."

"And whose fault is that?" Veronica taunted him, a sinister tone to her question. He felt himself wanting to lash out at her. "I assume you haven't checked the news lately," she said. "The lawsuit has your name all over it."

"None of that matters now."

"Why? Because a delusional kid broke into a house and brought you a fucking necklace? Or because you think that a social worker killed a girl who killed herself?"

Cole glared at her, unyielding. "The cross is a trophy, a memento of his kill." He paused. "I'm sure of it."

Veronica's gaze met his with a look of disgusted disbelief. "I really didn't want to think it was true when you started here, all the shit they said about you. The booze, the fuckups. But you really are nuts." She donned her hat and mitts. "And your little shoot-out last night will be the subject of an inquiry for sure."

"You're going to report that?"

"If I don't, someone who was there certainly will. That's if they haven't already."

"I was being assaulted by the crowd. People were tugging at my firearm."

"That's not what I saw. I watched a cop unload his weapon into the floor in a room full of unarmed people. A cop who looked completely out of his fucking mind."

"And where were you when they were all going mental?"

"Unlike you, I was keeping it together." Veronica dismissed her partner with a wave of her hand and headed for the door. "Did you know I found a bag of weed and a scale sitting on the back counter—no paperwork, no tags?"

Cole stood rooted, dumbfounded. He'd completely forgotten about the items he'd taken from Jardin's house.

"I'm so done," she declared, reaching for the door handle.

"What do you mean, you're done?"

"I mean, I'm not going down with your ship. I'm heading out to my family's cabin before the blizzard makes it too dangerous. I'll be staying the night there."

"You can't just leave me here alone. What about emergency calls?"

"The entire town is shutting down. Some places have already lost power. No one is going to be going anywhere before too long."

Veronica paused before opening the door, disdain evident in her every breath. "I got a call yesterday from a concerned citizen and I went to speak to her, and a few other people, after we put the preacher in cells last night."

"About what?"

"Take a look in the truck out back. I already sent the email. By Monday, when the weather clears, I expect there will be someone flying in to replace you."

Cole stammered through half a question, but Veronica stormed out, slamming the detachment door behind her.

Cole found himself desperately clinging to the leash of his anger. Against his better judgment, he decided to check his voicemail. Missed call, no message. His daughter's number. The second was from a police lawyer down in Ottawa. Her voice had a level of seriousness that made Cole cringe before she had even finished stating her name. "I assume you read the documents we sent. The lawsuit is going to trial. Things are going to move rapidly. We'll need to talk."

When Cole stood, the room seemed to tilt, and a sudden dizziness overcame him. He found himself clinging to the edge of the desk for support. He stumbled through the front door, and the preacher's incessant shouting from his cell was swiftly replaced by the howling of the wind.

Outside, Veronica's fading snowmobile tracks beckoned him to follow her into a colorless oblivion. The surrounding buildings had vanished in the swirling whiteness. Pulling his parka hood down against the stinging gusts, he rounded the back of the building, passing Pitseolala's vacant tomb. The doorway, agape since her body's disappearance, had filled with drifting snow. Everything around him seemed forsaken, everything inside of him collapsing. This week would likely mark the death knell of his career, any hope of redemption silently slipping away.

Reaching the police truck, Cole discovered an empty cab and an unoccupied prisoner seat. He moved around to the back and lowered the tailgate. A dark mass lay covered in a snowy shroud. He scrambled up into the truck bed with some difficulty and knelt down beside it. Without even lifting the tarp, he knew its grisly contents. He collapsed onto the dog's carcass under the weight of a lifetime of poor decisions, an avalanche of self-pity overwhelming him. In a few days, his career and his future would be buried alive. But tonight, as he stared out into the abyss beyond the town with nothing left to lose, he found the abyss staring back.

CHAPTER 33

Cole exited the truck into the frigid darkness. Several lights were on in Felix's house, but all the curtains were drawn. After scanning the deserted street, he cautiously made his way around the side of the house toward a dilapidated shed. Using his boot, he cleared away a small drift of snow before slipping inside and shutting the door behind him. He stood in the darkness for a moment listening to the caterwaul of the wind before turning on his flashlight. No windows faced the structure. He was safe from prying eyes. Even if Felix noticed his truck parked out front, he would assume that he or Veronica was sitting inside out of the cold. Still, the nape of his neck prickled in anticipation of being discovered.

He snapped on the flashlight and let his eyes adjust. Fuel canisters, old paint cans, and cardboard boxes filled the space. His breath sparkled in the narrow beam of light as it revealed a workbench covered in scattered power tools and various containers of odds and ends. Above it, a tool rack had been bolted to the wall. A closer look brought an ache to the back of his throat. Hanging among the implements was a set of rusted bolt cutters. He didn't need a forensic analysis to tell him they were large enough to sever a padlock. He shut off the flashlight. He had seen enough.

Cole's gloved fist pounded again on the outer door, icy needles pricking at his tender forehead, forcing him to squint. Cursing Felix for taking too long, he gave up hope just as a weak ribbon of light appeared between the curtains. The front door opened less than a foot, revealing Felix's face in the gap, flashing a look shifting from surprise to welcome. Apologetic offers of respite from the cold accompanied Cole into the house, where scents of cinnamon and frantic jazz notes erupted from the interior.

As Felix struggled to slam the icy door shut behind them, a once-organized shoe rack lay shattered on the floor, various footwear in a jumbled pile beside the discarded remains. Cole noticed a missing chunk of plaster where a coat hook once existed. Maliktu's words echoed in his mind: *He fell in the doorway.*

"That looks unfortunate," said Cole, pointing to the chaos at his feet.

"I slipped on the wet floor," replied Felix dismissively. "Clumsy."

Pointing to the gash on his own hand, an exhausted Cole deadpanned: "Makes two of us, I guess."

Felix, wearing a half smile, headed back into the kitchen to tend to the food he was preparing. "I decided to take the day off. Just making some lunch."

Cole removed his boots and followed Felix into the house.

"There's a blizzard rolling in," said Cole, pausing in the threshold between the living room and the kitchen, the tension solidifying.

"I heard." Felix flicked his chef's knife toward a small radio on the shelf. "When it rolls out, I'm going with it."

"Oh right, you mentioned. Somewhere warm for Christmas." Cole removed his gloves and hat, placing them on the table. "Where are you flying again?"

Felix ignored the question, scraping a cutting board of diced potatoes into a pot of boiling water with his back to Cole. "I thought we postponed a meal until after I got back."

"We got a call," said Cole, unzipping the top of his jacket and taking two steps closer. "Someone saw a kid breaking into your window."

"Yes, they smashed the glass, but they didn't get inside."

"So nothing stolen?"

"Nothing I noticed." Felix gestured around the room with both hands. "That's why I didn't bother reporting it." He rinsed the cutting board in the sink and placed an onion in the center.

"You mind if I take a look?"

Felix hesitated without looking up, his blade frozen in midair above the board. "At what?"

"The window. Just for the paperwork."

Their eyes met; both men appeared calm and cool. Felix picked up a remote control on the counter and silenced the jazz music coming from the speakers. "I said nothing was stolen. I'm not filing a complaint."

"Higher crime numbers mean budget increases for the detachment. No skin off your teeth, insurance-wise."

Felix resumed cutting the onion. "Sure. It's right through there." He pointed with his elbow toward the closed door behind him.

Cole crossed through the kitchen and opened the door to the narrow storage room. The window was covered with cardboard and duct tape. Standing in the dim light under the single bulb, a tingle rippled through his back, and he glanced over his shoulder, listening to Felix in the kitchen.

"Little bastards," shouted Felix. "Boys always getting into shit."

Cole backed out of the sealift room. The smell of frying garlic had filled the kitchen in his absence. He sat at the table before speaking again. "So it was a boy?"

"Probably. Nine times out of ten it is, around here. But you know that," Felix said, staring at Cole.

Felix set down his knife. He turned the knob for one of the stove burners and bent down to light a cigarette from a package on the counter. "Speaking of kids, I saw you driving with Pitseolala's little brother this morning," he said, nonchalant.

"You keeping tabs on me, Felix?" Cole held a serious face for a moment before offering a half smirk.

Felix chuckled, tight-lipped. "I was walking to the office." Felix waved his cigarette hand in a circle over his face, took a long drag, and exhaled as he pulled a coffee cup toward him, tapping his ash into it. "And he's a hard kid to miss."

"I thought you didn't go into work today."

"Oh, I did. Just to drop off Pits's file. And to tell them I was taking the day."

Cole noticed an ashtray on the table that wasn't present when he'd come for dinner. Three cigarette butts had been snuffed out in the bottom.

Felix offered a weak smile. "Do you know how he got those scars?"

Cole shook his head. "I've never asked him."

"Pits told me once. Winter camping with relatives. Maliktu was doused in fuel when an oil lamp overturned, catching the tent on fire. Their mother died trying to save them. Their father died of exposure on the long walk home. Only the two of them made it back to town."

"Survivors," said Cole.

Felix nodded in agreement, holding in a lungful of smoke before exhaling. He spoke without looking at Cole, rolling the cigarette between his thumb and forefinger, examining the burning end. "But it caught up with her in the end. I'm sure he's got his issues too—lighting fires, breaking into houses, telling lies. No one goes through childhood trauma like that without having it change you in a negative way."

"Like when your sister fell off that train bridge."

Felix glanced at Cole, wincing almost imperceptibly. He set the cigarette down on the edge of the sink and turned his attention to the burning food on the stove. He tossed the contents several times and added liquid from a bottle into the pan as he spoke.

"It's a full moon. You'll be busy tonight."

"Probably all weekend."

Felix picked up the butt and took another long drag once the food was under control, exhaling from the corner of his mouth. "You must get tired of it. Having to clean up the garbage around here."

"Someone has to do it."

"But why do people like us choose to be the ones?"

"We all make choices."

A wistful look washed over Felix's face. "I bet we both never would've thought all the choices we made throughout our lives would bring us up here, to this place, to this moment."

"No one ever does," said Cole.

"No, I guess not." Felix dropped the remains of the cigarette into the empty coffee cup, picking up his knife again. "How's your hand?"

"It's healing."

Felix scraped the chopped onion into the other frying pan, causing it to sizzle, and turned the burner down. "You should think about getting out of here too, before you do some damage that won't heal."

"The past always catches up with you," said Cole. "No matter where you go."

"You talking about the lawsuit? I saw the article this morning. You might be getting out of here sooner than you think."

Cole nodded without acknowledging him. Inhaling deeply through his nose, he braced his hands on the tabletop, stood up slowly, and moved into the adjoining living room toward the door.

"Just keep moving," Felix said with a smirk. "*Saudade,* remember?"

"Portugal, yeah." Cole nodded, hands in his pockets, staring at the wall of masks. "When did you say you were there again?"

"Around ninety-four to ninety-five. Chasing a girl. You know how it is."

Cole surveyed the living room casually. "No, not really," he said.

Silence lingered. Felix smacked his lips and wiped his hands on a dishcloth. "Well, I'd invite you to stay for a meal, but I wasn't expecting you—only prepared enough for one."

"That's fine. I only came about the window." He leaned in, his face inches from the white plaster mask of the drowned girl. Her expression calm, her eyes closed. Cole straightened up, turning his head toward Felix. "Why did she throw herself in the river?"

"Hard to say. Heartbreak, loneliness. Perhaps she grew tired of life."

Cole looked back to the death mask. There was something about her smile; it was as if she knew something he didn't. "Or maybe some lazy French cop didn't give a shit about a dead little girl."

"Sometimes life doesn't give us the answers we want. And some stones are better left unturned."

Cole walked back to the table. "Turning stones is part of my job. Even if they might have snakes under them."

Felix smiled, acknowledging the clever remark. "I know you claim not to believe in God, Cole. But are you a *spiritual* man?"

Cole spoke confidently and didn't hesitate. "No."

"I wasn't either. Until I went to Haiti. You should go visit someday, if you ever get the chance."

"Maybe," said Cole, his response rushed. He pulled the ashtray toward him, spinning it slowly with one hand, counterclockwise.

"Before I go, I wanted to let you know," said Cole, clearing his throat. "We have new evidence in Pits's case."

Cole fixed his eyes on Felix, waiting for his reaction.

Felix's face tightened, muscles contracting. He rotated his body straight on toward his guest. "Really?"

"Yeah, one of the crime-scene samples I sent away came back with DNA that wasn't hers."

"What kind of sample?"

"Epithelial DNA from the noose. I haven't reviewed the full report yet. They just said a second strand of male DNA showed up. The family has also agreed to allow us to exhume the body."

"And so, what does all that mean? In terms of your investigation."

"It seems she was also pregnant. The baby will give us DNA as well, both mother and father. But we won't know who that man is unless we can find a match. To do that, we'd need to get DNA from different persons of interest, see who matches. Might prove he was at the scene of her death."

Felix returned to chopping, lowering his head. "Interesting."

Another long silence dragged out between the two men, with delicate sounds of the outside storm and the cooking food in the background.

"Well, if you do notice anything missing, give us a call," said Cole, donning his hat and gloves.

"I'll do that." Felix didn't look up.

Cole picked up a cigarette butt from the ashtray. He turned it over in his hand, examining the brand name written on the filter.

"You can't get this brand in town. You order in your cigarettes?"

Felix didn't respond. The steady clack of the knife on the cutting board filled the room.

Cole continued, slow and measured. "When you leave, you should quit smoking. Get a fresh start."

Felix looked up. Cole hesitated until Felix acknowledged him and then slowly slipped the butt into his pocket, deliberately waiting for him to see the gesture. Tension seeped into Felix's skin, his face turned pale, and his back stiffened. Cole focused on the knife in Felix's hand for the first time since he arrived.

A look of recognition passed between them.

No turning back, thought Cole.

Cole squeezed the chest-mounted handset for his radio and never took his eyes off Felix. "Dispatch, it's Elderick Cole, Cape Dorset detachment, do you read me?"

Time stopped, both men frozen in place.

"I read you," said the operator, the connection crackling.

Cole spoke without breaking eye contact. "Just wanted to do a status check. I'm at House 625. I'm leaving right now. I'll be at the detachment in five minutes."

Now someone knows where I am if anything happens.

"Copy that. Over."

The thirteen steps to the front door with his back turned felt like a hundred. When he finished lacing up his boots, Felix, knife in hand, stood unwavering at the kitchen counter, watching. Despite Felix's wide smile, the storm Cole witnessed in the social worker's eyes matched the one raging toward their little town. The two men exchanged solemn nods; a new understanding had begun.

Outside, the night remained frozen. Cole trudged through a newborn snowdrift toward his truck but paused at the driver's side door. Scanning the monochromatic landscape around him, a mixture of feelings surfaced simultaneously—anticipation, dread, and uncertainty. He knew he had just stepped into a more dangerous territory.

Once settled in the locked vehicle, Cole stared at Felix's house. The still-warm engine turned over on the first try. The ball was now in Felix's court, and he had nowhere left to go. *Patience,* Cole told himself, but his racing pulse didn't dare slow until he was nearly home.

CHAPTER 34

The wheels of the abandoned car had been stolen by the first snowfall, and being no hindrance to traffic, the vehicle became a permanent fixture on the street. The children, perhaps not yet bored enough or saving their mischief for a particularly dull winter's day, hadn't smashed in its windows. Shielding him from the biting wind, it served as a perfect shelter for Maliktu to spy on Felix.

The devil had arrived roughly a half hour earlier at the house where Pitseolala had died. Maliktu had tracked his vehicle through the neighborhood on a hot-wired snowmobile. The sled was more suited to these dreadful conditions than Felix's cumbersome truck. As Felix unloaded items from the bed of his vehicle into the vacant building, his true objectives remained obscured by the blowing snow. The boy knew he couldn't be up to anything good. He thought of seeking out Cole for help but quickly realized that there wasn't time to locate him given the worsening weather.

When Felix finally drove off, Maliktu snuck out of the junked car and made his way to the front door. Shut but unlocked; he stepped inside. A small lantern on the floor of the main area illuminated the previously unlit house. The familiar and comforting smell of gasoline filled his sinuses. Taking several steps toward the kitchen, Maliktu remembered his previous encounter with his sister within these walls. The memory sent chills down his spine. He pushed his tongue into the space where his loose tooth used to be. Five red and orange jugs of different shapes and sizes lay on the kitchen floor. *Gas canisters.* Maliktu considered seizing the opportunity to burn down the cursed house once and for all. If a fire was what Felix wanted, then a fire he would get.

Pulling his lighter from his pocket, he grabbed the wastebasket he had doused in flammable products the last time and dragged it out into the center of the room. He dumped the contents in a pile between the gas cans and prepared to strike his flame.

But before he could light the blaze, the front door swung open with a resounding bang, and the blizzard's fury rushed into the house. Felix loomed in the doorway, clutching a jerrican of gasoline. Terror gripped Maliktu's heart; there was no escape, nowhere to hide.

Felix dropped the canister when he spotted the boy. Maliktu darted back toward the stairs, his footfalls heavy and frantic, with the man thundering after him. A hand seized his ankle halfway up the stairs, hauling him downward, forcing him to smash his knees against the wooden steps. Maliktu jerked his head sharply backward, catching a fleeting glimpse of Felix's sinister face in the dim light of the lantern. With an arm's length between them, Maliktu unleashed a wild mule kick, striking Felix squarely on the chin and sending him tumbling down several steps. The boy froze mid-staircase, holding his breath and hoping Felix would stay down.

But Felix quickly recovered, turning on a flashlight that flickered over his coat pocket as he produced a yellow canister that Maliktu immediately recognized as bear spray. As Felix struggled to activate the canister, Maliktu seized the opportunity, rocketing up the remaining stairs and around the corner into the nearest doorway. A pounding of boots followed him up the staircase. Blood and adrenaline surged through his little body as he fumbled in the darkened bedroom, desperately searching for a hiding place.

From beneath a small desk, Maliktu heard the thin, noxious stream of the bear spray discharge, followed by a torrent of profanity. An acrid smell filled the bedroom. Maliktu attempted to dash around

Felix as a flashlight beam swept across him. He bolted for the bedroom door and was almost through when Felix caught the arm of his parka. The man yanked the boy toward him and spun him around into a chokehold. The pressure on Maliktu's throat made it impossible to breathe. His eyes bulged and his arms thrashed. Felix arched his back and pulled the boy's feet off the ground, sinking his hold in deeper. Maliktu contorted his frame, twisting his body so that Felix's forearm shifted to the side of his neck. He bit down hard on Felix's exposed wrist, grinding his teeth into the tender flesh. He could taste the blood—rich and coppery like raw seal meat. Felix screamed and released his grip. Maliktu dropped to the floor in a heap, half crawling, half stumbling into the hallway at the top of the stairs. Winded and desperate, he turned to face Felix in the utter blackness. His little fists clenched tightly as he raised them stiffly in front of his face. Blinded by the flashlight beam, he charged his attacker with a frenzied wail. A calculated and well-timed kick by Felix when the boy lunged struck Maliktu in the jaw, and his skull hit the wooden floor with a resounding crack. His world went black.

CHAPTER 35

Through the window, Cole watched as the full force of the storm descended upon the town. Large drifts formed rapidly in the vacant streets, making walking even the short distance to the police truck difficult. In the heart of such a blizzard, color ceased to exist. There was only pure whiteness, no sense of direction, no sense of distance. A constant howling drowned out all other sounds. It was an all-consuming absence of everything.

Before leaving the house, he stopped near the door without consciously intending to and picked up the phone. He dialed his daughter's number. He expected the call to go to voicemail, like it always did, and he braced himself for the inevitable disappointment. But then, through a crackling connection, a voice broke through.

"Hello," she said, slightly winded, as if walking while she spoke.

Cole froze, caught off guard. Defenseless.

Her voice softened. "Dad?"

"I . . . I just wanted to check on you."

An image of her face—one unmarred by anger and shame—surfaced in his mind.

"I'm all right," she said, sounding only half certain. Cole hesitated to respond, waiting in vain for something more. A realization of how truly vast the distance was between them struck him hard and fast. All those miles, all those years. He closed his eyes, listening to the sound of her breathing, grasping for some fragment of her to hold on to for when he might need it most.

"I love you," he whispered.

"I know," Chloe said softly. "I gotta go. Someone's waiting for me."

He struggled for something meaningful to say, but all that came out was "That's good . . ."

She hung up, but the phone remained at Cole's ear. Momentarily lost, he stared out the window into the nothingness of the storm.

Once outside, Cole hoisted his exhausted body up into the driver's seat and struggled to shut the door. He started the vehicle, cranking the heater and using the dashboard vents to warm his stinging hands. There were no signs of approaching headlights in the fading visibility. As he pulled away from the station, he reached for the radio, hoping for a distraction. The same droning Bible reading in Inuktitut persisted. He fumbled to silence the unwelcome sermon as he rounded the turn toward the outskirts of the community. On a night that called for upbeat tunes and idle chatter, the airwaves delivered a prediction of the end of the world. He'd had enough evangelism for one day.

When he reached the edge of town, he pulled the bullet-riddled corpse of the dog out of the truck bed and dragged it to a steep embankment near the shoreline. Memories resurfaced of the first time he'd come here in the height of summer, sitting at the picnic tables beneath the towering arch of whale ribs erected to mark the spot. He tried to recall the last time he felt truly warm but came up with nothing. He heaved the frozen animal down toward the tidemark, the weight causing his lower back to seize. There might be witness statements and testimony about him killing the dog, but there certainly wouldn't be a body for forensics. Polar bears, foxes, and ravens would work together to make sure of that.

Sitting at the edge of town with his headlights pointed into oblivion, Cole stared out to the endless miles of nothingness and cold, contemplating the demise of his failed career. The realization that he would never get a chance to redeem himself came crashing down on his broken psyche. As he craned his neck to look in the rearview mirror, he hesitated before turning the ignition, paralyzed by the reflection of his own deathlike face. Unshaven, dark circles beneath lifeless, bloodshot eyes. He had never felt so truly alone.

But on the drive back into town, he felt a peculiar lightness, an almost liberating sensation akin to what a man on the chopping block felt knowing the axe was about to come down. The lawsuit, the suspension, the looming end of his employment—everything seemed predetermined and inescapable, and the tension of the unknown lifted.

An inferno greeted Cole as he pulled up to the house. Fueled by gale force winds, intense flames engulfed the social worker's home, destroying any potential evidence Felix might have left inside. The blizzard had intensified, forcing the local establishments and the health center to shut down. There was no one in the street to witness the blaze, and the volunteer fire department wasn't equipped for this type of situation, under these conditions. The little house was far enough away from the neighboring buildings that there was no danger of the fire spreading. Cole noticed that the social worker's truck was missing from the driveway. As the inferno consumed the house, his mind raced with possibilities. He grasped at straws as he stared through the cracked windshield into the raging whiteout. Where could Felix go on a night like this?

When he had almost run out of places to consider, the radio crackled to life with a familiar voice repeating Cole's name amid the static.

"I have the boy," said Felix, reaching out to him through the raging storm, beckoning Cole to a final confrontation. "You know where to find me."

CHAPTER 36

Cole guided open the front door of the abandoned house with his boot and slipped into the darkness within. Once out of the relentless wind, he pressed the door shut against the blizzard. A deathly hush descended on the room when the latch clicked closed. He pulled back the hood of his parka and switched on his flashlight. The sterile odor of cleaning products filled his sinuses—remnants of the crime-scene cleanup—but another out-of-place odor lingered in the air. He drew a long inhale despite the noxious fumes and held his breath for a moment. *Gasoline.* All he could hear were the muffled sounds of the storm outside and a steady pulse pounding in his eardrums. He let the breath go and withdrew his firearm, raising the gun slowly, keeping it close to his chest.

Holding the flashlight in an ice-pick grip, Cole brought it up underneath the gun to steady his aim. The bones of the house shook, timbers cracking and popping under the strain of a violent gust of wind. He waited until the noise subsided, then cautiously advanced, sweeping the gun and the flashlight side to side in a steady rhythm. The beam illuminated the long hallway, reaching into the black void of the kitchen. He half expected Pitseolala's hanging corpse to materialize. But there was nothing but reflected light and shadows.

Leaning his shoulder against the near wall, he felt for the edge of the doorframe. No sounds emanated from within the house. He inhaled deeply before wheeling around into the living room doorway, lumbering across the carpet and slamming his back against the far wall. Shadows undulated on the white walls as he swept the beam back and forth with the pistol leveled at arm's length.

Empty.

The structure creaked again from another powerful gust while he caught his breath. Cole hobbled down the corridor to the kitchen, his heavy boots shuffling across the linoleum. The combined weight of the flashlight and pistol took its toll on his arm muscles. He struggled to maintain a shooting position. The kitchen, like the living room, was empty. He checked the pantry—shelves of food, two stools, a chest freezer. No Felix. Was the radio call a trick? *Enough of this shit,* he thought, and was striding toward the exit when he heard a noise above him. A floorboard creaking? A door squeaking? He flicked off the safety on his gun and moved to the bottom of the stairs.

Concentrating his light on the vacant top of the landing, Cole tried to recall if Felix's name was on the list of registered firearm owners. *This could be a trap.* Instinct warned him to leave, but images of a helpless Maliktu clouded his judgment. Cole climbed the stairs with difficulty, leaning hard against the railing to ease the weight on his compromised knee. He climbed one step for every three labored breaths, never taking his eyes off the top of the stairs, gripping his pistol tighter as he approached the landing. Straining from such intense concentration in the low light, his eyelids fluttered rapidly.

At the top, the flashlight revealed the doorway of the nearest bedroom. Boarded-up windows blocked any ambient light from outside, rendering the house pitch-black. He clicked off the flashlight, lowering his cramping arms. *If I can't see, neither can you,* he reasoned.

Sliding along the wall, Cole reached the bedroom door. Slipping inside, he breathed quietly in the dark with only the sound of his thumping pulse inside his skull. He steeled himself and raised his gun, then snapped on the flashlight.

Empty.

His knee throbbed from the cold and the climb, pain making it hard to focus. Only adrenaline kept him upright. Cole pressed forward, keeping his body tight against the wall, as he advanced on the last of the upstairs bedrooms. He stepped into the room with his gun held high. Nothing but furniture. The whole unit was empty. He swore under his breath and lowered his cramping arms as he trudged to the top of the stairs and paused there with the butt of his gun resting on the newel post. *Where would Felix have taken Maliktu?* His mind drifted to the boy's imagined corpse, lying on the frozen ground somewhere, broken and bleeding, then to Pitseolala hanging in the kitchen, then to the Carter boy's lifeless body floating face down in the river. So much death. And everything he had done to stop it proved so futile. He clicked on the safety of his gun and swore again in a whisper. Then, realizing he was alone, he raised his head to the ceiling, screaming in utter frustration.

The piercing cry had barely subsided when another scream erupted from the darkness behind him. Cole spun around, only able to raise his flashlight and gun a few inches before the attacker struck him head-on. The force of the blow sent Cole stumbling backward, his left leg stepping out into the empty air above the top step. As his forearm smacked against the railing, the gun flew from his hand, and his legs flailed desperately for solid ground before his body plunged downward.

A white light exploded behind his eyes as the first impact of his skull on the hardwood stairs rendered him momentarily senseless. The flashlight tumbled from his limp fingers, clattering down with him. On the second bounce, his bad leg absorbed the brunt of the blow with a sickening crack. Muscles tore, ligaments ripped, and his kneecap dislodged. Tumbling down the remaining stairs, he landed in a deformed heap at the bottom.

Searing heat erupted inside his thigh, flooding his brain with firing synapses. A series of shrieks exploded from his lungs, fading only when he lost consciousness.

When Cole pried his eyes open, he found only darkness and agony. He had lost his bearings in the fall. When he struggled to sit upright, a hot poker of pain pushed deep into the head of his quadricep. Waves of nausea overtook him. His skin felt electrified, blood coursing through every vein. His tongue felt swollen and heavy. He opened his mouth to scream, but only gurgling sounds escaped.

Panic tore at his throat. He needed to get up, but the painful memory of his last movements left him paralyzed, too afraid to try. Grimacing, he lay back down, eyes watering profusely, grinding his teeth until he felt they might shatter. He steeled himself and pushed up onto his elbows. He dragged his mangled leg across the floor until he hit the wall.

As he slumped against it, his head awkwardly tilted forward, making it difficult to draw breath. He scanned the pitch dark for the beam of his lost flashlight, cursing everything. Fumbling around his body, his hands grazed an unknown object, and a sharp pain blossomed in his abdomen. A tingling sensation spread into his hips and lower back. He wrapped his good hand around the slippery handle of a knife. His fingers moved carefully down to the damp fabric of his parka. Blood. He pressed on the cloth around the blade, delicately, trying desperately to assess the damage in the dark. His sense of panic escalated; he needed light.

As if responding to his thoughts, a flashlight flicked on at the top of the landing. He reached for his holster and found it empty. Heavy footfalls descended the wooden steps, the beam lighting up the path ahead of them. The figure stopped midway on the staircase and pointed the flashlight into Cole's face. Blinded, he threw up a hand to block the light, averting his eyes downward to his body. The floor, his uniform, his hands—so much blood. A knife protruded from his lower abdomen. The person lowered the light and continued down the stairs. An acute burning sensation rushed up from Cole's leg into his torso. A violent spasm overtook him. His thoughts became singular. *The gun. The gun. The gun.*

His hands swept frantically around his limp body. His breathing grew rapid and shallow. Two more steps and the light reached the bottom of the stairs. Another wave of suffering seized him, and he moaned loudly when he turned his upper body too far to one side, reaching to grasp at shadows. The figure reached Cole's feet, pointing the center of the beam at his groin.

Acting solely on impulse, he gripped the knife's handle. His contracted abdominal muscles clung to the blade and the pain was excruciating as he heaved upward. The blade came free with a wet sucking sound; blood flowed freely out over his belly, soaking through his clothing, pooling beneath him. Cole pressed his compromised hand against the gushing wound and lashed out with the knife toward his unseen assailant. He whipped it back and forth, slicing only air. Without warning, the flashlight shone directly into his eyes, blinding him momentarily as an unseen object descended hard on his shattered knee. Cole released a series of prolonged and agonized screams until unconsciousness mercifully claimed him once again.

CHAPTER 37

Maliktu jerked awake at the sound of a booming crash. He rolled onto his left side in the impenetrable blackness. A shiver rippled up through his body; his extremities were numb from the cold. Struggling to move his hands, he realized they were bound behind his back. When he sat upright, his head brushed something soft—a familiar rattle of coat hangers jangled above him. No mattress beneath him, and a strange scent of unfamiliar perfume filled the dark space. Yes, but not his. He wiggled his hands beneath his buttocks and pushed his skinny legs through the loop of his restraints one at a time. When he brought his hands up to his face, the tape on his wrists scraped against his burn-scarred chin. His fingers found the tender lump on the side of his head, and flashes of memory clarified in his mind—Felix in the doorway, the chase through the house, then nothing.

A harrowing scream erupted from the floor beneath him, followed by a man's muffled, angry voice. Maliktu tore frantically at the tape on his wrists with his teeth. He wrenched his arms against the restraints during every break from gnawing until he was free. The taste of plastic adhesive filled his mouth, and his friction-burned wrists were raw and tender. Blowing into his frozen hands to warm them, he pushed himself onto his knees. When he tried to open the closet doors, they budged only an inch. Pressing one eye to the crack, he found it as dark beyond the closet as within. Pushing harder did nothing, so he braced himself against the back wall and extended his legs against the doors with as much force as he could muster. They yielded slightly, cracking under the pressure, but remained open enough for him to slip his hand through. Feeling electrical tape wrapped around the handles, he undid the Velcro and reached into the pocket of his parka. Gripping the bone handle of his *ulu,* he pushed the crescent-shaped blade between the doors and applied pressure until it sliced through the tape.

From downstairs, another scream reverberated as the closet doors burst open. Crawling out of the cramped space, he used the furniture and walls for guidance as he navigated his way out in the blackness. When he reached the top of the stairs, a soft glow emanated from below. He pulled himself to his feet with support from the railing, his legs aching and cramping from the cold floor of the closet.

Maliktu descended the first few steps silently, hugging the wall to avoid the creaking of the treads. The odor of gasoline nearly overwhelmed him. Pausing at the bend in the staircase, he knelt to observe the scene below through the railing posts.

CHAPTER 38

Maliktu watched as Felix set two heavy canisters of fuel down in the center of the hallway. A lone lantern threw faint shadows onto the surrounding walls. At the base of the staircase, a hulking figure lay slumped and defeated against the wall.

Cole surveyed the wreckage of his own body in the feeble light. Dark fluid pooled beneath his legs, his limbs were numb from the cold and blood loss, yet his abdomen throbbed with unrelenting heat. The possibility of any happy ending slipped away; one thought echoed on a loop in his fevered mind: *I'm dying.* With trembling fingers, he pressed on the open wound to stem the bleeding, producing shock waves of pain that nearly caused him to black out. The room spun out of control. Trying to quell the vertigo, he shut his eyes, only to be startled by a sudden onslaught of gasoline fumes.

Felix stood at the far end of the hallway, splashing fuel out across the floor. The social worker's voice droned on and on while he doused the room, but his words seemed garbled and distant to Cole. The spilled gasoline brought clouds of sparkling vapor up from the icy linoleum. After anointing the living room furniture with the remainder of the canister, Felix tossed the empty vessel into the mounted flatscreen with a loud crash. Cole made a desperate reach for Felix's pant leg as he swept past. The shift in weight caused him to moan in agony. Felix ignored him, focusing on his task.

Retrieving another full canister, he unscrewed the cap, his voice regaining clarity in Cole's ears: "You should have let her go. I gave her to you in a pretty little package."

He advanced on Cole in the lantern light, his face obscured by a strange black mask—featureless, yet terrifying in its ambiguity. His voice, though familiar to Cole, held an unfamiliar cadence, slow and melodic, and muffled by his sinister disguise. "Nobody would have missed her."

Setting down the canister, Felix squatted in front of Cole, burying the officer in his shadow. "You really shouldn't have pulled the knife out." He wiped a gloved finger through the growing pool of blood at his feet. "The blade was likely blocking severed arteries."

Cole, trembling and convulsing with shock and rage, struggled to draw a breath. Felix pulled Cole's zipper up tight against his neck. "You must be getting cold," he said, feigning concern before shaking a box of matches in Cole's face. "Don't worry, we'll fix that soon enough."

As Cole slouched, silent and helpless, his fragmented thoughts—the missing gun, the blood loss, the waiting gasoline, and, strangely, visions of the chained dog in the muzzle flare of his pistol—flashed through his mind. His head swirled with agony and confusion. No escape, no way to stop him. He reached out for Felix's masked face with clawed hands.

"That's not very nice," said Felix, batting the outstretched hands away with ease. He grabbed Cole's ankle and wrenched the injured leg, twisting the knee sideways. Cole groaned in agony, spittle draining from his lips, his face contorting grotesquely.

"*I'll kill you,*" whispered Cole through gritted teeth when he recovered from the assault.

"Ambitious," said Felix, rising to retrieve the remaining canister. "But highly unlikely." He set the third can of gasoline down in the entrance to the living room and tipped it over with a thud, sending the fuel sloshing out across the carpet. Cole scanned the surrounding floor in a panic. His flashlight was nowhere to be seen. He might be able to crawl to his gun if he could only find it. *Pepper spray.* He frantically searched his belt for the weapon. *Gone.* Along with his radio handset and collapsible baton.

"You were unconscious, so I took the liberty of removing them," said Felix in a matter-of-fact tone as he watched Cole search for the missing items. He squatted in front of Cole again, lifted his mask, and offered a mocking frown. "Have no illusions. This is the end."

Cole's head lolled under the weight of the circumstances, confusion and pain clouding his every thought.

No way out. No way to stop him. No way to—

In the midst of his panic, a diminutive figure emerged from the shadows on the stairs behind Felix, defiant and silent—Maliktu. The boy and the policeman locked eyes in silent understanding. Cole, his strength momentarily renewed by the boy's presence, glared at Felix. He spoke as loud as his weakened lungs would allow, determined to keep Felix distracted.

"Why Pits?" he shouted, eyes closed to brace for another wave of pain.

Felix, engrossed in adjusting his wristwatch, ignored the question. Cole persisted, his voice growing louder. "Why her?"

This second shout prompted Felix to pause for a moment. He smiled slightly. His face and his voice softened: "She killed herself."

"Bullshit." Cole punctuated the word by spitting blood onto the floor. "I want to know why she really died."

Taking advantage of the distraction, Maliktu slipped along the far wall in the shadows and moved into a position directly behind Felix.

"She stepped up on the chair herself," said Felix, almost wistful at the gruesome memory. "She even put the cord around her neck. So frightened up there. Trembling like a little wounded bird." His gaze drifted off as he relived the experience. "I told her that she was close to Jesus—just one step away. All that pain, all that suffering, would be"—he blew imaginary dust from his open palm—"gone."

He shook his head, looking disappointed. He sighed heavily, his breath crystallizing in the cold air. "But she couldn't go through with it; I could see it in her face. So I helped her along. You should have seen her face when the chair tipped over, her little feet dancing." Felix sounded as if he were about to cry. "So beautiful."

Cole, unable to contain it any longer, convulsed in a fit of brutal coughing, deep and wet. Maliktu had moved entirely behind Felix, blocked from Cole's view.

"I was careful, but apparently not careful enough," said Felix. "The broken condom, it accelerated things."

"She wasn't the first," said Cole, half question, half statement.

Felix smiled knowingly, looking into Cole's eyes for the first time since he squatted. He shook his head.

"Who are you really?" asked Cole.

"I've had so many names over the years, it gets hard to keep track."

Cole grabbed the fabric of Felix's pants and hung on with all his remaining strength. Felix had just opened his mouth to speak again when the floor creaked loudly behind him. He spun around to face the noise. Maliktu stood opposite him, holding his *ulu* aloft with both hands trembling. Fear rippled up through him as he pointed the blade at Felix. Gasoline fumes that saturated the air in the darkened area caused his eyes to water.

"Get to the door," Cole shouted, groping in vain as Felix pulled away from his grip. He collapsed onto his side, moaning in agony from the attempt.

Maliktu held his ground, staring down the man who killed his sister. Felix stepped toward the boy, then stopped abruptly, holding his palms up in mock submission.

"Put the knife down," said Felix gently. "We can talk about this." He took a second step forward, extending to reach for the weapon. Maliktu responded with a series of wild two-handed slashes, forcing Felix backward. His retreat gave Maliktu confidence, and he lowered his guard. Felix lunged ahead at the opportunity, knocking the blade aside and shoving Maliktu violently into the wall. The force of the blow knocked the air from the boy's lungs; the *ulu* tumbled from his limp fingers into the shadows. Maliktu's vision swirled in a kaleidoscope of white and gray. He crumpled to the floor like a marionette with its strings cut.

Felix pounced, straddling the boy's inert body, pummeling him about the head with his fists. Maliktu raised his arms in defense, taking several blows on the forearms before a punch to the temple left him reeling. He feigned unconsciousness to end the assault, as he had done with bullies many times before. Felix stumbled backward, leaning against the wall for support, panting heavily from his efforts. He looked back and forth between the fallen man and boy.

"This house will burn to the fucking ground. With a disgraced cop and a pyromaniac inside, there will be no end of theories. It will take them months to figure out what happened. I'll be long gone before they start sifting through the ashes."

Felix laughed, leaning forward with his hands on his knees, but his unsettling cackle abruptly ceased as he stood upright. Through squinted eyes, Maliktu noticed Felix's expression change dramatically as he peered into the darkness of the kitchen. He appeared confused, as though he'd seen something that deeply unsettled him.

CHAPTER 39

Cole removed the prehistoric talisman from his chest pocket with a trembling hand. He rubbed it between his blood-soaked fingers before locking his fist in a death grip around it. Tears welled from the intense pain and noxious fumes. Half-formed thoughts emerged from the chaos in his head—blood loss, gasoline, death. Unable to focus or move, he spit a mouthful of blood onto his shattered leg. Shadows around him seemed to constrict at the gesture. He stared helplessly into that narrowing void. So dark, so cold.

While Cole struggled to remain conscious, Felix stammered and shouted in a foreign language—guttural sounds like swear words—while heaving a large canister of gasoline into the living room. Taking advantage of his absence, a recovering Maliktu rolled onto his side and scrambled up onto unsteady legs. Ripples of nausea coursed through him as he regained his balance. Unconsciously, he reached into the wide pocket of his parka and found a forgotten object in his grasp. The discovery brought a sudden surge of determination within him, pushing out the hopelessness that had overwhelmed him just moments before.

Cole remained slumped against the wall, drifting in and out of consciousness. He struggled to concentrate on the muffled voices and the dark silhouettes moving through the gloom around him. Everything he could make out appeared charred at the edges, hazy and backlit. All hope of redemption, any chance of saving his career, his life, his soul—if such a thing existed—drained out of his body without so much as a whisper. In one last primal effort to survive, he lurched to one side, toppling over in an effort to crawl outside. Pain, instant and fierce, clarified his vision when he hit the floor, catapulting him back into reality.

Lying on his side in the doorway, he watched as Felix reentered the room brandishing a wide smile reminiscent of a wolf before its meal, teeth bared in anticipation. He saw the boy standing stock-still in the center of the room with his bright orange flare gun pointed directly at Felix's skull. The killer's once-gleeful expression wilted into a petulant scowl at the sight of Maliktu before settling into a look of pure smugness. Felix snatched the stolen pistol from his waistband, leveling it at Maliktu's head before disengaging the safety with a flick of his thumb. Cole mirrored the movement, extending his arm toward Maliktu, the boy's eyes, filled with desperation and panic, fixated on Felix.

An eerie silence descended on the room. Neither gunman wavered an inch as they faced each other. Cole watched in horror, motionless. As he searched for the strength to right himself, a sudden awareness overwhelmed him, a realization that if either gun fired, the gasoline fumes would erupt in an inferno that would likely kill them all. The house, a death trap.

As the trio remained motionless and silent, the timbers of the building cracked and popped with every gust of the blizzard, windows rattling in anticipation of the mayhem to come. But somewhere behind it all, a familiar melody emerged from the keening of the wind and the clattering percussion of the shifting house. Maliktu recognized his music slipping into the room, whirling through like an errant draft, and he drew a deep inhale through his nose, pulling the gasoline fumes deep into his lungs, feeling the weight of the flare gun in his hands and the pure and vengeful swell of the fire to come.

Felix opened his mouth to speak, but words never materialized. Maliktu watched as his gaze drifted again to the open doorway of the kitchen, fixated on some subtle change in the shadows. The killer blinked twice, slowly and deliberately. His pistol dipped an inch as his attention wavered. Maliktu fixated on Felix's exhale, a cloud of ice crystals momentarily obscuring his face.

One breath.

Felix raised the handgun again, his focus snapping back to the boy.

"If you shoot," he said calmly, "your flare gun will ignite the fumes."

At the mention of ignition, Maliktu's entire body trembled, adrenaline coursing wildly through his veins. The muscles of his outstretched forearm burned under the weight of the flare gun, and the hairs on his neck bristled as another cloud of frigid white formed around Felix's head.

Two breaths.

Felix lowered his own gun and took a cautious step forward, narrowing the gap between them. Maliktu remained motionless, eyes wide, fixed on the killer's mouth.

"It will kill us all," said Felix, reaching out, palm up, toward the flare gun pointed at his face. He exhaled, a billowing puff of whiteness escaping his lips.

Three breaths.

Across the room, Cole bolted upright in a surge of adrenaline. His face was pale and gaunt, his expression bewildered, as if he couldn't comprehend where he was. In a swell of pain—or perhaps frustration—he screamed with every ounce of energy left, a primal, incoherent, utterly desperate cry. Felix snapped his head toward the sound. In that fleeting moment, Maliktu shut his eyes, and as the fourth unseen breath began to flow from Felix's mouth, he squeezed the trigger.

A white-hot fireball blazed from the barrel, lighting up everything in a blinding flash. The molten projectile struck Felix in the side of the head before careening into the living room and igniting the gasoline with a bomb-like rush that sucked the oxygen from the room. The concussive force of ignition threw both of them sprawling to the floor. Darkness and shadows gave way to the harsh and unforgiving light of an inferno. Felix clawed at his burning face with both hands, wailing in agony, barely audible over the relentless crackle of the flames as they ripped through the house, feeding on the gasoline that had been poured on every surface.

The arm of Maliktu's parka burst into flame. He pulled the coat over his head in one swift move, throwing the burning garment at Felix's crumpled form. The intense heat on his body approached unbearable levels, stealing his breath and singeing his eyes. Meanwhile, a resurrected and panic-stricken Cole made an anguished bid for salvation, face down near the floor, dragging his crippled frame inch by inch toward the door—a distance of mere feet that seemed a monumental task.

Ravenous flames consumed everything in sight, racing throughout the house, bent on total destruction. The scorched air swarmed with fireflies of burning debris. Somewhere a window imploded. Maliktu sidestepped Felix's thrashing legs as he writhed in agony. The killer's screams were muffled by his hands clutching his still-smoldering face. The boy scrambled toward the foyer and grabbed onto the wide collar of Cole's parka. Crackles, hisses, and pops exploded around them. The heat overwhelmed him as he dragged the injured policeman toward the front door, flames singeing his bare arms and shoulders while he struggled. A ceiling of smoke descended rapidly, reducing visibility to near zero. A noxious wave of burning plastic threatened to asphyxiate them both. Maliktu kept his head low and held his breath. Overcome by his exertion and his injuries, Cole sank once again into limp silence.

Undeterred, Maliktu yanked the front door wide open, letting the oxygen of the roaring blizzard outside feed the hungry inferno within, intensifying the blaze. He threw his weight backward, glancing over his shoulder into the swirling storm. The effort proved too much, and he crashed onto the snow-covered porch with Cole's body snagged on some unseen obstacle.

Maliktu righted himself, staring into the heart of the raging furnace, seeing Felix, his face blistered black and swollen beyond recognition, clutching Cole's ankle with both hands. Cole jerked to life when Felix squeezed his injured knee. A split second later, he screamed, pushing himself up onto his elbows, lashing out savagely with his good leg. His heel missed Felix's disfigured face by a finger width each time. Maliktu locked his forearms under Cole's armpits and heaved backward with all the strength he had left.

Cole's eyes widened and fluttered shut repeatedly as he tried desperately to focus on the blurred contours of Felix's face. In the midst of the struggle, a spectral figure seemed to emerge from the maelstrom of black smoke and embers behind Felix. Long hair whirled in the updrafts from the open door as the shadowy presence crawled through the fiery chaos toward Felix's prone body. With the last of his strength, Cole jerked his good leg upward, driving his boot down into Felix's head, forcing him to let go.

Maliktu tumbled backward at the sudden release of tension and dragged Cole's inert body with him in a clatter down the icy steps. Gasping for breath, he collapsed at the bottom on his back in the knee-deep snow next to Cole. His eyes grew wide as he lay there, transfixed by the blinding streetlamps, the swirling snow, and the towering cathedral of flames above. The Arctic wind drove the fire higher into the night sky, a column of pitch-black smoke blotting out even the brightest stars.

Freed from the threat of burning alive and nestled in the snow, both Cole and Maliktu allowed themselves to sink into a helpless oblivion.

CHAPTER 40

Winter was a time of darkness for the Inuit. Before the white man came, the only sources of light were celestial bodies and the flames of the *qulliq*—a stone basin filled with precious whale oil used as a lamp in the *iglu*. Maliktu's grandmother had told him how her own mother would rapidly grind bone tools together to create enough heat to spark dried moss collected before the snow arrived. The smoldering moss would ignite the oil, and the tiny flames would heat and light the *iglu* during the long winter. The *qulliq* was kept burning throughout the cold months and carefully tended. It was difficult to relight and without its warmth, a family could easily die.

Maliktu awoke in an unfamiliar bed. Fitted wool blankets weighed heavily on his bones. Strange machines hummed and whirred around him, their lights blinking in time with the beat of his own heart. He pulled an arm out from beneath the covers. It hurt to move. His eyes traced the tube taped in the crook of his elbow up to the plastic IV bag hanging from its metal frame. Foreign sounds drifted in through the slightly open window. Through the glass, a cityscape glimmering on the distant horizon cast a pale light into the otherwise dark room, far too many streetlamps for Cape Dorset or even Iqaluit, the glow like a long-forgotten dawn.

He strained to reach for the lighter propped upright on the nightstand. It hurt to breathe. He flipped it over and over between his fingers, the motion comforting him when he shut his eyes. Images and sensory experiences flooded his brain—the gasoline fumes, the blood-soaked snow, the blinding light of the burning house.

Horizontal plastic curtain strips clattered when the heating fan kicked in. A dark figure slumped in a chair stirred in the corner of the room. Maliktu craned his neck from the pillow and opened his eyes as wide as he could to see more clearly in the gloom. Pingwatsiak, his grandfather, sat sleeping. His eyes remained closed as the curtains continued to rattle. The old man cleared his throat and shifted slightly beneath his blanket. Maliktu closed his eyes and looked again, reassuring himself that Pingwatsiak was really there. He let his head drop back onto the pillow, relieving his aching neck. A slow smile spread across Maliktu's face, and his eyes focused on a point in the blackness on the ceiling above the bed. Shadows coalesced into a familiar form. His sister's face, her dark hair splayed out, shifting in blackness, spreading out across the ceiling before fading into nothingness.

The room brightened as the moon emerged from behind a cloud, burning with relative brightness through the windowpane. Pitseolala's image had disappeared, but the feeling of her presence remained, energizing the air around him. He turned back to the window. The stars around the moon flickered in the swirling snow like sparks from a raging fire. Maliktu's thoughts drifted randomly back to a teacher who told him that the moon had no light of its own. The sun hid on the other side of the earth at night, and the moon merely reflected its light, a giant mirror in the emptiness of space. An elder from another community had once told him that the sun and the moon were born into the same family. The sun's face was so beautiful that the moon could not resist her beauty. He lusted after her endlessly, but she knew it was wrong for him to do so. She distracted him one day with a bowl of hot soup made from her breast milk and her blood and ran from their home. She sprinted as fast and as far as she possibly could. When he realized she was missing, he chased after her, and he has been chasing her around the sky ever since.

Maliktu wasn't sure he believed either version. He wanted to ask Cole what he believed. The policeman and he had shared the medevac plane, their stretchers positioned across the narrow aisle from each other as they headed south, the little aircraft shuddering violently in the terrible winds. Cole had been in bad shape—covered in blood, unconscious—when he was lifted from the snow beneath the burning house. But on the plane, his face looked calm, serene, like that of a child resting in his mother's arms. They had been wheeled into the hospital together but separated since then.

He watched as his grandfather continued to sleep soundly in the corner, his snoring deep and rhythmic. Maliktu knew he would feel better if he also rested for a while. There were doctors here who could get him more pills to settle his scattered mind. Then he and his grandfather could go home, and go hunting again out on the frozen ocean, without fear of visions beneath the ice haunting him.

Cole was likely down the hall, he told himself, sleeping in a room like this one, in a bed like this one. The boy focused again on the spot in the darkness above the bed where his sister had appeared to him. But she was gone—where, he didn't know, but he felt certain her suffering was over. Music slipped in beneath the closed door. Not his music from the hills, but a faint melody from a radio down the hallway. As he focused on the sound, trying to identify the tune, he drifted off into a deep and dreamless sleep.

CHAPTER 41

Cole had grown accustomed to myriad noises in his Arctic house: ravens dancing on the corrugated steel roof, the drone of distant snowmobiles, the furnace pushing warm air into the cold ductwork to make it thump like a poltergeist in the walls. But now, lying on his unmade bed, he slowly became aware of an eerie silence that unsettled him. He opened his eyes and sat up, swinging his legs around to plant his feet on the floor. No sting of cold hardwood on the calloused soles of his bare feet. No chill in the bedroom. Dreamlike moonlight filtered in through the frosted windowpane. He touched his bad knee, then caressed his face, then his damaged hand, a vague memory of his childhood surfacing—a little boy awkwardly learning to make the sign of the cross.

Hazy images wafted up from the depths of his mind. The burning house. The dark fuselage of a small plane. The harsh lights of the emergency room. All accompanied by distant echoes of shouting voices. He curled his toes into the warmth of the carpet before taking a few hesitant steps, feeling his way in the blackness toward the bedroom door.

No limp. No pain.

He reached for the door and found only empty space. Turning around, he saw that his bedroom had disappeared into a murky void. He caught sight of a tiny, warm glow flickering in the far corner of the room, seemingly a hundred feet away in the distance. He stepped toward the glimmering light, toes brushing through the thick rug as he shuffled forward with hands outstretched, walls and furniture suddenly absent, surrounded only by shadows.

After several steps, he paused and ran his hands down his chest. Feeling fabric, he realized he was wearing his uniform, the utility belt buckled once more around his waist. He explored the shirt covering his abdomen with frantic fingers.

No wound. No knife.

His thoughts drifted to the boy. He rubbed his eyes and looked up toward the missing ceiling. The night sky sparkled with emerging stars. Now somehow outside, he drew a deep breath, holding it, wondering how a dream could feel this real. The icy ground crunched beneath his shoeless feet. As he approached the light, it revealed itself to be an *iglu,* lit from within, illuminating the cracks between the blocks of compacted snow. He circled the dwelling, marveling at this dark underworld in which he found himself, before dropping to his knees at the entrance and crawling into the heat of the narrow tunnel.

Inside, Pitseolala sat at the *qulliq,* tending its flame with a slender piece of caribou bone. She didn't acknowledge him as he entered. He knelt across from her with the stone lamp between them. The tiny row of flames flickered, and their shadows trembled on the *iglu*'s walls. She set down the bone tool beside the *qulliq* and raised her head. Her eyes grew wide at his arrival, her expression free of the tension and pain he had seen in it so many times. Her face, impossibly young and healthy, radiated beauty. Happiness and calm washed over him as he stared at her immaculate face.

Tears welled in his eyes, and he wiped them away with trembling fingers. She reached out to him and he took her fragile hand. She looked angelic in the light of the *qulliq,* vibrant and peaceful. He ran his thumb across her warm, soft palm. She smiled at his touch, her gentle smile that had touched Cole's heart.

He whispered her name.

And then she leaned forward and blew out the flames.

ACKNOWLEDGMENTS

I would like to extend a heartfelt thanks to my agent and friend, Gideon Pine at Inkwell Management, for believing in me as an unknown author. He and his father, Richard Pine, have provided representation beyond what I could ever have hoped for.

Thanks to Amy Einhorn and Shannon Criss at Crown for bringing this book to life in such a spectacular way.

A special thanks to Austin Parks, Abby Oladipo, Andrea Lau, Heather Williamson, Maureen Clark, Elora Weil, Hannah Perrin, Greg Kulick, and the entire team at Crown for making this book possible.

To my wife, Joy, who had faith in me from the very beginning. Your love, encouragement, and support made this dream possible. I love you so much.

I want to express my gratitude to Andrew Mahar, my brother, my best friend, and my silent partner in writing crime. This book wouldn't exist without you.

Thank you to Lorraine Lazier, who told me to put my feet on the floor and changed my life.

I am grateful for the friendship and support of Osvaldo Croci, Rosemary Thorne, Bob and Sheila Schneider, Aaron and Vashti Cumby, Michael Chandler, Anne Bishop, Jan Morrell, Loukas Crowther, Andrew Cooke, Chris Fedora, Sammy Davis, Liberty Halaca, Curtis Jones, Mike Drake, Mark Palermo, and Adam Hawboldt.

Thanks to Richard Thomas, Suzy Vitello, Chuck Palahniuk, the late great Jack Ketchum (Dallas Mayr), and every other author who read parts of what would become this book and offered advice.

I would like to thank the people of Cape Dorset who welcomed me into their homes and lives, including those who are, tragically, no longer with us.

I am also grateful to the police officers I met over the years while working in the North who candidly shared their stories, struggles, and friendship.

To my parents, Malcolm and Roberta Kempt, thank you for your unwavering support in my quest for a life less ordinary. I love you both dearly.

To my sister, Cynthia, whose love and support mean the world to me; your life and success are a constant source of inspiration.

Lastly, I want to remember Little G, who died shortly before I signed my book deal. I kept hoping you'd live forever. You were perfect. I miss you terribly.

ABOUT THE AUTHOR

MALCOLM KEMPT worked as a criminal lawyer in the remote Arctic for seventeen years before leaving to write full-time. He now lives on the island of Newfoundland. *A Gift Before Dying* is his debut novel.